1.50

BURIED ALIVE

J. J. Alexander got to his knees, feeling groggy. He felt the girl pulling on his arm, and finally stood.

"Where are we?"

"In the mine tunnel. They're going to blow it up with black powder!"

"Then we've got to get away from the blast. The concussion could kill us."

He grabbed her in the dark and pulled her farther back into the tunnel. As he hurried he stumbled over rocks and the ore-car rails.

And then a bright light suddenly shot through his brain and he felt as if he had been hit in the back with a battering ram. Thick, choking dust billowed around him. Rocks began raining down on him.

And then everything went black . . .

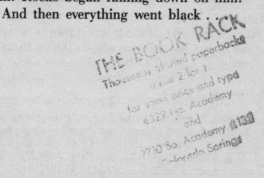

TALES OF THE OLD WEST

SPIRIT WARRIOR (1795, $2.50)
by G. Clifton Wisler
The only settler to survive the savage indian attack was a little boy. Although raised as a red man, every man was his enemy when the two worlds clashed—but he vowed no man would be his equal.

IRON HEART (1736, $2.25)
by Walt Denver
Orphaned by an indian raid, Ben vowed he'd never rest until he'd brought death to the Arapahoes. And it wasn't long before they came to fear the rider of vengeance they called . . . Iron Heart.

WEST OF THE CIMARRON (1681, $2.50)
by G. Clifton Wisler
Eric didn't have a chance revenging his father's death against the Dunstan gang until a stranger with a fast draw and a dark past arrived from West of the Cimarron.

HIGH LINE RIDER (1615, $2.50)
by William A. Lucky
In Guffey Creek, you either lived by the rules made by Judge Breen and his hired guns—or you didn't live at all. So when Holly took sides against the Judge, it looked like there would be just one more body for the buzzards. But this time they were wrong.

GUNSIGHT LODE (1497, $2.25)
by Virgil Hart
When Ned Coffee cornered Glass and Corey in a mine shaft, the last thing Glass expected was for the kid to make a play for the gold. And in a blazing three-way shootout, both Corey and Coffee would discover how lightening quick Glass was with a gun.

Available wherever paperbacks are sold, or order direct from the Publisher. Send cover price plus 50¢ per copy for mailing and handling to Zebra Books, Dept. 1915, 475 Park Avenue South, New York, N.Y. 10016. Residents of New York, New Jersey and Pennsylvania must include sales tax. DO NOT SEND CASH.

TOMBSTONE LODE

BY DOYLE TRENT

ZEBRA BOOKS
KENSINGTON PUBLISHING CORP.

ZEBRA BOOKS

are published by

Kensington Publishing Corp.
475 Park Avenue South
New York, NY 10016

First printing: October 1986

Printed in the United States of America

Chapter One

He knew the first time he saw her that she was phony.

Oh, she had all the markings of a gentlewoman, with her well-cut traveling suit of tan covert cloth, neat curly blond hair, and lips with not too much artificial color.

But he detected a barely discernible hardness around her eyes. And when she stepped out of the stagecoach, she showed a little more ankle below her long skirt than was necessary so that every man watching knew she had shapely legs. Every man within seeing distance was watching.

She had come to the end of a journey over rocky mountain roads in a four-up stagecoach—jammed in between five big men—and still she managed a smile. He had to admire her for that.

Two of the men retrieved their luggage from the top of the coach. There were a couple of tin suitcases and a bag made of heavy carpeting. Then, when the hostler handed down a large overland trunk, the men helped lower it gently to the ground.

"Thank you. Thank you so much," she said.

He tried to place her voice, but the few words she had spoken gave him little to go on. It did have a hint of a Midwestern twang. Not strong, just a hint. She was probably from the Midwest, like him, James J. Alexander III.

The two men, both wearing suspenders to hold up their baggy wool pants, carried the trunk across the plank sidewalk and into the plush New Windsor Hotel. She followed, carrying a small leather case. He followed too but hung back as the young woman signed her name in the hotel register. He saw the desk clerk's eyebrows go up, saw his lips form a silent whistle as he looked at the signature and then at her.

Alexander watched her climb the carpeted stairs behind the men carrying her trunk, noticed her slender, straight back and small waist. She climbed the stairs like a lady, holding her skirts just above her feet, head up, shoulders square.

He waited until the desk clerk turned his back to open the mail sacks that had come with the stage, and sneaked a look at the register. Yep. He could have guessed. Miss Josephine Dobbs. From St. Louis, Missouri.

A smug smile spread over his face. She was the first. There would be others, but she was the first. He would earn his salary, and the Pinkerton National Detective Agency would be proud of him. All he had to do was prove that she was not whom she claimed to be. How? Just watch her. Sooner or later she would do or say something that didn't fit her assumed identity, and he would accost her and make her admit she was an imposter. He knew how to do it, having been well trained in direct and cross-examination.

6

Miss Josephine Dobbs indeed. And from St. Louis. Wouldn't you know it? It would be extremely difficult for authorities at El Tejon in southwestern Colorado to trace the origin of anyone from that far away. And pretty. Sure. That would make it easier for her in a territory where women, especially pretty ones, were few and far between.

Alexander was chuckling to himself when he saw the two well-dressed men come hurriedly in from the street and approach the mahogany hotel desk. They wore coats that came down to their fingertips, cravats at their throats, fancy vests, and trousers with a crease down the front. The short one even wore spats.

They too looked at the signature on the ledger, then called the desk clerk over, and all had an excited, whispered conversation. While they whispered, they looked up the stairs in the direction the young woman had gone as if they hoped to see her coming back down.

Sure, they would be excited. Alexander chuckled to himself again. The short man was president and principal stockholder of the Bank of El Tejon, and the tall man owned the mercantile store down the street, the Top Hat saloon, and no telling what all else.

They would naturally be excited about the arrival of Miss Josephine Dobbs. Anyone named Dobbs would stir excitement in El Tejon.

Alexander fished his room key out of the pockets of his new denim pants and started toward the stairs himself. He stopped suddenly when he saw two more men hurry in, cross the marble lobby floor, and take a look at the register. There was Sheriff Boyd Hutchins, with his walrus mustache, roll-brim hat, roll of fat

7

around his middle, and jackboots. And there was Calvin Stewart, who owned the hotel and most of the grasslands east of El Tejon, with his high-heeled riding boots, high-crown silver belly hat, and well-creased pants.

They were all men Alexander had learned about by asking questions and listening in the hotel lobby and at the Top Hat saloon.

Now the four men were whispering excitedly and glancing up the stairs. They reached a decision. Sheriff Hutchins walked away from the group and headed for the stairs. He had no doubt been assigned to approach the young woman and learn what he could about her.

Alexander acted quickly. He was closer to the stairs than the sheriff was, and he hurried up the steps a short distance ahead of him. At the top, he stopped at room 204—his room—inserted the key in the lock, and hesitated, watching out of the corner of his eye.

The sheriff walked past him and stopped in front of room 206 next door. Alexander stepped through his own door but left it open a crack. His ears strained as the sheriff tapped lightly on the door of room 206.

The young woman took her time answering. The sheriff coughed nervously and tapped again. Finally she opened the door.

Sheriff Hutchins spoke in a hesitant and drawly but polite fashion. "I'm sorry to bother you, Miss, but I saw your signature on the book downstairs and, uh, I was wondering if you're maybe related to the gentleman we knew as Buckshot Dobbs?"

"Yes," she answered quickly. "He was my father."

The sheriff shuffled his feet, trying to think of what

8

to say next, and she interrupted his thoughts. "You're the sheriff, aren't you? I was planning to see you later today."

"Yes, ma'am. I'm Sheriff Boyd Hutchins. I'd be tickled to be of service to you."

There was a pause, and Alexander imagined her looking him over, studying his face, trying to determine whether he was friend or foe. He coughed nervously again. Finally, she spoke.

"I heard about my father's death, but I don't know how he died. I want to know all about it."

"How did you hear about it, Miss?"

"A letter from a Mr. Henshaw. Clarence E. Henshaw."

"Henshaw," Hutchins repeated, as if trying to remember the name. "Henshaw. Could that be the gentleman we know as Bear Tracks Henshaw?"

"I don't know him, Mr. Hutchins. I just received a letter from him three weeks ago. If you'll wait just a moment, I'll show it to you."

Another long moment of silence. Alexander was afraid to look and see what the sheriff was doing. He would be caught eavesdropping, and that would be embarrassing. Then she spoke again. "Here it is. It was postmarked at Rosebud, Colorado, June 25, 1899 and I didn't receive it until July 18. What puzzles me is Mr. Henshaw said my father died here and owned property here. Why wasn't the letter mailed here?"

Another pause. Alexander imagined the sheriff was reading the letter. Then, "I don't know, Miss Dobbs. Old Bear Tracks, uh, Mr. Henshaw don't stay in one place very long. I've been tryin' to locate him. He's one of the few people that knew anything about Mr.

Dobbs, uh, your dad. Would you mind, Miss, if I ask where this letter caught up with you?"

"At home. In St. Louis."

"Yes. Uh, Miss Dobbs, I would appreciate it if you would be kind enough to come over to my office as soon as you feel like it. Not right now, of course. You prob'ly want to rest up after your long trip. But as soon as you feel like it, we've got some important things to talk about. You, uh, prob'ly knew Mr. Dobbs died intestate and owned some valuable property."

"Yes, I knew he owned a gold mine."

"How did you know that?"

"My mother received two letters from him. The second one came last February, I believe. He said he had—how did he say it?—'struck a vein'—and had more money than he could spend. He wanted my mother, my sister, and me to join him here."

"Was you aimin' to do that, Miss?"

"No. That is, my mother wasn't. My sister and I wanted to but Mother was opposed to it. Mr. Hutchins, my mother and father were not the best of friends. The reasons are very personal."

"Yes, ma'am." The sheriff cleared his throat. "Wal, whenever you feel up to it, come to my office. Mr. Webber over at the bank will want to talk to you too. He—the judge made him administrator of your father's estate."

"Oh, yes, I suppose there does have to be an appointed administrator. Yes, I do indeed want to meet Mr. Webber."

Alexander heard the sheriff shuffle his feet, heard the creak of leather as he shifted his gunbelt. "Come in whenever you feel rested, Miss Dobbs."

"Thank you, Sheriff."

Alexander closed his door quietly two seconds before the sheriff walked by.

Now he was puzzled. Could she really be the old prospector's rightful heir? She had a letter from Bear Tracks Henshaw. Henshaw, he had learned, was probably Buckshot Dobbs's best friend. Buckshot Dobbs was a man who had few friends. No, judging from what he had been able to find out, he was a man who had no friends. He was a loner, a hermit, a jack-of-all-trades who took up prospecting after gold was first discovered in these parts.

But while Dobbs had no close friends, he did have an acquaintance or two and Bear Tracks Henshaw was one of them. Yes, Henshaw probably knew him as well as anyone. He was the one the authorities sought when they tried to find a next of kin. If Dobbs had a next of kin, Henshaw could possibly know about it. According to what the Pinkertons had been told, Henshaw couldn't be located. Now it appeared that he had not stayed around after Dobbs's death and had gone to Rosebud where he had mailed that letter.

"Umm." Alexander sat on the narrow bed in his room at the New Windsor Hotel and pulled off the new lace-up boots. He sighed with relief. The boots were not broken in yet and the left one pinched his big toe. This is all very interesting, he mused. That letter.

Well, he would have something to write about to the superintendent at the Chicago bureau. About time. He had been in El Tejon three days and until now he had had nothing to report.

11

He wished they had a telegraph in El Tejon. It was a new town and there wasn't much there yet. A lot of money and a lot of new construction, but none of the modern conveniences. Talk had it the Denver & Rio Grande was planning to lay track through El Tejon, and with that would come the telegraph. But until then, he'd have to use the painfully slow U.S. Mail.

He was digging through one of his two Gladstone bags for a pencil and stationery when he heard her door open and close. Light footsteps went past his door toward the stairs. She was leaving.

Boy, would he like to get a look at that letter. The superintendent would be pleased if he could report to him exactly what that letter said and all about it. Why not? How to pick a lock was one of the things he made it a point to learn after he joined the agency. The Pinkertons frowned on it, but he had talked an older agent into teaching him. He even had a specially made pick. Let's see. Where was it?

He rummaged through his luggage again until he found the pick, a rounded length of steel four inches long with a flattened hook on one end. Still in his sock feet, he quietly opened his door, looked up and down the hall, then tiptoed to her door. He squatted and squinted through the keyhole. Yep, it should be easy. After another look up and down the hall he slipped the steel into the keyhole, probed, pulled, pushed, and turned. The lock opened.

It occurred to him that he was breaking and entering, and that was a felony in Chicago and probably everywhere else. He could be sent to prison for what he was doing. That was something he had learned at Harvard before he dropped out. He hesi-

12

tated and started to turn back. But a detective had to take risks. That was something he was taught by the Pinkertons, not by Mr. Blackstone at Harvard.

OK, he would go ahead with it. Moving silently, he entered, closed the door behind him and crossed the room. His mind was trying to think of a plausible lie he could tell if he was caught, but nothing came to mind.

Would she scream if she found him there? If she did, what would happen? Would armed men come running and shoot without asking questions?

He tried to push those thoughts out of his mind and concentrate on finding that letter. Her clothes were hung carefully on an oak clothes tree beside the one window. The window was open a couple of inches, allowing a small breeze to ruffle the long dresses and petticoats. A hand mirror lay on the chiffonier beside a box of face powder and a round box of rouge. A small amount of the powder had been spilled. Beside those items was a letter.

Fingers trembling a little, he picked up the letter and read the address on the envelope. It was written with a lead pencil in a sprawling, barely legible handwriting. "Missus Margaret Dobbs, 10252 River Street, Saint Luis, Mizoura."

He took out the letter. "Deer Missus Dobbs," it began in the same lead pencil handwriting, "I am terrible sorry to tell you your husband Buckshot Dobbs died day before yesturdy at El Tehon in Colorada. I knew about you becuz I knew him and about you when you lived on Antler Crik about 12 or 13 yers ago. I am the man that lived up on the mountain. I know Buckshot sent you a letter last

13

winter and tol you about his find. I got yor adres out of his cabin. I do not know if any body els knows about you and your childrun. Missus Dobbs I am shur sorry to have to tell you about him dyin', but I bleve he want me to tell you. Yer frend. Clarence E. Henshaw."

For a long moment, Alexander looked at the letter. It told a sad story, really. An old prospector dies. Nobody knows much about him. Only one man, an old acquaintance, even knows he has a next of kin and the old acquaintance does what he has to do and breaks the news to his widow.

Alexander carefully refolded the letter, put it back in the envelope, and placed the envelope exactly where he had found it. It was a very sad story.

Suddenly, he remembered that he was breaking the law and he hurried in his sock feet back through the door, quietly closed it behind him, and tiptoed to his own room. He lay on his back on the bed, put his hands behind his head, and stared at the plaster ceiling.

The letter indicated that Mrs. Dobbs had children. Were they Buckshot Dobbs's children? Yes, they would have to be if Clarence Henshaw knew about them. Lived at a place called Antler Creek. Wonder where that is? And how old are her children? The woman who calls herself Miss Josephine Dobbs is in her mid-twenties.

This was something he had to report to his superintendent at Chicago. He wished the U.S. Mail wasn't so damnably slow. He stood up, picked up a sheaf of stationery and a pencil, sat in a chair by the window, put a suitcase on his lap for a desk, and began to write. He wrote two lines and paused, his head cocked to one side, thinking.

The widow had children. The young woman has a letter written to the widow by an acquaintance of the deceased. She claims to be one of the children.

Mr. Joseph Webber, bank president and appointed administrator of the estate, had hired the Pinkertons to find an heir, if there was one. No one knew. No one in El Tejon even knew Buckshot Dobbs's real first name. In fact, no one in El Tejon knew anything about him at all.

Alexander was assigned to El Tejon to discreetly, without making himself known, appraise all who arrived claiming to be the rightful heirs. She was the first, and, because he had been warned to be suspicious, he was suspicious. Now, he wasn't so certain.

"Dammit," he said aloud, "is she or isn't she?" He would certainly have to find out.

Chapter Two

The next time he saw her was the same day, evening rather, in the hotel dining room. The New Windsor Hotel was the newest and fanciest in southern Colorado, and Alexander had to put on a bow tie with a boiled shirt and dark finger-length coat to enter its dining room without being scowled at by the waiters.

He took his usual table in the far corner where he could watch the door and the entire room. Why? Well, he figured that's what a Pinkerton agent ought to do. It made him feel more like a detective.

The room held only ten tables but there was room for more if more were needed. The tables were covered with white linen cloths. Only two other tables were occupied. Alexander wondered if the hotel was making a profit with its fine restaurant. The hotel itself always had vacancies.

She came in alone and was immediately escorted to a table by a white-coated waiter with a thin, neat mustache. Another waiter hurried to her table and filled a crystal water glass from a crystal pitcher. Still another handed her a handwritten menu. Miss Josephine Dobbs had changed clothes, but she was still dressed like a lady in a gray dress with ruffles at the top, just over her ample bosom, and at the bottom just over her dainty black slippers. Her hair was parted on one side, with blond curls that hung down nearly to her shoulders. A striking young woman, thought James J. Alexander as his eyes took in everything about her.

She sat facing him, halfway across the room, head down, studying the menu. When she glanced up, she caught him staring at her, and for a second her eyes were puzzled as she stared back. Then she lowered her gaze and resumed reading the menu.

Were her eyes blue? Or gray? Or blue-gray? She had seemed interested in him for a second. Or was she merely puzzled because she caught him ogling her? Oh well, she was no doubt accustomed to being ogled. An attractive young woman like her had to be accustomed to that.

James J. Alexander III of the Chicago Alexanders was no ladies' man. There was nothing about him to catch a pretty young woman's eye. Average height, slender, a straight mouth, and a fairly firm chin. His face was smooth-shaven and pale, obviously not a face that had battled the elements. In fact, on any street in Chicago and on the campus at Harvard, he looked like an average young man from an influential family. Only one thing about his appearance worried him. Though only twenty-six, his hairline was beginning to recede, and he knew that in a few years he would be as bald as his father and his father's father. Brother

17

Jonathon was the lucky one. He had inherited his hair from Mrs. Alexander's side of the family and it was thick and wavy.

His steak Orlando was served with a bow and a flourish by the white-coated waiter, and he picked up his knife and fork and went to work on it. Every now and then he sneaked a glance at her. When her French onion soup was served, she took the sterling silver spoon in her right hand and began to eat.

But not as expected.

Instead of daintily lifting the side of the spoon to her mouth as any proper lady should, she was eating hurriedly, shoveling the soup into her mouth. In less than a minute she had devoured the soup and was wiping her lips with the linen napkin. A lady would merely dab at her mouth, fearful of smearing lip rouge. Interesting.

And when her steak was served, she smiled sweetly at the waiter, watched him retreat, then picked up her knife and fork, and dug into it, chewing rapidly.

Now that, Alexander thought, is a puzzler.

She dressed like a lady, walked like a lady, and talked like a woman with a fair amount of education. But she ate like a waterfront stevedore.

Again, she caught him staring at her, and again she stared back, only this time she held his gaze for several seconds. Were her eyes blue-green or just green? Her frankness embarrassed him. He felt as if he had been caught peeping through a keyhole, and he smiled a weak smile in an attempt to cover his embarrassment. She quickly looked away. When she resumed eating, she did it with class.

His first appraisal of her was right, she was not

what she had appeared to be. A pity. She was so pretty.

Determined not to stare at her again that evening, Alexander concentrated on his meal. The steak was definitely on the tough side, and he was grateful that his family dentist had kept his teeth healthy. The boiled potatoes could have stood a little more boiling. But the gravy was good. And the wine was good. Some French brand. Alexander's former roommate could have told him all about it, but Alexander himself could never find anything particularly interesting about wine.

He left the dining room ahead of her and went out onto the plank sidewalk. The August sun was warm in the high country, but the evenings were cool. He liked that. So much better than the steamy sidewalks of Chicago and Boston. The air was clean and fresh and invigorating. He walked briskly down the four-block length of Main Street and back up the other side, past the livery barn and feedlot, the general store, a blacksmith shop, the laundry. As he passed the livery barn he noticed the heavy ore wagons parked in a row in a vacant lot east of the barn. There were six of them. Strange he had never seen any of them on the street. He stopped to watch two horses in a feedlot rear, paw the air, and bite at each other playfully. One squealed a high-pitched squeal, wheeled, and kicked at the other horse with both hind feet.

So that was the weird noises he had heard the first night he spent in El Tejon. It was horses in a pen, squealing as they bit and kicked at each other. He had imagined it was a wounded panther or an Indian's battle cry just before he pounced on some poor

19

unsuspecting settler. Everybody in Chicago knew about the bloodthirsty Indians Out West whose favorite recreation was scalping palefaces. He was happy to note that there were no Indians around El Tejon. And he could understand why most of the men who rode into town carried guns.

Back in the hotel, Alexander bought a copy of the *Rosebud Gazette*, which had come in on the stage, and took it up to his room to read. He settled into the chair by the window, opened the newspaper, and noted that it was dated August 15, 1899, two days earlier. The biggest headline yelled at him: RAILROAD COMPLETED; FIRST TRAIN EXPECTED.

The story told how rail construction was finally completed by the Denver & Rio Grande Railway Company, and the first train was expected to arrive the next day. That would make it yesterday. A hundred or more people from forty miles around were expected to be on hand to see the first train steam its way into the new railroad depot. The mayor would be there, and the Elks Club band would be there too.

Alexander chuckled to himself. A train puffing into the station might be something special out west, but in Chicago and Boston it was so commonplace that people paid no attention to it anymore. He read through the paper and was disappointed that there was no national news and no news of the war in the Philippines. He put on his pajamas, the striped ones his mother had given him, blew out the lamp, and got into bed.

He lay for a long while on his back with his hands under his head, thinking about her, wondering what the morrow would bring. When he dozed off, he dreamed he was in the middle of a gun battle and a beautiful blonde was with him.

Breakfast in the hotel dining room was served with the same white-coated bows and "Yes, sirs" as dinner and lunch, but the meal was bland. It was French toast, common in the East, but served in El Tejon as if it was a delicacy. The bacon was good, however. Must have been home-grown without as much fat as the bacon that came from the large packing houses in the East.

Alexander sipped the last of his coffee, wiped his lips, left a dime tip, and went out into the hotel lobby, intending to step outside and take in some morning air. He didn't get that far.

The banker, Joseph A. Webber, accosted him.

"Pardon me, sir, are you by any chance Mr. James J. Alexander?"

Alexander stopped and turned toward him. "Yes, sir, I am."

The banker held out his hand. "Allow me to introduce myself. I am Joseph A. Webber, president of the Bank of El Tejon."

They shook. The banker had a firm grip and he smiled a friendly smile. "I'm told, Mr. Alexander, that you are perhaps looking for investment opportunities in our city."

He remembered then that he had told the few men he had met in El Tejon that he was looking for business opportunities. He had to give some reason for being in town and asking questions. "Oh, why yes.

21

It occurred to me, Mr. Webber, that since the town is comparatively new I might find a way to make a profit here. I like the town, sir, and I like this invigorating mountain air."

The banker, dressed in his dandy clothes, was shorter than Alexander and had to reach up to put a hand on his shoulder. "You are absolutely right, Mr. Alexander. El Tejon is booming, what with more gold being discovered and a new, larger sawmill being planned. And I'll let you in on a little secret, sir." He glanced around furtively, as if he didn't want to be overheard. "The D&RG railroad is building a spur line to El Tejon. That will make us an important shipping center for valuable ores, cattle, sheep, and lumber. Any investment you make will pay dividends, you can be sure of that, sir."

His words puzzled Alexander. "I can't help noticing, Mr. Webber, that the town seems to be, uh, well, on the quiet side. Not much seems to be happening."

The banker's smile widened and he winked. "Things will happen, Mr. Alexander. Indeed they will. You just watch us grow."

"I'm sorry, I don't understand."

"I'll tell you something else that is not common knowledge, sir. The biggest industry now is the Josey Mine. It is closed temporarily because the owner died recently and a legal heir has not been found. I happen to know that the heir is now in town, and the mine will soon be reopened." He glanced around and winked again. "When that happens, sir, you can bet your last double-eagle that economic activity will grow by leaps and bounds."

"Ummm. I see." Alexander pretended to ponder

that bit of intelligence. "Then the mine cannot be worked without the heir's consent?"

"That is correct. The court appointed me administrator of the deceased's estate, but I do not yet have authorization to resume taking ore out of the Josey. But I soon will have. Yes, sir, we'll be hiring people and opening up that mine within a few days."

"Tell me, Mr. Webber, are you sure the person who claims to be the heir is what he or she claims to be?"

"No doubt about it. She has a letter written to her mother by a friend of the deceased. It surely is proof enough. If not, we'll find more proof. I have the Pinkerton Detective Agency working for us."

"I see." It was difficult not to smile. His guise was working.

"Do yourself a favor, sir, and come over to the bank when you have a moment. I can steer you onto some good investments. You can be among the first to see the extraordinary value in real estate in this city, and there are plenty of opportunities for opening a business."

Alexander thought it over and said, "Yes, I may do that, sir. Any particular time?"

The short banker pulled a biscuit-sized watch out of a vest pocket, looked at it, and turned to leave. "Almost anytime, sir. I must be excused now, however. I have an appointment to meet the new mine owner at the bank. We have arrangements to make. Good-day, sir."

"Good day."

It started as a good day. The air was so clear and clean that he could imagine it sparkling. He stood on the boardwalk, inhaled deeply, and let his eyes rove over the pleasant scenery, the high pine- and aspen-covered ridge to the north and the wide grassy meadowland to the east and south.

This could certainly cure a man's physical ills. It could cure a man's financial ills too. The banker was probably right, a new town with several active industries around it and a railroad would be a good place to invest.

Yes, a railroad would make the town prosper. And it was headed this way. He knew from reading the newspaper that it had already reached the town of Rosebud about twenty miles east. The newspaper seemed to be uncertain about the D&RG's future plans, but Mr. Webber appeared to have some inside information.

Those thoughts were going through his mind when Miss Josephine Dobbs brushed past him on the sidewalk. He tipped his beaver hat, but she didn't notice. She was headed toward the bank, no doubt to meet with Mr. Webber. He would have given anything to hear their conversation. He followed, but discreetly.

Whoever built the bank had spared no expense. A marble floor, wrought iron and brass around the tellers' cages and the clerks' desks, etched-glass shades on the lamps. She was sitting at a desk, just inside a low iron railing.

He watched her fidget with her purse nervously as she sat there alone, no doubt waiting for Mr. Webber. She ought to be nervous. She was playing a role, pretending to be a lady and doing a good job of it too, but actually not always so ladylike.

But only Alexander knew that.

Now she was joined by Mr. Webber, who took a seat

across the desk from her. He smiled. She returned his smile, apparently at ease now. She wore a small, black lacy hat on top of her blond curls. Alexander moved forward, trying to be unobtrusive, until he was standing at the rail. By straining his ears he could catch a little of the conversation.

"Now, Miss Dobbs," the banker was saying, "first let me offer my condolences on the death of your father. Mr. Dobbs was one of our most valuable citizens, and was well liked by everyone." He saw the banker look up at the doorway, saw his mouth fly open, saw him grab hurriedly at a drawer of his desk. Alexander glanced back the way the banker was looking and saw the two masked men and the big pistols in their hands.

A shot was fired, and a deep masculine voice bellowed, "Hands up, ever'body. Don't nobody move. Move and we'll shoot."

A woman screamed. The masked men looked at Mr. Webber and pointed their pistols in that direction. Alexander soon discovered why. The banker had a silver-plated revolver in his hand and was pointing it at the masked men. Alexander saw the danger, and he moved as quickly as he had ever moved in his life.

With one long step he was over the railing, and in two more he was beside her. In another motion he shoved her off the chair onto the floor and fell on top of her.

Guns boomed. The woman's screams reached a hysterical pitch.

Two more shots were fired, one from a large-caliber gun and the other from a smaller caliber. The noise filled the building and stung the ears.

Footsteps. Quiet. But only for a moment.

A man said, "Oh, my God." The woman resumed her screaming. Another man yelled, "They're gone. Get the sheriff. Hurry, somebody."

Alexander raised his head. The masked men were gone. Mr. Webber was standing at his left, holding the silver-plated pistol, looking down at him. Alexander looked into the face of the girl under him. Their noses almost touched.

She was soft and feminine and her breath smelled of violets and roses and everything nice. She said, "Get the hell off of me, you—you masher."

He was shocked. He had never heard a lady swear. "I'm sorry, Miss. I didn't mean to, uh . . ."

She squirmed. Were her eyes green now? And suddenly she smiled. The anger was still in her eyes and the smile was a forced one, but it was a smile just the same. Her teeth were not so perfect after all. But, my God, she was beautiful.

"Sir, would you mind removing yourself?"

"Huh? Oh, yes. Certainly. I'm, uh, I'm sorry."

He got to his knees and then to his feet. He offered her a helping hand and she took it. She straightened her dress, patted her hair, reset her hat.

He continued stammering, "I, uh, really didn't mean to, uh—" Suddenly he exclaimed, "Look. Look here." He pointed to a splintery hole in the back of the chair she had been sitting in. "It's a bullet hole. You were almost shot."

"Oh, my." She examined the hole. "My goodness." The blue eyes turned on him. Or were they blue-gray? "I'm fortunate that you did what you did, Mr., uh—"

"Alexander. James J. Alexander."

She smiled sweetly. "I owe you my life, Mr. Alexander. If there is any way I can repay you . . ."

"It was a pleasure, Miss, uh, Miss . . ."

"I'm Josephine Dobbs." She held out a white-gloved hand, and he shook it, careful not to exert any pressure. He was tempted to ask her to dinner, but that wouldn't do. After all, he was a detective and he might have to be the one to blow up her little scheme. It wouldn't do to be too friendly with a suspect.

Around them, people were talking excitedly. The woman who had been screaming was now sobbing uncontrollably. Someone asked, "Was anybody shot?" There was no answer. Alexander turned to the door.

Sheriff Hutchins burst through the door a split second before Alexander got to it and they almost collided.

"What happened?" the sheriff yelled. "Somebody said there was a robbery."

Chapter Three

It occurred to Alexander that he ought to hang around the hotel lobby until the stage arrived and check out the new arrivals, if there were any. A handful of people stood near the clerk's desk discussing the attempted robbery.

"It took a lot of courage for Mr. Webber to shoot it out with them," said a man in a business suit and muttonchop whiskers. "He's mighty lucky he didn't get himself shot."

"I can assure you that Joseph Webber is a man who will not be scared off by a few ruffians." The speaker was the tall man, the owner of the mercantile and the Top Hat saloon. "Were it not for his courage those hoodlums would have made off with some of the town's capital."

"We're all very fortunate that no one was injured," said another man who looked very much like the first one but without the whiskers.

Alexander sidled up to the front desk, eyeing the clerk and listening to the conversation.

"And that girl," said a woman standing with the group. "What a terrifying experience. Had it not been for some young man who pushed her onto the floor she surely would have been shot."

"Why, that was the young man who—" the tall man looked around and spotted Alexander. "Why, there he is now." He hastened to the desk and stuck out his hand. "You're the fellow who saved that young woman's life. Allow me to introduce myself. I am John Bokhauser, one of the property owners here."

He shook with him. The man's handshake was firm and he pumped Alexander's arm up and down vigorously. "I've seen you around town but I haven't had the pleasure of being introduced."

Alexander introduced himself and told the same lie. "I'm looking for investment opportunities, and when I came here a few days ago I became interested in the town."

The man's eyes grew shrewd for a moment and then he smiled. "I can assure you, Mr. Alexander, that you could not have found a better place. Come up to my office soon and I can tell you about some very fine opportunities."

"Your office, sir?"

"Yes. Just over the Pine Valley Mercantile. I have a suite of rooms there."

"I'll do that, Mr. Bokhauser."

"Fine. I'll be looking forward to seeing you again. Good day, sir."

"Good day."

Bokhauser went back to his group, and slowly they drifted out onto the sidewalk. The stage from Rosebud arrived with a few shouts, a loud "Whoa," and a rattle of trace chains. Four passengers disembarked, and two of them entered the hotel, signed the register,

29

and were assigned rooms.

Alexander tried to look them over without being obvious. He waited a few minutes after they climbed the stairs and then looked for the desk clerk. He was out of sight.

Furtively, feeling like a sneak thief, Alexander stole a look at the register. He had never learned to read upside down, so he took another glance around and turned the book toward him.

One name wasn't interesting. The other was. Oh boy. Charles E. Dobbs. Kansas City, Missouri.

"Sir?"

Alexander stiffened. The desk clerk was back.

"Is there something?"

"Uh, no." He had to think fast. "I was expecting someone on the morning stage and I wondered if he had arrived."

"Only a Mr. Dobbs and a Mr. Winette," the clerk said. "Mr. Dobbs is the second person named Dobbs to arrive in two days."

"Umm. Strange, isn't it? But they are not the gentleman I was expecting. Perhaps his trip was delayed. Thank you very much." He walked away and went upstairs.

As he walked past room 202 he looked hard at the door, wishing he could see through it. Charles E. Dobbs. In room 202. A Dobbs in 202 and a Dobbs in 206. One on either side of him. A woman and a man. Could they be related? One of them from St. Louis and the other from Kansas City. It's possible, he thought. But, he mused to himself, I'll bet a cartwheel they don't even know each other.

He would give anything to be on hand when the two

met, to watch their faces. Wouldn't that be great? How could he manage it? Was she in her room? Yes, she had gone directly to the hotel from the bank. Could he manage it? He decided to try.

His knock on room 202 was soft at first, and when he got no answer he knocked louder. He heard bedsprings squeak. The man had been resting after his trip. He knocked again. Soon the door opened a crack and a bloodshot eye peered through at him.

"I'm very sorry to bother you, sir, but I couldn't help seeing your signature on the hotel register. I wonder if you are perhaps related to an acquaintance of mine, the late Buckshot Dobbs and his daughter?"

"Huh? His daughter?" The door opened wider, and the man who had signed the register as Charles E. Dobbs stood in his sock feet, suspenders hanging down over his baggy-at-the-knees pants. He had short black hair trimmed high above his ears, a thin mustache, and a surprised look on his face. "My father had no daughter. I have no sister."

Alexander's eyebrows went up. "Is that right, sir? Well, may I introduce you to Miss Josephine Dobbs of St. Louis, Missouri?"

"Huh?" The man, about Alexander's age, mulled it over, then said, "Certainly." Suddenly he smiled an easy smile. "If I have a sister, I would certainly like very much to meet her. Where can I find her?"

"Just two doors down." Alexander nodded in the direction of room 206.

"Will you wait till I make myself presentable?"

"Of course."

The door closed. Alexander smiled to himself. Oh, won't this be great? Now to approach her. He waited

31

until another patron of the hotel, a stout man in gray business clothes, walked past and started down the stairs, then went to the door of room 206.

She answered his knock readily and appeared to be ready to go out onto the street. "Oh," she said, surprised to see him. "Mr. Alexander."

"I'm very sorry to bother you, Miss Dobbs, but I was wondering if you happened to be related to a man I knew, a Mr. Buckshot Dobbs?"

"Why, yes. He was my father. Where did you meet him?"

He evaded that question by asking another. "I was wondering too, Miss Dobbs, if you happen to be related to Mr. Charles E. Dobbs."

The blue-gray eyes were puzzled. She pondered the question. "I don't know, sir. I have cousins on both sides of the family that I have never met. Charles E. Dobbs. Ummm. My father had a brother somewhere and he could have a son."

There was no alarm in her eyes. No fear.

"Would you care to meet him? He just checked in, right down the hall?"

"Oh yes. I'd love to meet him. I have always wanted to meet all my relatives." Still no alarm.

The door to 202 opened and Charles E. Dobbs stepped into the hall. His hair was combed and he had put on a dark coat that came just below his waist. He wore black shoes with pointed toes and gray suede ankle-high tops. Alexander motioned him over. This was going to be fun.

"Miss Dobbs," Alexander had to force the chuckle down before it came up, "I would like to introduce you to Mr. Charles E. Dobbs." He watched their faces. He was disappointed.

The man kept his face straight and even had a touch of humor in his expression. She put out her hand to shake his.

"What a pleasure to meet you," she gushed. "You just have to be a cousin. I knew my father had a brother somewhere, but I, we, never knew what became of him."

The man's eyes wrinkled with humor. "May I ask, Miss Dobbs, who was your father?"

"Why, John Dobbs. Also known as Buckshot Dobbs."

The man's face broke into a smile. "Unless our fathers were twins with the same name, that can't be. My father was John Dobbs."

Her eyes widened in surprise. "You're father's name was John Dobbs? Are you sure about that?"

"Absolutely."

A frown replaced the look of surprise. "That's strange. Are you very sure? You couldn't be mistaken?"

"I'm certain. I know my father's name."

"Oh, my." She turned those blue eyes on Alexander. Wide blue eyes. "Mr. Alexander, what should we do? You appear to be a learned man. Should we visit the sheriff?"

"I think Miss Dobbs, that you had better visit a barrister."

"A barrister? But I have no funds to employ a barrister." A deep furrow appeared between her eyes. Were they gray now? "I was just going to visit Mr. Webber at the bank again. He is the legal administrator of my father's estate, and we never got to finish our conversation. Perhaps he will have a suggestion."

She started to walk past Alexander, then stopped and looked him in the eye with those blue-gray eyes of hers. "Your father's name was John Dobbs?" She was talking to Charles E. Dobbs but looking at Alexander.

"Absolutely."

"How strange. We should have a long visit and get acquainted very soon." She left, walking gracefully down the stairs, back straight, holding her skirt with one hand.

The two men stood looking at each other a moment, then the new arrival spoke. "What do you make of all this, Mr. Alexander?"

"Sure beats the tar out of me."

"Could it be—I'm almost afraid to even think such a thing, but could it be that she is an imposter?"

Alexander smiled. "Beats the pee-wadding out of me."

He stepped around the young man and went to his room, unlocked the door and went inside. He closed the door behind him, shutting off Mr. Charles E. Dobbs, or Mr. Keister Spieler or whatever his real name was. He sat on the edge of the bed, smiling.

One of them was an imposter, no doubt about that, and whichever one it was was a damn fine actor. Probably him, but how to prove it? She does have that letter. Wonder what he's got? Has to have something. Can't just blow into town, say he's Buckshot Dobbs's rightful heir and take over a gold mine.

Chuckling, Alexander pulled out a dresser drawer, took out his stationery and wrote another letter to his superintendent in Chicago.

That done, he changed into his new denim pants and new flat-heeled lace-up boots. He winced when he put his foot into the boot that was a shade too tight, but when he stomped down on it, it didn't feel too bad. A checkered wool shirt went on next, then a large dark-blue bandana and a wide-brimmed hat with a high crown pinched in at the top.

After a careful look at himself in the dresser mirror, he went out onto the boardwalk, heading for Ma Blessing's cafe. It appeared to be where the laboring men ate, those who didn't have wives to cook for them and couldn't stand their own cooking. With his new duds, he hoped he could mingle with them and learn things.

"Howdy, Easterner," said Ma Blessing, taking in his new unshrunk pants and the new unsoiled hat. He was disappointed to realize that he stood out like that.

"Hello, ma'am. Could I see a menu please?"

"Ain't no menu 'cept in my head. If you don't like beef roasted in the oven, then you'll go hungry in here." He guessed she was around fifty-five but prematurely aged. Her gray hair was pulled back in a bun. Her face was round and pleasant, and her eyes wrinkled with good humor.

He sat on a stool at a rough wooden counter and looked at the men around him. It was noon, but there were only six other customers in a room that could easily accommodate twenty or thirty. There were miners in their narrow-brim hats and baggy wool pants, timberjacks in their Scotch caps and red suspenders, and a cowboy. Alexander guessed he was a cowboy. He had spurs with large rowels on his boots.

Ma Blessing stood with her hands on her plump

hips. "Well, are you or ain't you?"

"Oh, pardon me," he said, smiling. "Yes, I'll have the beef roasted in the oven, if you happen to have any."

Her wrinkled, plump face grinned just enough to show misshapen teeth. "Just happen to have some. Want some gravy on it?"

"I, uh, I'm not used to eating much at noon, ma'am. Could I have a sandwich? I'll have the gravy for dinner tonight. For supper, I mean."

"Yep. With my own homemade bread." She squinted at him. "Mebbe it'll put some color in your face." She went to the kitchen.

When the cowboy got up and walked to the counter, Ma Blessing came out to meet him. He paid her and walked to the door, his spurs clinking loudly on the wooden floor. Alexander turned to watch the man leave, admiring him. His denim pants were faded and had shrunk so that they fit tighter and his gray hat was soiled, with the brim rolled up on the sides.

Alexander had always admired cowboys. The few he had seen. As a child, he once told his father that he was going to be a cowboy when he grew up. Mr. James J. Alexander II immediately sat him down and had a father-to-son talk with him, telling him about how the family tradition of practicing law had to be carried on.

Just the same, Alexander had always admired cowboys and wished he could be one. He would have given anything to get acquainted with the cowboy who had just left Ma Blessing's cafe.

The sandwich came and Ma Blessing leaned against the counter and watched him eat it. "Delicious," he said after taking a bite, and it was. "Better than the food at the hotel."

She smiled. "Them fancy chefs and such don't know how to cook for a man. Me, I've cooked for ever'thing, includin' a brandin' crew, a bunch of lumberjacks, and a rail-layin' crew. Nobody ever left my kitchen hungry. How long you been in town?"

"A few days. I wish I'd discovered this place sooner. They don't seem to know what to do with a steak at the hotel."

"Listen," Ma Blessing leaned closer, "all them gents know how to do is wear them tall white hats and talk about their kordon blue and filay migyon or whatever it is they feed folks over there. Listen, if you want a good steak, come back tonight. Our beef ain't fed so much fattenin' grain and stuff like they do it in them Eastern cities. You ain't never et a good steak till you et a good grass-fed one."

He chewed heartily, enjoying the sandwich. "I'll be here, Mrs. uh . . .?"

"Blessing. Call me Ma. Ever'body else does. Where you from, young man?"

"Chicago."

"Well, it ain't none a my business but I'm real curious about folks, how come you're out here?"

"Business, Mrs. Blessing. I'm an entrepreneur."

"A what?"

"An investor. I'm looking for good investments." An idea came to him. "I'm particularly interested in gold mining and I heard that gold is being discovered around here." He could only hope that she would take an interest in that subject. She did.

"Gold. That's what makes men crazy. Plenty of

gold found around here, but the way I hear it, it's peterin' out."

"Really?"

"Yep. Only mine that's got a good vein left is the Josey and she's shut down."

"Oh? Who owns it?"

"A old sourdough name of Buckshot Dobbs owned 'er, but he's dead. And they can't open 'er up till the next of kin is found."

"That's too bad. Did you by any chance know this Mr. Buckshot Dobbs?"

"Prob'ly as much as anybody, but nobody knowed him much. Lived over west in a cabin he built hisself and he never came to town 'cept to buy a few groceries. Didn't come in here but twict, and he ate like he thought somebody was gonna take his plate away from him. Wanta know what I think? I think he was touched in the head a little."

"But he found gold?"

"Oh yeah. He got lucky. Ever' onct in a while one a them old roosters strikes it rich." Ma Blessing wiped the counter top with her work-worn hand. "Yep, he was rich."

"What did he do with his money?"

"Well, at first he hid it, and then Shurf Hutchins went to see him and talked him into puttin it in the bank. Told him about the robbers and such."

"Sounds like an interesting character. Where is his cabin?"

" 'Bout three miles west on the road to New Mexico Territory. On the north side of the road. Can't miss it. Stinks like a packin' house."

"Is it a log cabin?"

"Logs, boards, tarpaper, gunny sacks, anything he could find. He wasn't much of a carpenter." Ma Blessing left to take the money from another customer who had finished his meal.

"Powerful good chuck," the customer said. "Wish that old Chinese at camp could cook like that." He left, and Ma Blessing turned back to her kitchen. "Got a heap of dishes to warsh," she said over her shoulder.

Alexander's mind went over what Ma Blessing had said. Lived in a cabin about three miles west. Wonder if anyone has searched it for clues to his relatives? Surely, someone has. Could they have overlooked anything that a trained detective might find? Probably not.

But out on the street again, he made up his mind. Three miles. Not too far to walk. There surely weren't any Indians this close to civilization. He started walking, wishing he had some old comfortable shoes.

Chapter Four

The noonday sun had reached its peak, and the flies were buzzing around his face and arms. There were big, black horseflies that were merely bothersome and little, green deer flies that stung like a wasp. He walked past two horses standing in a small pen on the outskirts of town, stomping their feet and shivering the hide on their legs and shoulders to keep the flies off. He wished he could make his skin shiver like that. He walked on down the road, over rocks and wagon ruts.

He wondered if there were any rattlesnakes. He had read about the rattlesnakes Out West. Their bite was usually fatal and they were under every rock and bush.

The narrow road curved into a stand of magnificent ponderosas. Among them were the ever-trembling leaves of the aspens. A light wagon pulled by two horses came around the curve toward him, and, when the horses saw him, they stopped suddenly and tried to spin around in their harness. The driver, a man in bib overalls, hauled on the lines and yelled at the horses. "Prince, you, Joe, get back in thar."

The horses straightened out, but their ears were pointed at Alexander and their nostrils flared. They refused to move toward him.

"Joe. Git up thar." The driver had no whip and all he could do was yell at the horses. They pranced but refused to move forward. "Mister," the driver said, "you're scare-spookin' my team. Would you step aside?"

At first, Alexander didn't understand why the horses were afraid of him, but then he remembered reading about the wild mustangs Out West being captured and half-tamed. He stepped off the road into the timber. The horses went on by then, snorting at him and stepping lively past him. The driver gave him a friendly wave.

The next vehicle he saw was a bicycle, a big one with a huge front wheel and a small rear wheel. The rider, wearing knickers and a cap with a bill on it, said "Howdy." The contraption was unsteady, and the rider was having a wobbly time keeping it upright on the rocky, rutted road.

How much farther? Another mile? Alexander's big toe in the tight boot was hurting again. He walked on and eventually came to a place where the trees had been cut down, creating a small park full of stumps. The cabin sat back on the far edge of the clearing. He stopped and studied the cabin, a one-room shanty. No sign of life.

Walking carefully, watching for rattlesnakes, and hoping there were no unfriendly Indians around, Alexander approached the cabin. He stopped a few yards from the door and said timidly, "Hello."

No answer. The door was made of planks with a

board nailed across the top and bottom to hold them together. There was no knob or lock, just a homemade latch. It was a short length of wood that fit into two horseshoes, one on each side of the door frame. He lifted it out of the horseshoes, and the door slowly creaked open on rusty hinges.

Timidly, he peered around the half-open door. Inside, it was dark. He took a step inside and stopped. He made out a few pieces of furniture and a window. The window had a piece of canvas hung over it and no light came in. He pushed the door in farther and waited until his eyes became accustomed to the gloom, then stepped to the center of the room.

The floor was wood, and so was everything else except the small stove with two cooking lids on it. Gradually, he began to see better, and he made out a wooden bunk with wooden legs on one end of the room and a cabinet made of boards nailed together and nailed to the wall on the other end. The table was made of rough-sawn boards with sections of aspen trunks for legs, and so was the one chair in the room.

Alexander stood still and looked around carefully. Exactly what he was looking for he didn't know. Ma Blessing was right, it stunk. Lord, how it stunk. Why were the bed legs sitting in tin cans? And what was in the cans? Coal oil? And what in the name of Job was in that flour sack hanging from the ceiling? Meat, that's what it was. Rotten meat. Alexander almost gagged. But he had walked three miles to get a look inside the cabin. Breathing shallowly, he turned slowly and surveyed the room carefully.

The stove was lopsided, and he could see why. One leg was broken and the stove was propped up on two rocks. A few cans of vegetables stood in the cabinet, and a can of Arbuckle coffee. A coffee pot and a dirty skillet sat on the stove. Another skillet hung from a nail on the wall, and a towel made of an empty flour sack hung on another nail beside the table. What was in that gallon can on the table? Oh, molasses.

Alexander felt as though he was invading someone's privacy, a dead man's privacy, and he felt a little chill. He listened carefully for possible footsteps and heard none. Still moving cautiously, he went to the window and lifted the canvas, letting in more light. A canvas mattress and a dirty wool blanket were on the bunk. When he felt of the mattress, he could tell it was filled with hay or grass. And when he picked up the blanket, he knew why the bunk legs were sitting in cans of coal oil.

Bugs. Big ones. Vicious looking.

He had heard about bedbugs, and he shivered at the sight of them. How could anyone live there?

He had a strong urge to leave. The authorities had no doubt already searched the place and there were no clues. He stepped to the open door and looked out to be sure he was alone. No one. He stood in the doorway and looked around the room again. Aha. One corner of a canvas bag showed under the bunk.

With a little fear in his heart, Alexander touched the bag, half expecting something live to spring at him. When nothing happened, he dragged the bag out from under the bunk and stood back a moment. Then, summoning his courage, he fumbled with the leather drawstring, opened the bag, and peered in. All he could see were old clothes. Finally, he picked it up and dumped the contents onto the floor. Just old clothes. No papers, nothing of interest.

Disappointment pulled down the corners of his mouth. The thought of going through the pockets of the greasy old overalls was repugnant, but he did it. One at a time he held them up and put his hands in all the pockets. A corncob pipe and a sack of Bull Durham tobacco were all he found.

He poked around among the cans of fruit and bags of dried fruit in the cabinet, then eyed the wooden box beside the stove. It had "Dynamite" painted on it. The box held no dynamite, only a few sticks of firewood and an old Montgomery Ward catalog with many of the pages torn out. The pages had no doubt helped start fires in the stove.

Idly, he picked up the catalog and thumbed through it. A stub of a lead pencil fell out, and he saw the two sheets of brown wrapping paper folded inside between the pages. He unfolded the sheets and discovered handwriting on them.

Curious, he carried the paper to the open door where the light was better and tried to read the writing. It was a childish scrawl, written with the lead pencil and barely legible. It reminded him of the letter written by Bear Tracks Henshaw, only this was even more childish.

Let's see, umm. Reading it was like working a puzzle. He made out the word "finest," then "imported," and then "silk." That was all. What in the world? Oh. It came to him. The writer had copied words from the catalog, trying to learn to write. Just a pathetic attempt at trying to learn to write.

Buckshot Dobbs was illiterate. Alexander wondered how he could have written letters to Mrs. Margaret

44

Dobbs in St. Louis, telling her about his mine. Or were there really such letters?

He turned the page over and discovered more childish penmanship. Let's see. The word "Dobbs" was there in several places. There were several false starts and then the wife's name, Margaret Dobbs. Below that was Josephine Dobbs. Looked like he was practicing writing his family's name. Half a page down was the name Etty, which was crossed out. The name Ettie was written under it. His daughters? Near the bottom of the page was the name Fred Dobbs, and beside that was the misspelled name Fredrik Dobbs. Who was Frederick Dobbs?

The letter written by Henshaw indicated that Buckshot Dobbs had children, but it didn't say how many or what sex.

Alexander searched through the catalog for more wrapping paper and found none. He decided to leave the cabin. He folded the two sheets of paper and put them in his hip pocket, closed the door behind him, put the length of wood back inside the horseshoes to hold the door closed, and walked rapidly back to the road.

He didn't realize he had been breathing shallowly until he got back on the road and away from the stink of the cabin. Then he let his breath out with a whoosh and gulped in the clean air. Whew! And the old man was rich and didn't have to live that way. He could have bought the New Windsor Hotel and had the best bed in town and the best food. Ma Blessing had to have been right, Buckshot Dobbs was touched in the head.

But he must have been a pathetic old man, trying

so hard to learn to write. Must have wanted very badly to communicate with his family. Must have missed his family something terrible. Wonder who they are and where they are. The woman who calls herself Josephine Dobbs hasn't really proven anything. And that young dandy who calls himself Charles Dobbs— Alexander chuckled to himself—he hadn't proven a thing either. A legal battle was brewing.

Walking back toward town on the rocky road through the pines, his sore foot making him limp slightly, he thought back to the young woman.

And then there she was right in front of him.

The first thing he saw coming around a curve among the trees was the horse, then the two-wheeled buggy it was pulling. Alexander stepped off the road, fearful that the horse would shy away from him. But it only turned its head and pointed its ears at him and otherwise kept trotting along. It stopped when the driver said "Whoa."

The driver was Sheriff Hutchins, and sitting beside him as prettily as could be was Miss Josephine Dobbs. "Taking your daily constitutional?" the sheriff asked in a friendly drawl.

"Why, yes," Alexander lied. "It's a beautiful day and I can't get enough of this mountain air and scenery. We don't have trees like these back in Chicago, you know."

"Seems kinda warm to me," Hutchins said, "but I reckon if I was from one of them Eastern cities I wouldn't think so."

Alexander tipped his hat at the young woman. "Hello again, Miss Dobbs."

"Nice to see you again, Mr. Alexander."

He wondered where they were going, but he didn't want to appear nosy, and he didn't ask. They said nothing more. Hutchins clucked at the horse, and the animal moved into its trotting gait, pulling the buggy behind it. He watched it disappear and guessed that they too were going to the cabin. Yes, that was it. She would want to see where her father lived or at least pretend to be interested. He wondered where the Josey Mine was. Was it on the same road? Could they have been going there? Another thought occurred to him: he had taken what could be considered evidence out of that cabin. It was the second time since he had arrived in El Tejon that he had done something illegal.

It was turning dark in the thick woods when he came out of them at the outskirts of town. His big toe was hurting more with each step. The hotel room would look good to him. He walked past a long tin building and saw men sitting on the ground outside. They were working men in rough working clothes. All but one. Alexander nodded at them and saw the one man leave them and come his way. The man was young and well dressed. It was Charles E. Dobbs. He waved at Alexander and yelled, "Oh, say, Mr. Alexander."

Alexander stopped and waited for him to approach. "I would like a word with you, sir, if you don't mind."

"Certainly, Mr. Dobbs."

"I, uh, I've been asking around and I have been told that my father's mine is about four miles down this road. Have you seen it?"

"No, sir, Mr. Dobbs, I have not."

"Oh, I thought you might be able to tell me, uh, are

47

there any wild animals in this territory? You see, I don't know how to ride or drive a horse, and I was wondering, is it safe to walk around in the woods? I mean, I see you have just returned from a walk in the woods."

Alexander smiled. "I don't know how to advise you, Mr. Dobbs. I have been here only a few days myself, and I don't know. My walk was just a short one and I saw nothing to fear."

"May I ask, sir, what is your business?"

"I'm an entrepreneur. I thought there might be an opportunity here."

"Oh, I see. Then you have money to invest?"

"I have some investment funds, yes."

"Are you by any chance interested in gold mining? I will inherit a very valuable mine soon, and, frankly, I know nothing about mining and I don't care to learn. The mine will be for sale."

"Then you are the legitimate heir of the late Mr. Dobbs?"

"Yes, sir."

"Do you by any chance have a brother named Frederick?"

Alexander noticed the wary, cornered-animal look that crossed Charles E. Dobbs's face. It was quickly replaced by a smile.

"No. That is, not that I know about. You see, sir, my mother and father lived together for only a short time in Kansas City. That was just before he came out here to look for gold. I was born after he left, and I doubt he ever knew about me."

"What was your father's real first name?"

"John. John Dobbs. That's what my mother said."

"Tell me, Mr. Dobbs, how did you know your father had died?"

"A friend, an old family friend, said he heard about his death while visiting the city of Rosebud."

"What is your mother's name?"

A look of exasperation quickly crossed the young man's face, then disappeared. He shrugged. "That is something I am prepared to tell the authorities, Mr. Alexander, and not something I like to discuss with strangers. However, I will tell you. Her name is Margaret. Mrs. Margaret Dobbs. She never married again."

It was pure speculation on Alexander's part, but he was almost certain he knew how the young man had learned the widow's name. He pulled off his boots in his room at the New Windsor Hotel and sighed with relief as he wriggled his sore toe. He sat in the chair by the window and mulled it over.

The man named Bear Tracks Henshaw wrote a letter to the widow of the late Buckshot Dobbs. The letter was mailed in Rosebud. So Bear Tracks had gone to Rosebud after his friend's death and had probably told someone all about it. That someone told someone else and eventually the story got as far as Kansas City.

If it got as far as Kansas City, it could have traveled to St. Louis too. The superintendent at the Chicago bureau was right, the word would spread and soon some con man or con woman from somewhere would appear at El Tejon in the state of Colorado and try to make the authorities believe he or she was the rightful heir.

Alexander had his work cut out for him. He chuckled. He had wanted to do something different. He had wanted adventure, and he had wanted to come Out West. He was getting what he wanted.

But, boy oh boy, if that superintendent knew about his illegal activities, he would be fired from the Pinkertons so quick it would make his head swim. What to do next? Easy. Go to Rosebud, hunt up Bear Tracks Henshaw, and pump him for all he was worth. Alexander stretched out in his chair, wriggled his sore toe, and made plans to do just that. A knock on the door interrupted his thoughts.

Limping badly now, Alexander went to the door and opened it. Sheriff Boyd Hutchins stood there, a stern look on his face.

"I want to talk with you, young feller. You've been nosin' around where you had no business."

Chapter Five

Alexander stepped back to allow the sheriff to enter, but Hutchins made no move in that direction. "Not here. In my office. Right now."

"What? Why?"

"In my office. You know where it is." The sheriff turned to leave. "In five minutes. Don't make me come back for you."

Asking why and what were dumb questions, Alexander knew. Going into that cabin was an illegal act, and the sheriff somehow knew he had been in there. Marks on the dusty floor, something. No use compounding the crime by pretending innocence, and no use incurring the wrath of the local authorities by being uncooperative. He intended to keep his real mission in El Tejon a secret, as instructed, but O.K., he'd go see the sheriff in his office.

He picked up his boots, then immediately ruled them out. His big toe still hurt. The patent-leather slippers would have to do. His stomach growled, reminding him that it was dinner time, but dinner would have to wait.

The sheriff's office was in a two-room stone building with a larger, wood-frame building attached to it at the rear. The sheriff was waiting inside behind a huge roll-top desk. His feet were propped up on an open drawer. It was after sundown and cool and the light was not too good inside the room. A heavy iron door separated the sheriff's office from the jail in the side room. Wanted flyers hung on the walls beside a calendar with the dates crossed off up to the current date.

"Yes, sir," said Alexander, speaking very respectfully.

"Come in and shut the door, son. Set over there." Hutchins nodded toward a wooden chair. Alexander closed the door and sat, eyeing the sheriff fearfully. He had read about the lawmen Out West who were sometimes quick on the trigger.

"Now then," Hutchins put his feet on the floor and tilted his chair back on two hind legs. "Just who are you and what are you doing in El Tejon?"

"Why, I'm here looking for investment opportunities, Sheriff. My name is James J. Alexander the Third."

"Yeah, that's what you've been tellin' folks, but I'm not so sure. That young lady told me about how you arranged a meetin' between her and that other young feller that came in on the stage today. He claims he's Buckshot Dobbs's son and she claims she's his daughter, and they never met before. Now what I want to know is what are you claimin' to be. A nephew or somethin'?"

Alexander almost smiled with relief. So that was

52

what worried the local authorities. The sheriff thought he was another imposter trying to get a piece of the dead man's estate.

"No, Mr. Hutchins, I'm in no way related to the late Buckshot Dobbs. But I am curious. Ever since I came here I've been hearing about the Josey Mine and how someone was going to claim it, but no, I have no claims on it at all."

"Then what was you doin' in Old Buckshot's cabin?"

Alexander did smile then and spread his hands in a gesture of harmlessness. "As I said, Mr. Hutchins, I am curious. I have been offered a share in the Josey Mine and I just wanted to see it. I didn't find it, however, but I did find the cabin which I was told belonged to the deceased."

"Just curiosity, huh? And who offered to sell you a piece of that mine?"

"Why, the gentleman who said his name is Charles Dobbs." It was true, although it didn't happen in that order. Alexander hoped the sheriff wouldn't know that.

Then the sheriff grinned. "Now you seem to be a well-spoken, educated young man. You didn't just hand over some cash, did you?"

Alexander was indignant. "Of course not. My family didn't gain its wealth by being stupid, Mr. Hutchins. But I am interested in gold mining. I would like to learn more about that particular mine."

Hutchins's chair came down on all four legs. "Wal, you'll have to wait till somebody proves he has the right to open 'er up, and that'll take awhile. Meantime, I ain't gonna arrest you for trespassin', but I

53

could, you know."

"I appreciate that, and I won't do it again. Uh, would you mind telling me, does this Charles E. Dobbs have anything to prove that he is who he says he is?"

"Yeah, he's got a letter that Old Buckshot wrote to his estranged wife. Says she lives in Kansas City, but her health is bad and she can't travel, so he came out here to take over Old Buckshot's property."

It was hard to do, but Alexander managed to hold back a snicker. He had to cough and hold his hand over his mouth to hide it. He coughed again, cleared his throat, and asked, "A letter, you say? From the deceased?"

"Yeah, that's what he claims."

"Did you see it?"

"Sure. He showed it to me."

"Is it authentic?"

"How in thunder would I know? He's got a letter, she's got a letter, and as far as I know they're both on the con. Howsomever, I'd b'lieve her before I'd b'lieve him."

"Why?"

"Instinct, son. But that won't hold up in court."

"Do you think it will come to a court battle?"

"I know it will. Old Joe Webber over at the bank is the legal administrator of the estate and he ain't gonna turn loose of nothin' 'less the Honorable Judge Rutherford says so."

"Judge Rutherford," Alexander said. "A state district court judge?"

"A circuit court judge, and he ain't due here for, let's see—" Hutchins squinted at the calendar on the

54

wall "—six or seven days. Let 'em fight it out in court. Judge Rutherford'll find out which 'un is lyin'."

Alexander had to cough again to cover another suppressed giggle. He already knew the man was lying, and in all probability, the girl was too. A letter from Buckshot Dobbs indeed.

He stood up. "Anything more, Mr. Hutchins?"

"No. Go on about your business, but if I was you I wouldn't go stickin' my nose where it don't belong. Some of these boys around here are a leetle bit spooky about strangers and they got itchy trigger fingers."

"I appreciate the advice, Mr. Hutchins. I'll be more discreet from now on."

He didn't want to wear his city shoes to Ma Blessing's cafe, so he went back to the hotel, changed out of the denim pants into something more dignified and went to the hotel dining room. Dinner over, he went back to his room feeling restless and lonely. He wanted to talk to someone, yet he didn't. What he had found out he had to keep to himself. They didn't tell him about the loneliness that went with being a special agent. He tried to read one of the Charles Dickens books he had brought but soon gave that up. He paced the floor, sat in the chair awhile, and finally put on his pajamas and got into bed.

Tomorrow he would take the stage to Rosebud, hunt up the man named Bear Tracks Henshaw, and find out all he could. Then he'd send a telegram to his superintendent. They had to have a telegraph at Rosebud, and that would be better than waiting for the U.S. Mail. Yes, that's what he would do.

But when Miss Josephine Dobbs entered the hotel dining room next morning, his plans underwent an

55

abrupt change.

He had gotten there first and was sipping his second cup of coffee when he saw her. She paused in the doorway just long enough to catch him staring at her, then made straight for his table. "Good morning, Mr. Alexander."

He hastily wiped his mouth with the linen napkin and stood as she approached. "Good morning, Miss Dobbs. Beautiful morning."

"Yes, isn't it. A trifle cool, however, even in August."

"Oh, yes, this high altitude air is cool this early in the day, but the sun will warm things up."

"Oh, I hope so." She seemed to be waiting for something.

"Would you care to join me, Miss Dobbs?" He pulled out a chair for her.

"Why, yes, thank you." She sat and folded her hands in her lap. "I hate eating alone, and you seem to be a nice young man, and I do owe you my life."

"Oh, no, you don't owe me anything."

A white-coated waiter appeared and handed her a menu. She looked at it and frowned. "I don't see any eggs. I always have eggs for breakfast."

"No, no eggs this morning. The waiter said he expected a shipment today, but they have none to offer this morning. The toast and marmalade are very good."

She ordered toast, orange marmalade, bacon, and coffee. "I do hope you have cream for the coffee," she said to the waiter. "I always have cream in my coffee.'"

"Yes, ma'am," the waiter said. "We always have cream."

Alexander chuckled after the waiter left. "I'll bet they have their own cow out back. That's why they always have cream."

She smiled. Her eyes were the clearest blue he had ever seen. "Would you mind if I ask where you are from, Mr. Alexander? Pardon my curiosity, but you obviously are not a frontiersman."

"Chicago." He couldn't stop smiling at her.

"Are you a sales representative?"

"Oh, no. I'm an entrepreneur."

Her eyebrows went up. "Really? And do you believe there are investment opportunities on the frontier?"

She was no ignoramus. She knew what the word entrepreneur meant. "Yes. A lot of money is being made in the mining towns. My family commissioned me to find a business to invest in." He leaned forward. "Everyone tells me that a certain mine, which they call the Josey Mine, is very rich and will soon be operating again. And they tell me that you are the legal heir to that property."

Miss Josephine Dobbs looked down at her hands demurely, then turned those blue eyes on him again. "I am, Mr. Alexander. However, there seems to be some dispute about that. The gentleman you introduced me to yesterday, the man who claims to be Charles E. Dobbs, says he is the rightful heir."

Alexander smiled, enjoying the moment. "Yes, I know. I was offered a share in the mine by that gentleman. Of course I didn't buy it, and I won't until the courts award it to the rightful heirs. I mean, I

57

believe you, Miss Dobbs, but I must protect my investment legally."

"Of course you must. Tell me, do you know anything about gold mining?"

"Not a thing."

"I don't either. I wish I did. I must have another look at the mine."

"Another look?"

"Yes. The sheriff drove me there yesterday and to my father's cabin, but I would like to go back. I saw an old desk in the uh—what did Mr. Hutchins call it—the 'office shack,' I believe. I would like to look through it."

"What would you look for?"

"I don't know. Anything. As you said, Mr. Alexander, I'll have to prove that I am a daughter of the late Fred Dobbs, and I'd just like to see what I can see."

"What?" He was astonished. "Did you say the late Fred Dobbs? Why just yesterday you said your father's name was John Dobbs."

Smiling sweetly, she said, "Yes. And didn't the other gentleman repeat the name after me?"

Her breakfast was served then, and she shook out her napkin, placed it carefully on her lap, and took a sip of her coffee. "Ooh, it's hot." She avoided his eyes and took a dainty bite of her toast. "Umm, good." Now she was concentrating on her meal, ignoring him.

Alexander was trying to understand. She was the first to mention the name John Dobbs, and the other man repeated it. Now she was calling Buckshot Dobbs Fred. "Did you by any chance get a look at any papers or anything at the mine yesterday?"

She stopped chewing long enough to answer. "No. I wanted to go through that desk, but the sheriff said it was getting dark and we had to leave. He said everything had been searched anyway. Would you like to see the mine?"

"Huh? Oh, why yes. I would like very much to see it."

"Would you care to accompany me there?"

"I certainly would. But how are we to get there?"

"Can you drive a horse, Mr. Alexander? I think we can rent a horse and buggy."

"Sure. I've handled horses many times." But could he? He had driven a horse on the streets of Chicago, but not Out West. He remembered the way those mustangs behaved on the road yesterday, and now he wasn't so sure of himself. "That is, I have handled gentle horses. I uh—"

"We could walk."

"Walk? You?"

"Why not? It's only four miles, according to the sheriff, and I walked that far every time I went to school or to the theater in St. Louis."

"You walked?"

"Yes." Her eyes were serious.

"But what about the trams?"

"She looked down then, but only for a second. "Will you take my word for it, Mr. Alexander? I can walk."

"He shrugged. "O.K., if you can I certainly can. But have you heard about the Indians and panthers and rattlesnakes on the frontier?"

"That's bunkum. The Indians have been chased onto reservations, panthers don't attack people, and the altitude is too high for poisonous snakes."

"Oh," he said, feeling foolish. "I knew that. I, uh, I just wondered if you knew it." Was it really true, that there were none of those dangers? And was she suddenly someone else, no longer the demure Easterner?

She took the last sip of her coffee and dabbed at her mouth with the napkin. "Shall we get started? Suppose I meet you in the lobby in, oh, say twenty minutes. I'm almost ready."

"Sure. Twenty minutes." He watched her leave, admired the way she walked, wished he knew more about the out of doors and the Wild West. And about her.

Chapter Six

What to carry with him? The bowie knife, for one thing. He located the knife and its belt sheath in his luggage and again tested the blade. Sharp. After the sporting goods clerk had talked him into buying it— "Everyone who goes Out West must have a knife and this is the finest, a genuine bowie knife"—he had handed it to the scissors sharpener who came by the house with his pushcart asking for business. And now it had a razor edge.

What else? Matches. That's something else he had been talked into buying when he decided to come to El Tejon. He found the wooden matches in their thin metal case. What else? A compass? He wished he had brought a compass.

The new boots still hurt his left big toe, but he couldn't go for a long hike in the mountains wearing low, thin shoes. He grimaced as he pulled the left boot on and laced it up.

She kept him waiting fifteen minutes. Just like a woman, he muttered to himself. When she appeared, she was dressed the same as the day before, gray bell-shaped skirt and a white shirtwaist with ruffles on the sleeves. A wide straw hat sat securely on her head, and her gloves were of kidskin, silk-stitched, fancy. Her shoes were the high-top, lace-up kind, but with low heels and round toes. She waited for him to open the door for her, said "Thank you," then took off like a race horse.

The lady set a pace that was hard for a man with a sore toe to match, but he gritted his teeth and managed to keep up. She wasn't talking, only looking straight ahead, and her heels made a rapid staccato on the boardwalk. Not until they reached the end of the walk and started up the slight incline into the woods on the west side of town did she slow down.

Breathing heavily now, she said, "I'm not used to this altitude anymore."

He was panting for breath too and relieved that she had slowed her pace. "This—high, thin air—takes some getting used to." He finally caught his breath and asked, "Did you say you're not used to it anymore? Were you once?"

"Yes. I was raised in the mountains."

"You were?"

"But that was a long time ago." She walked on, leaving him with unasked questions.

He walked faster to catch up and looked at her, trying to think of a way to learn more about her background. She ignored him and concentrated on walking, stepping over the rocks and wagon ruts. Oh, well, they were going to spend most of the day together, and he would find a better time to ask.

The road was deserted that morning and seemed steeper than it did the day before. Alexander looked up at the high ridge on the north and quipped, "I hope we don't have to climb over that."

"No, we'll go around it. The mine is in a little quakie valley."

"A what?"

"A valley with a stand of quaking aspen."

"Oh. Is that what you mountaineers call aspen? Quakies?"

"Sometimes."

"You said you were raised in the mountains, where?"

"On Antler Creek, near Rosebud."

"That letter from Mr. Bear Tracks said Buckshot Dobbs had children. How many? Do you have a brother?"

She stopped and faced him. "You're just full of questions, aren't you?"

"Yes, well, I suppose it's none of my business, but I have this curiosity that won't quit."

"There's a little rhyme I learned when I was a kid, Mr. Alexander. It goes like this, 'Ask me no questions and I'll tell you no lies, keep your mouth shut and you'll catch no flies.'"

"O.K.," he said with a weak grin. "I've been properly chastised." Sore toe and all, he took the lead then and didn't look back. Let her catch up. Up to now he had been letting her set the pace. He had asked all the questions and done most of the talking. Let her break the quiet if she wanted to. And if she didn't want to, well, that was all right too.

When they walked past the stump-filled clearing and the cabin, he didn't even look in that direction but concentrated on his walking. He could hear her breathing hard behind him. Good. Served her right.

Soon he realized that they had walked around the end of the high ridge. The road went downhill a little for a short distance, then climbed again. Suddenly, they broke out of the pine forest and stood on the edge of a narrow valley full of aspen trees. He stopped and she stopped beside him.

"Are you angry with me, Mr. Alexander?"

"No." But he said it without conviction.

She moved in front of him and faced him. "Let me ask *you* something. Will you tell me who you really are?"

"Why, I—I told you."

"That's more bunkum."

"What? What are you saying?"

"You're a Pinkerton agent."

"How—how did you know?"

"You took the liberty of going into my room and reading my mail, so I went into your room and read your mail."

"You did?"

She shook her head affirmatively.

"How did you get in?"

"The same way you did. I picked the lock. With a hairpin."

"With a hairpin? That's all it took?"

Again she shook her head affirmatively, a smug little smile on her face.

"Well, I'll be—"

"Damned?"

"Yes. Yeah. Damned. How did you know I went into your room?"

"A little face powder spilled on the floor and a footprint. Not a shoe print, a footprint left by a man

64

in his stocking feet. That means it had to have been someone from one of the other rooms."

His mouth opened but he said nothing.

"And back there you said that Bear Tracks's letter mentioned my father had children. Nobody told you that."

Alexander shrugged and finally grinned. "O.K., so you know who I am. I suppose there's no use asking who you are. Anyway, now you know why I ask so many questions."

"I could report you to the sheriff, you know."

"Why didn't you?"

"I had a mind to, but I got to thinking I might need additional proof of my identity, and you might be of some help."

"I see. You're asking my help knowing that I might turn out to be your worst enemy? That's not very smart, Miss, uh, whoever you are."

Another sweet smile turned up the corners of her mouth. "Well, I'll just have to prove to you that I am Josephine Dobbs, one of two daughters of the late Fred "Buckshot" Dobbs."

He digested that, started to say something and changed his mind. Stupid, she definitely was not. If she could get him on her side, she would have a valuable ally. Finally, he said, "We'll see about that. Now show me that mine."

It wasn't much farther. A narrow wagon road branched off the main road and cut through the aspens. A few of the aspens had fallen across the road since it had been used.

"Those trees grow fast and die fast," she commented. "Here's where we tied the horse yesterday."

He saw the buggy tracks, horse tracks and a small pile of manure where the animal had been tied to a tree. "I see. I see the mine too. I guess that's what it is."

What he saw were four tin shacks and a big steam boiler behind one of them. A tall headframe with a large pulley at the top stood over that shack. Another had the word "powder" painted in a sloppy fashion on the side, and another had "office" painted in the same fashion on the door.

The next thing he saw was a ten-foot-wide hole in the side of a high steep ridge with wooden steps leading up to it. Narrow rails came out of the hole and an ore cart was sitting on the rails. Fractured rock had been dumped off the side of the hill where the rails ended.

He stopped and took a long look around. The only sign of life was a tiny striped chipmunk that scampered under one of the tin shacks. She led the way.

"Here's where I saw the desk," she said, leading the way to the office. "Right in here."

The door to the shack she went to was already half open, and he followed her inside. The desk sat beside a small wood-burning stove. A wooden chair sat beside the desk and another chair sat just inside the door. She went to the desk, paused, looked back at him and said, "No telling what kind of rodents might have made their home in here. But, uh, here goes."

"Want me to open it?" He didn't really want to but he thought it would be the gentlemanly thing to do.

"No, I'll do it." She lifted on the top front and it rolled up, exposing a half-dozen pigeonholes and a flat work space. He stepped up beside her, half expecting a rat or something to come out of one of the pigeonholes.

"Are there rats around here?" he asked.

"Yes. When people move out of buildings, the pack rats move in. They're harmless though."

"I see. Then why don't you take a look in those?" He nodded at the pigeonholes.

"I will." She reached out a hand, carefully pulled a sheaf of folded papers out of one of the holes, blew the dust off, and began fumbling the papers open. "I can't quite make them out. Looks like business papers."

"Let me see." He took them from her hands and examined them. "Business papers, all right. Here's a bill of lading for some iron single-jack drills, whatever they are. And this one's for a dozen eight-pound sledges and a half-dozen square-tipped shovels. All written in a good hand. Definitely not Buckshot Dobbs's hand."

She stood close and looked across his arm at the papers. "How do you know it isn't my father's penmanship?"

Casting a sidelong glance at her, he said, "I know, that's all."

She took his arm and turned him toward her. "Oh you do, do you? You think you're so smart. Well, let me tell you something, I know my dad was illiterate, and I also know he was trying to learn to write. Don't you think it's possible he did finally learn? He wasn't stupid, you know."

He had to grin at her outrage. But he obviously knew more about Buckshot Dobbs than she. "No," he said, "he never did learn."

"How do you know so much?"

He didn't answer and instead reached into another cubbyhole and took out another sheaf of papers. "More bills of lading, written in the same hand. Uh, oh, here's a signature. Let's see. Bertrum Wingate. Yep, Bertrum Wingate."

He turned to her puzzled. She wore a puzzled frown too. Suddenly, she brightened. "Oh, now I know. Bertrum Wingate was Dad's employee. He is someone he hired to do the paperwork. Maybe you're right. Maybe Dad never did learn to write."

"Then where is this Mr. Wingate?"

"Dead, probably. The sheriff told me two men were killed in an accidental blast in a tunnel and my dad was one of them. Mr. Wingate was probably the other one."

"Makes sense, all right. Otherwise, he would be the one the authorities would talk to, to learn more about your, uh, Mr. Dobbs."

"And," she added, almost to herself, "that would explain why those letters my mother got last winter were so legible. Mr. Wingate wrote them. Yes, this looks like the same hand."

"Umm. Well, if he did any correspondence by mail, someone had to do the writing. And I can understand why your, uh, Mr. Dobbs would want to conceal that fact."

"That explains it. Mother couldn't believe Dad had learned to write that well."

"Then there really are letters from your dad to your mother?"

"Of course." Suddenly she frowned again. "There were. They were destroyed in a fire."

"In a fire, you say? Then you can't produce them?"

"No."

"Uh huh."

"What are you thinking, Mr. Alexander?" Her eyes were green now. "That I just made up a story about those letters? Well, let me tell you something, there really were letters."

He met her angry gaze for a moment, then looked away. "O.K., if you say so. But," he glanced at her again, "that's a pretty handy reason for not being able to produce them."

She snorted, "Huh," and turned away angrily.

No longer thinking about rats or any other possible danger, Alexander went through the other cubbyholes and found more business correspondence, including copies of two orders for dynamite. The orders were to be shipped to Mr. Frederick Dobbs at El Tejon, Colorado. Fred Dobbs. There was no doubt now that Buckshot Dobbs's real name was Frederick.

Next Alexander opened the two drawers in the desk and riffled the papers he found in them. A book he opened listed the names of the employees and their wages. He counted the names. Forty-eight. The Josey Mine employed forty-eight men. Yes, it probably was the biggest business around there. Closing it had to have been an economic blow to the community of El Tejon.

Alexander turned to look over the rest of the room—and froze instantly. The young woman heard his sudden intake of breath and looked in the direction he was looking.

She let out a shriek.

Two men stood in the doorway. They had big pistols in their hands, and the pistols were pointed at Alexander and the girl.

Chapter Seven

For a long moment no one spoke. Alexander stood petrified. He had never looked down the barrel of a gun before. The girl's next shriek stuck in her throat.

Finally, one of the men looked at the other and broke into a giggle. "Caught 'em in the act," he said between giggles.

"Yup," said the other, deadpan. "Found 'em snoopin' where they don't belong."

Relief swept over Alexander. These men were guards, hired to guard a valuable gold mine. He smiled with relief. "Listen, we have a right to be here. This is Miss Josephine Dobbs, daughter of the late Buckshot Dobbs. You gentlemen don't know it, but she could very well be your next employer."

The giggler giggled again. The other man raised his pistol and pointed it at a spot between Alexander's eyes. "That ain't funny. She ain't never gonna be no boss of mine."

"Listen." Alexander wasn't so sure of himself now. These looked like the same men who had tried to rob the bank. "Listen, we haven't taken anything. We were just searching for papers with her father's name on them, that's all."

The giggler shuffled his feet and spoke, "He's a talker, a real spieler. Wonder if he's got any spendulics in them brand-new britches." He was slender with nervous eyes. Both men wore slouchy hats, bib overalls, and heavy jackboots.

"Turn your pockets inside out," the other man said. He was husky with a dark face, heavy black eyebrows, and thick lips.

"Why?" Alexander couldn't keep his voice from revealing the fear that went through him. "What do you want?"

The husky man took two long steps toward Alexander and let him have a closer look at the bore of the gun. "You do as you're told, city slicker, or I'll shoot another hole in your head."

He had no choice. He turned his pants pockets inside out, allowing his change to drop out of a side pocket.

"Turn around."

Alexander did as ordered. The giggler lifted his wallet out of a hip pocket and opened it. "Look at this," he said, holding a card up to the husky man's eyes.

"What is it?"

"I don't know." The giggler turned the card over, frowned at it, and began to spell: "P-I-N-K-E-R-T-O-N. Pink-er-ton. Pinkerton. That's what it says. He's a Pinkerton."

"That so?" the husky one asked.

"Yes."

"What you doin' here?"

"That's none of your business."

The husky man's pistol came up and hit Alexander on the side of the face. It happened so fast he didn't have time to dodge it. He staggered back, stunned, his face numb.

"Oh," the girl cried as if she had been hit.

"Don't talk to me like that," the husky one said. "When I holler, you jump. Savvy?"

"Teach 'im some respect for his elders," the giggler said.

They both glared at Alexander for a moment, then the giggler turned his attention to the girl. "Now her."

"Oh, no," she said, backing away, horror in her eyes.

"Leave her alone," Alexander said.

"You want some more, city feller?"

"No. I mean, please don't hurt her."

"What you gonna do about it?"

"I—I don't know."

"What if I put this gun down and gave you a good whuppin'?"

Alexander had hope then. He had learned to box. He could take care of himself in a fair fight. "I certainly would defend myself."

The giggler giggled. "Whup 'im. He's too purty. Make 'im look like a man."

But the husky one seemed to be thinking it over. "Naw. It wouldn't do to leave 'em all beat up. Wouldn't look right."

"Why not?"

" 'Cause we got to make it look like a accident. We don't want 'im found with two black eyes and his teeth knocked out."

73

After a second the giggler had to agree. "Yeah, wouldn't look right. They want it to look like a accident."

"Oughta be easy, the way they been snoopin' around. That drift's ready to cave in anyhow."

"Yeah, it'll look like they poked around in there and bumped into a timber and the whole damn hill came down on 'em."

"All right, you two, outside." The husky man's gun didn't waver.

"Where—where are we going?" Alexander was almost afraid to ask.

"Just walk where I tell you to."

They walked, two guns behind them. "Up there," the giggler said, nodding in the direction of the wooden steps that led to the big hole in the hill. They climbed the steps, walked past the empty ore car, and stopped at the entrance to the tunnel.

"Wait here," the husky man said. "Don't move. If they move a inch, put a forty-five slug in 'em," he said to the giggler.

"You know where they keep the powder?" the giggler asked.

"Yeah. Over there in that shack." The husky one went down the steps and headed toward one of the tin buildings.

"What—what are you going to do?" Alexander asked. The girl was quiet.

"Berry ya. Just like we done Ol' Buckshot and his sidekick. A little powder and you"ll never git out of there alive."

"You—you buried them? Murdered them?"

The giggler giggled.

Alexander glanced back into the tunnel. The horror of what was planned knifed through him like a cold wind. They were going to be marched into that hole at gunpoint, and the hole was going to be blown up. That's what happened to Buckshot Dobbs and Bertrum Wingate. They didn't die of an accident. It was murder. What could he do?

Trembling with fear, Alexander shot a glance at the girl. Her face was white and she was trembling too. They were about to be murdered. He had to do something.

The giggler looked back downhill and yelled, "Find it?"

"Yeah." The other man was coming out of the shed, carrying a small wooden keg.

He had to do something and he had to do it now.

Swiftly, he stepped in front of the giggler, jabbed at his face with his right fist, and grabbed for his gun hand with the left.

The giggler was startled enough that he staggered back, cursing.

Alexander got a grip on the gun and continued jabbing with his right fist. The giggler twisted his head away, staggered back again, and stumbled over a large rock. With Alexander's fist in his face, he went down hard on the seat of his pants, yelling now for help.

Alexander concentrated on twisting the gun out of the man's grasp and finally succeeded. But the gun was knocked out of his grasp too and went sliding down the hill. The giggler struggled to get up.

Trained in the manly art of self-defense, Alexander allowed his opponent to stand, then went into his stance. He kept his elbows down and his fists pointed upward, left fist out ahead of the right one. He stood with his left foot ahead of the right foot too, ready to jab and punch with his left fist while watching for an opening for his right.

He had control of the situation now. No one not trained in pugilism could be a match for him.

The giggler stood still for a moment, puzzled at what confronted him. Then with an angry growl he ducked his head and charged.

Alexander's left fist connected solidly, but with the top of the man's head. A sharp pain went through Alexander's hand and up his forearm, leaving it numb.

A split second later, the man's head crashed into his face, knocking him backward. He tried to throw punches, but the man was too close. His head was right in Alexander's face.

Again, Alexander was butted, and then the man had him in a bear hug, pushing him backward. Blood spurted from Alexander's nose and ran into his mouth.

Suddenly, the man's hold loosened. Suddenly, he was dancing a jig, trying to ward off blows from the young woman. She had picked up a rock and was beating at his head furiously.

"Leave—us—alone."

All the man could do was stagger back and cover his head with his arms.

Alexander's left hand was still numb, but he got in a lick with his right fist.

Then a bright light and a blinding pain tore through his brain, and he felt himself falling.

* * *

He was vaguely aware of being dragged by the arms across a rocky surface. He could hear men panting with exertion, and he could hear someone whimpering. A woman. He blinked his eyes and shook his head, trying to clear his brain. A woman whimpering? What was happening?

A man spoke. "This's fur enough." He was dropped onto his back. He couldn't see. "Mebbe I oughta lay her out with a gun barrel too."

"No, she'll stay put. And this'n ain't goin' nowheres."

"Yeah, I hit 'im hard enough that he won't wake up for a long time. Mebbe never."

"Let's go."

He heard footsteps going away, but still he couldn't see. The girl was whimpering again. He felt her hands on him. "Mr. Alexander. Please."

What was happening? He shook his head and blinked again.

"Please, Mr. Alexander. They're going to kill us. Can you hear me?"

He willed his lips to move, but all that came from them was a groan. He tried again. "Uh, uh, what . . . ?"

"They're going to blow up the tunnel, Mr. Alexander. They're going to kill us."

"Huh? What . . . ?" Move, lips. Talk. "What's going on? Who's . . . ?"

"Those two ruffians. They killed my dad and Mr. Wingate and now they're going to kill us."

He reached up and touched his head. One side was

covered with something sticky. Blood? "What happened?"

"You were hit on the head with a gun. One of them ran up behind you and hit you on the head while you were struggling with the other. You were unconscious when they dragged you in here."

"Where—where are we?"

"In the tunnel. They're going to blow it up with black powder."

He sat up, feeling groggy. "We have to get out of here."

"We can't. They're waiting out there with guns. If we try to leave, they'll shoot us."

"We can't just sit here and wait. We have to move." He got to his knees, felt her pulling up on his arm, and finally stood. His knees were trembling, but he said, "Come on."

"I'll help you, but I'm afraid of those men, those guns." She kept her hold on his arm. She was no longer whimpering.

He took a step, two steps. He could see the end of the tunnel now. "We can't just sit here and wait for them to—Did you say they're going to blow it up?"

"Yes."

"My God. Then we have to get back. Get away from the blast. If we get closer to the entrance the concussion will kill us. Come on." He grabbed at her in the dark and pulled her farther back into the tunnel. As he hurried he stumbled over rocks and the ore-car rails, and he repeatedly glanced back at the entrance to keep himself oriented. She was breathing hard, trying to keep up.

For the second time a bright light shot through his

brain, and he felt as if he had been hit in the back with a battering ram. He pitched forward onto his face and almost lost consciousness again. Rocks rained down on him, pummeling him.

The girl screamed.

Covering his head with his arms, he lay there helpless until the rocks stopped falling. She was moaning. Dust billowed in toward them. Thick, choking dust. It was pitch dark.

Coughing, he turned over on his back. He tried to see but everything was black. She was coughing now. Good. At least they were both alive. Groping with his right hand, he found one of her feet. She was lying on her stomach.

For a long while they both lay there, coughing, trying to get a lungful of clean air. He was the first to move, getting to his knees. Then she struggled to her knees. They stayed in that position for several minutes, too weak to stand.

Finally, he managed to speak. "You O.K.? Are you hurt?"

"No." The word came out with a gasp from a tortured throat. "I—I don't think so."

Gradually, the dust settled and breathing was easier. He managed to stand and move his arms. No bones were broken. He could move.

"Mr. Alexander? Are you all right?"

"Yes. Can you stand?"

He heard the rustle of her clothing as she struggled to her feet. "Yes. I'm standing."

"Can you see anything?"

"No, not a thing."

"I guess they did what they said they were going to

do. We're sealed in here."

"Oh." She was silent, then a whimper came out of her. "I'm sorry. I can't help it." She was crying softly.

"It's excusable, Miss Dobbs. We're in a bad fix."

"We're going to die here, aren't we?"

"That's what they think." He groped for her, got a hand on her shoulder. "Go ahead and cry, but don't use up any more oxygen than you have to."

She sniffled, "Why?"

"If we're sealed in here the air won't last long. We'll die of suffocation."

"Is there—is there anything we can do?"

"I don't know. Can you walk?"

"Yes."

"Let's see, which way was the opening?"

"I think it was that way. Why? Are you turned around?"

"I am disoriented. I thing it was this way."

His head hurt, but he was thinking clearly now. He groped for her and found an arm. "All right," he said without enthusiasm, "let's walk in this direction."

They shuffled their feet and carefully picked their way, often stumbling over shattered rocks. They went fifteen feet and ran into a wall.

"Oh, God, I wish I could see," he said. "Well, let's go this way then." He turned and started picking his way.

"Wait. Take my hand, please. I don't want to lose you." She wasn't crying anymore.

Taking her hand in his, he continued walking, groping with his feet, straining his eyes, trying to see. It couldn't be much farther. When he collided with a wall again he made a half-turn and kept going. How deep was the mine? Probably plenty deep. Well, at least they wouldn't run out of air for awhile.

"Do—do you think we're going in the right direction, Mr. Alexander?"

"I don't know. If we don't come to where the entrance used to be pretty soon, then we'd better turn around."

"What will we do when we find the entrance? I mean what used to be the entrance."

"Dig. With our hands. That's all we can do. Maybe a miracle will happen and we can dig out."

"You're right. That's all we can do."

They shuffled on.

"Mr. Alexander?"

"Huh?"

"I think we're going the wrong way. We should have come to something by now."

"You're right. Let's turn around. We're probably just going deeper into the mine."

They turned around and went back the way they had come, walking faster now. He held onto her hand.

"Mr. Alexander?"

"What?"

"I'm sorry I got you into this. It's my fault. It's me they want to kill. You just happened to be with me."

"How do you know that?"

"The way they talked. They were carrying out someone's instructions."

He was concentrating on his walking. "Yeah."

Twice she tripped and would have fallen had he not kept his grip on her hand. Once he fell onto his knees. He got up feeling as if his knees were raw ground beef.

Again he collided with a wall, and he shifted his

direction obliquely. It seemed they had gone farther in this direction than they did in the other direction. They had to come to something soon.

He tripped and fell again, and when he got up he tripped again. He put out his hands and discovered a huge pile of fractured rock in front of them.

"Here it is. This has to be the place where the tunnel opened."

"Yes. It feels like it might be."

"It's not a solid wall like the others we ran into. I wish I could see." He heard her grunt and strain. "What are you doing?"

"Trying to pick up one of these rocks. Wonder how many there are?"

"Thousands. But, well, let's get started."

A rock clattered behind him. "I've already started," she said. Another rock rolled down onto his hand.

"Let's start at the top, or as near as we can get. Throw them behind us."

Without answering, she climbed as high on the pile as she could and started dropping rocks off the pile. He climbed until he could feel the ceiling with his hands and started picking up rocks and throwing them.

Grunting, eyes stinging from dust, they worked. Two hours later his arms felt numb and his fingers were raw. Fatigue forced him to stop for a moment. She was quiet.

"You O.K.?"

"Yes. Tired though. Very tired. Do you think we have a chance in the world of digging out of here?"

"I don't know. It's the only chance we have."

"My gloves are worn through already and my

fingers are sore."

"Mine too."

"Do you think we'll run out of oxygen?"

"I don't know. Not for awhile. There has to be a lot of air in this mine."

"Perhaps we should have gone on into the tunnel. Maybe we could find some tools there."

"I thought about that, but I don't know what good a pick and shovel would do. These rocks are too big to pick up with a shovel."

She sighed. "You're right. The only thing that will do the job is our hands."

"Yeah." He straightened up, picked up more rocks, and threw them behind him. She did the same.

They worked for several more hours, breathing heavily. His arms felt like lead weights, and his hands had lost all feeling. When a long groan came from her, he stopped and sat on his haunches.

She spoke in a strained voice. "I can't—I just can't do it anymore."

"Rest a minute."

"I'm sorry. I ache so much." Her voice cracked. "We're going to die, aren't we?"

He allowed a long sigh to escape. "I wish I could tell you everything was going to be all right, Miss Dobbs. But there's no telling how many tons of rock we have to move to get out of here. Maybe more than we can possibly move."

She started crying softly again. He wanted to touch her, put an arm around her. Why not? Groping, he found her shoulders and hugged her to him. He caressed her hair. He remembered how soft and lovely she was that day—how long ago?—when he had

83

thrown her to the floor in the bank and had lain on top of her. "Oh, God," he said. He felt like crying himself.

Then a horrifying realization came to him: it was getting hard to breathe. Were they running out of air? "Oh, God," he said again, releasing her and straightening up.

Grabbing at rocks furiously, he ignored the pain in his arms and hands. "Not much time left," he grunted. "Got to move this—this damnable pile of rocks. Got to hurry."

She too realized what was happening, and she too resumed working furiously.

Grunting, straining, crying with frustration, they worked. Was there no end? Damn it, there had to be. Move, you damnable rocks, move.

He heard her groan and heard a clatter of rocks. "Miss Dobbs? Josephine? What happened?"

Her groan came from below him, and he realized that she had collapsed and slid down to the floor of the tunnel.

"Josephine." Fear welled up in him. She had collapsed with fatigue and would not be able to go on. Thinking about how it was all up to him now, he managed to renew his attack on the rocks, grunting, cursing, grabbing, and throwing rocks. Then his feet gave out from under him and he felt himself sliding down to the tunnel floor. He tried to scramble back up, but his knees gave out and he could only sit and moan.

It was over now. They were both too weak to do anymore. Breathing was becoming more and more difficult. How long? Less than an hour. Maybe not that long. Probably a half-hour.

He found her hand again and held it tightly. Her fingers moved slightly but she was too exhausted to move her arm. She was right, they were going to die.

He wondered how long it would be before their bodies were found. If they were ever found. Yes, they would be. Sooner or later the mine would be reopened and they would be found. The mine was too valuable to remain abandoned. Funny. They were in a valuable gold mine and they were dying in the midst of gold. Funny.

Only not so funny.

Wearily, he raised his head and looked up at what used to be the entrance to the mine. Lights were shooting through his brain again, just as they did when he was hit by a gun. He must be losing consciousness again. His eyes were seeing sparkles. Why fight it? Just lie back and let death come. It wouldn't be long now.

Chapter Eight

Wait a minute. Wait just a gosh darn minute. Sparkles? Lights? He opened his eyes and looked up again. A light?

He blinked, shook his head, and looked again. The light was still there. Tiny. And very dim. But definitely a light.

Hope gave him new strength and he scrambled to his feet and crawled up the pile of rocks. Yes, daylight was coming through near the ceiling. Wonderful daylight.

Working feverishly, he clawed at the rocks and opened a small hole. He put his face to the hole and breathed deeply. Wonderful, beautiful, delicious fresh air. It gave him strength. He clawed at the rocks again and opened the hole wider. He could almost put his head through now.

They were going to live.

"Josephine!" His voice was excited. "Josephine, look! Look up here! Daylight!"

No answer.

With a knot of fear in his throat he slid down to her. He could see now, but only vaguely. He got an arm under her shoulders and raised her to a sitting position. She groaned.

"Come on. You've got to get up. There's fresh air up there. Come on." He got his hands under her armpits and straightened her up. She got her feet under her, trying.

"Come on, Josephine. Please. Try harder. We're going to live."

Unintelligible noises were coming from her throat, but she was trying to stand.

"Climb up here. It's not far. Up here the air is clean and fresh. Come on, please."

He pushed and she climbed. She was like a large rag doll, ready to collapse if he let go his hold. "Uh," she grunted. "I can see it."

They had to stand precariously on the side of a huge mound of broken rocks to get their faces up to the hole, but the fresh air was reviving. It was like a drink of cool water to a couple suffering from dehydration.

"Ooh, nothing ever felt better," she said. When he looked over at her he saw that her blond hair was down in her face and her face was dirt-streaked. Still, she was beautiful.

"Now let's get out of here," he said, moving back and grabbing at rocks. "Won't take much more and we can crawl through."

She helped, clawing at rocks and pushing them down to the tunnel floor. Gradually, the hole widened.

"I think we can get through now," he said. "You go first and I'll follow."

She got her head and shoulders through and was stuck. Alexander pulled on a large rock that was under her shoulders and finally moved it. "That ought to help. Try again." She squirmed, wriggled, and kicked with her feet and finally got her hips through. Her long gray skirt was filthy and one of her high-topped shoes was partially unlaced.

"Can you see anything?"

"Yes. I can see the buildings and the trees and the grass. It's a wonderful sight, Mr. Alexander."

"O.K., when you get outside I'll follow you."

"I'll have to slide down this pile of rocks head first, but I'll make it."

"Where are we in relation to the opening in the tunnel?"

"Just inside a little ways. Some of the logs holding up the entrance are askew."

"Be careful."

When her feet went through the hole he knew she was upside down, but she was outside and safe. Her voice came back to him as if from far away. "I'm all right. Can you get out?"

"I'm a little bigger than you, but I think I can get through."

He put his arms through the hole and his head followed. But he couldn't get his shoulders through. "I'll have to move some more rocks, but it won't take long." He pulled back and clawed at the rocks around the hole until the hole was enlarged. "I can make it now. I'm coming."

"Let me help you," she yelled.

He could hear her moving rocks on the other side of the hole, and he put his arms over his head again, preparing to reach through. Then he felt the rocks under his feet shift, felt himself sliding back down, heard her scream, and saw the opening close.

Thick dust billowed up around him, and again he was in total darkness. The whole pile of rocks shifted, and he felt himself being borne downward, down to the tunnel floor. Rocks slid down with him, and he covered his head with his arms.

He knew immediately what had happened. Her weight on the other side of the pile had caused it to shift and that brought more of the tunnel down on him. Maybe on her too. Again, he was sealed inside the mine.

And again he felt helpless. His arms were too weary and his hands too sore to dig anymore. For a time he sat with his knees drawn up and his head resting on his knees. How many more rocks would he have to move? Could he do it? Another long groan came from his lips.

For the second time he thought about death. They would at least find his body, now that the girl was outside. How would his family take it? Very, very hard. They were a close family. He couldn't remember hearing about any of his relatives dying young. He would be the first. Well, he thought with chagrin, that's the way it should be. He was the adventurer, the one who had quit law school and become a private detective, the one to go Out West.

Did he do something unbelievably stupid, quitting school? He had had an opportunity that ninety-nine percent of the young men of the nation could only dream about. He had hurt himself, and he had hurt his family very much. Why? He didn't know. It was an unexplainable itch, an itch to do something different. Something on his own.

And now it was all over. His mother would suffer terribly.

A sob formed in his throat, and for a second he felt like crying. But with determination, he managed to force down the sob, and he stood up slowly. By George, they would know he died trying.

Willing himself to move, he slowly climbed, clawed, and scrambled up to the roof of the tunnel. If only he could see. His fingers were raw and when he touched rocks with them the pain was unbearable. Any kind of tool would be better than using his fingers again.

He remembered the bowie knife he carried on his belt and took it from its sheath. The blade was long enough that he could dig with it—he hoped. He tried but got nowhere. The rocks were too big to shove aside with a knife blade. But dammit the knife ought to be good for something.

Working by feel, he cut off a piece of denim from the bottom of his right pants leg and wrapped it around his right hand. It helped. He could handle the rocks with less pain now. Next he cut a piece from his left pants leg and wrapped it around his left hand. He put the knife back in its sheath and worked with both hands, moving rocks and dropping them down to the tunnel floor.

At least he had more air. The hole had let in fresh air while it lasted. He wondered if Miss Dobbs was safe or lying under a pile of shattered rocks. If she was safe, she'd go for help. If. The most important word in the English language. Working automatically, without feeling, he continued pulling, pushing, and rolling rocks.

Finally, he had to quit. He just couldn't raise his

arms anymore, and the denim padding was worn to shreds. He was thinking more and more about the girl, wondering if she was safe and whether she would bring help. Or would she run into those cutthroats again? If she was dead, then he was as good as dead. He slid down to the tunnel floor and sat on his haunches. He sat there for a long time. The air was stifling, and breathing was becoming difficult again. He was too tired to care.

At first, when he felt and heard rocks and dirt sliding down from the pile, he thought nothing of it. But then he heard a noise. Something went "thunk," and more rocks rolled down. His head came up. What was it? There it was again. Thunk. A pause, then, thunk.

Someone was digging from the other side. She had found help. Someone was working to free him from the other side.

He managed to get up and climb to the ceiling. He tried shoving rocks, but his fingers felt like bare bones. More thunks and then he saw daylight. He yelled, "Hey." His voice was hoarse and weak, but he yelled again. "Hey."

"Mr. Alexander?"

It was her. She was on the other side.

"Hey."

"I'm breaking through. It won't be long now, Mr. Alexander."

Thunk. The hole opened wider. Thunk.

"Are you all right? Can you hear me?"

"Yes. I can hear you."

Thunk, thunk. Now he could see through the hole. She was standing on a large timber that had fallen horizontally across the mine entrance, and she was swinging a pickax. With every swing, she grunted with exertion, but with every swing the hole grew wider.

"I'm getting it, Mr. Alexander. Thank God, you're all right."

"If I can just move these two big rocks," he said, "I think I can get through."

With sore fingers, he managed to loosen two large rocks and send them rolling and sliding down the pile. The hole was big enough then.

"O.K., I'm coming out. Is anyone with you?"

"No, just me. Be careful, Mr. Alexander."

When he got his head and shoulders through, she pulled on his arms and helped him. His hips and finally his knees came through. He was upside down, but he was outside, and the timber she was standing on seemed solid. He got his hands on it and then his knees. And then he was standing beside her.

At first he couldn't talk and couldn't move, only stand there and stare at the scenery around him. It was near sundown, but he could see the tin shacks, the headframe and pulley over one of them, and the trees. Finally, he looked at her.

"Do you know something, Miss Dobbs? You're the most beautiful sight in the world."

The corners of her mouth turned up slightly and her hands went to her hair. "I'm a sight, all right. I know I'm a mess."

Moving sorely, he climbed down from the timber and held up a hand for her. When they were both safely on the ground just inside the mine entrance, he had an urge to take her in his arms and hug and kiss her, but he didn't think she would appreciate that. Instead he put one hand on her shoulder and said, "Josephine, you're wonderful. I thought you'd be gone long before now."

"I couldn't. I thought at first that I should hurry back to town and get help, but I wasn't sure there was enough air in there. I found that pick and decided to try to dig you out."

"You saved my life. I couldn't have done it by myself."

She took a tentative step and stopped. "Ooh, every bone in my body aches. Oh, I wish we had a ride back to town. That bathtub at the hotel will be wonderful."

He took her hands in his to help her walk and noticed their pitiable condition. Her nails were broken, her fingertips were raw, and the palms were blistered.

By helping each other they climbed down the wooden steps and off the side of the hill. She stopped and knelt to tie her shoe, but her sore fingers couldn't handle the strings. He knelt and tied the shoe for her. It would be a long walk back to town.

"I remember seeing a brook over there in the woods," he said. "A drink of water would taste good."

"Yes, I remember."

They found the creek, a narrow rivulet that came out of the side of the hill and meandered through the aspens. They had to lie face down and put their lips to the water to drink. He straightened up first and looked down at her. She had strong shoulders for a woman, a slender waist and—he forced himself to look away.

When she sat up, he noticed for the first time that she had lost the hat she had left town with, and he realized that he had lost his hat too.

"Your poor face," she said. "And your head. For a time there I thought the blow had killed you."

Managing a crooked grin, he fingered his head, found the dried blood on the side of his head, and found the dried blood on his upper lip. He knelt beside the rivulet and washed his face. The cold water made him feel better.

She did the same.

"I think I can go on now," she said. "Wouldn't it be wonderful if somebody came along in a wagon and gave us a ride back to town?"

He grinned. "Yeah, that would be wonderful."

By the time they had walked back to the main road, dusk had come and with it cooler air. They limped along through the trees, each step a struggle. His big toe was hurting again. The sound of horses' hooves clattering over the rocky road gave them hope for a second—but only for a second. The horses were coming around a bend and through the trees ahead of them. Not behind them.

"I have to rest awhile," she said. "Just let me sit here on this rock for a few minutes." She sat on a knee-high boulder at the side of the road. She put her elbows on her knees and her chin in her hands.

"Sure, rest awhile. We'd probably scare the horses anyway if we stood in the road." He was looking at her, feeling sorry for her and wishing he could carry her to town when suddenly she sat up straight and let out a small scream.

He looked where she was looking and saw the two horsemen ride around a curve in the road. It was the two ruffians, the giggler and the husky bully.

The horsemen were talking and didn't see the man and woman until they were within twenty feet of them. They reined up suddenly. The giggler squawked in surprise and grabbed for the gun on his hip. The husky one said, "What the hairy hell—?" and grabbed for his gun too.

Alexander acted without thinking. At least he was not aware of thinking. But he remembered the team of horses he had accidentally scared on the same road, and he acted.

With a wild whoop he jumped toward the horses, waving his arms and whooping at the top of his voice.

The giggler had his gun out and he fired, but his aim was spoiled by the horse he was riding. The horse snorted, ducked backward, and went in the opposite direction, kicking at the sky with both heels. "Whoa," the giggler yelled. "Whoa, you stump-headed sonofabitch."

The husky man's horse did a toe dance, forcing its rider to concentrate on staying in the saddle. Alexander whooped, waved his arms, and jumped toward the horse.

The animal, thinking some kind of wild beast was attacking, spun around and tried to catch up with the giggler's horse. Its rider fell onto its neck, dropped his gun, and grabbed for the saddle horn.

"Run," Alexander yelled to the girl. "Through the trees."

She ran, holding her long skirts up above her shoe tops. He caught up with her, took her arm, and helped her along as they ran through the trees, around boulders, over fallen timbers, and across gullies. He expected to hear the horses come up behind them any second. They ran.

Twice she stumbled, and he held her up, but the third time she tripped they both went down. Their breathing was coming in gasps, and they couldn't talk. She started to struggle up, but he pulled her down, trying to tell her that they were in a gully and might be safer than up and running.

When he heard the horses coming he crawled on top of her and shielded her body with his own. The horses came on at a gallop, and the giggler was swearing. Alexander buried his face in her hair and waited for the bullet that would end his life. Instead the horses went on, and the giggler was still cursing the horse, the darkness, and that "damn old powder."

For awhile he felt safe. He got to his knees, then sat on the ground, and hugged his knees. She raised herself up too and looked around.

"Are they gone?"

"Yeah, I think they are."

"I hope they don't come back."

"It's getting darker. In a few minutes, they won't be able to see us."

"Shall we stay here?"

"Yeah. Until it's good and dark."

They sat, hugging their knees, watching the woods turn darker. Eventually, he stood and helped her up. "Which way?" she asked.

"Back that way," he answered.

They started walking, and heard the horses coming again. They ducked back into the gully. They heard one of the men curse the "damned tree limbs and this barrel-headed sonofabitch that runs under ever' damn tree limb he can find."

The husky one was grumbling, "Should of gone back sooner, before dark. Should of knowed that old powder didn't have enough kick."

"We gotta find 'em," the giggler said.

By the time their voices faded into the darkness it was night and so dark that Alexander could barely make out the shape of the trees. He stood again and helped her up.

"What should we do?" she asked.

"We'll have to stay off the road. They're looking for us. We'll cut through the trees and get back to town that way."

"Do you know which way to go?"

"I think so. It has to be this way." He led her by the arm in what he thought was the right direction. But in his mind he knew he could be disoriented again.

Chapter Nine

Trees, low-hanging tree limbs, tree roots, rocks, boulders, hills, gullies, and darkness all combined to make traveling extremely difficult. After running into tree limbs and stumbling over roots for the twentieth time, they stopped. She dropped to the ground and sat on her feet. He dropped beside her.

It was time to tell her what had been going through his mind. As much as he hated to, he had to tell her. "Uh, Miss Dobbs. Josephine."

A weary "Yes," came from her.

"I hate to tell you this, but I have no idea where we are."

"I guessed as much."

"I turned left back there, thinking we would have to come to the road. I thought we could follow the road and, if we happened onto those men, we could escape again in the dark. Now, I'm afraid that I can't even find the road."

She was silent, and he feared she was crying silently. But when she spoke finally, her voice was calm. "I suppose it was foolish of us to wander around in the dark. We'll have to wait for daylight."

"Yeah." He looked at the sky, what little of it he could see through the treetops. "There's a three-quarter moon. If we could find our way out of these woods, it wouldn't be so dark. But you're right, we'd better stay still until daylight."

Sitting there, not moving, he realized that the temperature had dropped about twenty degrees since dusk, and he shivered audibly.

"It's so cold," she said through clenched teeth. He unbuttoned his shirt, a heavy muslin shirt, and put it around her shoulders. "Here, this will help."

"Oh, no. You'd freeze." She shrugged it off.

"No, I have an undershirt. Besides it isn't cold enough to freeze."

"I can't take it." She pushed it back to him.

He tried to think of something he could do to keep her warm, but he could think of nothing. He groped the ground for firewood but found none. She had an idea. "I'm wearing a petticoat under this wool skirt, and I can take the skirt off and wrap it around my shoulders."

"Won't your, uh, legs get cold?"

Shivering, teeth chattering, she said, "Not as cold as my—the rest of me. The petticoat is a long one."

She stood and unbuttoned her skirt. He could barely see her in the dark as she stepped out of it, though her white petticoat was plainly visible. "That's better," she said as she sat down again. "You'd better put your shirt back on." He did.

Twice during the night he heard a rustling in the grass and pine needles on the ground. He had no idea what it was, but he was too tired to be afraid of anything. He lay back on his side and pulled his knees up against his chest, and finally, in spite of the cold, he dozed.

The ponderosas were visible in a cold, gray light when he awakened. He awakened with a start, and it took him a few seconds to remember where he was. When he looked around, he saw the girl lying in the same position, her knees drawn up and her hands between her knees. Standing was painful. Every muscle in his body groaned. He shivered and waved his arms to get the blood circulating.

They were in a grassy spot among trees that reached forty to sixty feet into the sky. Moss-covered rocks seemed to grow out of the ground. The ground sloped sharply upward ahead of them.

He looked at the sky. There was no sign of the sun, only a dim gray light. He wondered how long it would be before the sun came up and warmed things up. He wished he could stop shivering.

Away off in the distance he heard a dog howl, and that gave him a flicker of hope. Where there were dogs, there were people. But when it howled again, he knew it wasn't a domestic animal. The howl had a crazy, hysterical tone to it. A wild sound. It had to be a wolf. Or a coyote.

Fear added to the cold made him shiver again. He had read about the wild coyotes and wolves Out West. The animal howled again in a high, eerie octave, and ended its high notes with a series of yap-yaps. Another animal joined in, yap-yapping wildly. They sounded like hysterical laughter. Now he knew there were more than one. A pack of wild wolves. He had read about how they could kill a large buffalo. A puny, unarmed man and woman would be easy game for them. They had to move.

"Miss Dobbs. Josephine."

Her eyes came half open and she grunted. Then she said, "Oh," and her eyes opened wider. Sitting up, she looked around fearfully, saw him, and asked, "What? Where are we?"

"I don't know, but there are some wolves around here. We'd better get going."

"What?" she asked, still not fully awake.

"Wolves. Or coyotes. I heard them."

She stood up and listened. It came again, a series of hysterical barks and yap-yap-yaps.

"I think they're coyotes," she said. "They're harmless."

"Are you sure?"

"Well, I—I think so."

"You're not sure. We'd better move."

"Do you think those—those ruffians are still looking for us?"

"I don't know. Our problem right now is to find our way back to El Tejon. But we'll have to keep our eyes open for them."

"Perhaps they've given up." She waved her arms and stamped her feet. "Brrr, it's cold." She looked down at herself, at her white petticoat. "Oh, I'm—would you please turn your back, Mr. Alexander."

"Huh? Oh sure." He turned around while she stepped into her skirt and buttoned it. The hysterical sounds came again, only this time farther away. That made him feel better. The wild wolves hadn't gotten wind of the human prey. "Let's go. It's too cold to stand around here."

"Which way?"

"Well, I, uh, I don't remember climbing any steep hills so I don't think we should go that way. Let's go downhill until we get out of these woods and then maybe we can see where we are."

"Anything is better than standing here freezing."

He took off, walking briskly in spite of sore muscles and a sore toe. He waved his arms while he walked, trying to get warm. When she stumbled, he took her arm and helped her along.

"Oh this—this gosh-danged skirt," she said. "I can't help tripping over it."

He didn't blame her for using foul language. In fact, it was a relief because now he could swear too when he felt like it. "I hope we get out of these damnable woods soon."

The character of the woods gradually changed as they walked along until they left the ponderosas and tall spruce and were in thicker woods of lodgepole pines. No grass grew among the lodgepoles and they walked on a floor of dried pine needles. They slid down a deep, rocky ravine, climbed out, and went on.

Now they were in a stand of aspen, and tall grass and wild flowers of every color grew among them. A short time later they were on the edge of a wide, treeless valley where the grass grew in bunches and four deer a half-mile away raised their heads and watched them. Away off in the distance a high ridge of mountains, white in places with snow, caught the morning sun. They stopped.

"Do you see anything familiar?" she asked.

He answered with a sigh, "No."

She dropped to the ground and sat on her feet in the tall grass. "We're lost, aren't we?"

He sat beside her. "Yeah. I'm sorry."

"You're not to blame."

He was silent, trying to think. She added, "It's me. They wanted to kill you only because you were with me. If anyone is to blame, it's me."

"You can't be faulted. It's their fault, those two cutthroats."

"They killed my dad and now they want to kill me."

Her words brought his head up. "Yeah, that's what they said, didn't they?"

"Yes. They thought we were going to die so they didn't care what they said."

"What did they say when I was unconscious?"

"They said they were going to put us in the mine and blow it up and make it look like an accident. They said the timbers were about to collapse anyway. And they said they blew up my dad and Mr. Wingate."

"Yeah, they said something like that before I, uh, was hit. And didn't they say something about—what was it? Didn't they say something that would indicate that they were carrying out instructions?"·

"Yes. I remember. The two men said 'they,' meaning someone else, wanted it to look like an accident."

Their immediate problem was forgotten for the moment and Alexander worried over what she had just said and what he remembered hearing. Buckshot Dobbs's death was murder, and someone wanted her killed too. Was someone else planning to take over the Josey Mine? That was the only answer. Someone had a scheme for taking over the mine, and to do that he had to have the owner and his heirs murdered.

Was it the man from Kansas City, Charles E.

Dobbs? Not unless he had been in or near El Tejon around June 21, the day Buckshot Dobbs was killed. If not he, who?

Suddenly, Alexander chuckled without humor. All this meant that the girl sitting beside him was the real Josephine Dobbs. Too many things pointed in that direction. But that wasn't news. He had been calling her Josephine ever since they were sealed inside that mine. Up to now he hadn't really admitted to himself that his first impression of her was wrong, but in his heart he knew it. Now he had to admit it.

"Josephine, I'm sorry I doubted you."

"That's your job."

Yeah, he thought, that was his job. Now he had two jobs. He had to check out anyone else who claimed the estate, and he had to find out who ordered the murder of Buckshot Dobbs and his daughter.

And whoever it was would damn well pay the penalty.

With that in mind he jumped up, ignoring the sore muscles and fatigue. He wanted to get started. Now he was angry. Some damn body was going to pay.

He reached out a hand for her and helped her up. "Let's go. Let's do something."

"What?"

"Well, let's think." He looked around and saw the sun shining above the tops of the trees behind them. "O.K., that's east. When we left town, we walked in a southwesterly direction. At least I think that was the direction we went. What do you think?"

"I think you're right. I remember it was still early and cool and the sun felt warm on my back."

"Then we went west. The road was full of curves

where it went through the trees and around the ravines and boulders, and if I'm not mistaken, we turned south more often than we turned north."

"So, if you're correct, we are southwest of El Tejon."

"O.K.," Alexander said, looking in a northeasterly direction, "let's go that way."

"There's a high peak over there," she said. "Perhaps we can climb to the top and see the town. It's in the right direction."

She pointed and he saw the peak off in the distance. It was bare of trees and a spot of white snow showed near the top. "It's a long way, no telling how many miles. But it's in the direction we want to go. Let's go."

With renewed determination he set off. When she fell behind, he realized that she could not match his pace, and he slowed down. His head hurt, and his toe was killing him, and she had to be hurting too. But they had to keep going.

The next time they stopped to rest, his big toe hurt so much he had to take his boot off. With his bowie knife he cut a slit in the boot toe where it put too much pressure on his big toe. On second thought, he cut a hole in the boot. Who cared if he ruined it? It felt better when he put it back on.

His stomach reminded him that they had not eaten in over twenty-four hours. She must be starved. What could he do? He had read about outdoorsmen setting traps for rabbits and squirrels and things, but he hadn't seen any rabbits or squirrels. What would he do if he caught one? Skin it? Those deer he had seen were too far away for even a good rifle shot, let alone a man armed with nothing better than a bowie knife. If they kept going, maybe they would soon get back to civilization.

For a long while it seemed that the high peak ahead of them wasn't getting any closer, but by mid-afternoon he could see it more clearly. There was snow in some of the crevices near the top. There were no trees on top and that meant it was above timber line. From up there a person ought to be able to see a long way. But it was beginning to look as though they would never get to it.

She was walking more slowly, and he was feeling weaker too. Now they were climbing and that made it worse. It would be easier to go downhill, he thought, but the way to civilization had to be ahead of them, and that meant going uphill.

By late afternoon they were back in the timber, a mixture of ponderosa, lodgepole, and spruce. Once they skirted a deep hole in the ground, and he stopped to wonder about it. It was man-made. A prospector's hole? Yeah, that's what it was. He had read about how the prospectors dug a lot of worthless holes, trying to find a vein of gold.

Another mile, and the girl stumbled and fell. She was too weary to move or even to talk, and could only lie on her side and gasp for breath. He knelt beside her and had an urge to just lie down with her. She was finished, and he couldn't leave her.

Would a rest help? Probably not. They both needed food more than anything else. A combination of food and rest would give them the strength to go on. He stood up and picked up a fist-sized rock. With luck he could kill a bird or something and dress it with his bowie knife. He had matches in the little tin box in his shirt pocket, and he could build a fire and cook something. Looking around, he realized that no living creature was in sight. According to all he had read about the woods and the mountains, wildlife was supposed to be all around.

Alexander walked away from the girl, looking at the trees for birds and at the ground for rabbits. He saw the cabin.

Chapter Ten

At first he could only stare at it, wondering if his eyes were playing tricks on him. The cabin was built of logs and it blended in with the woods. It had a dirt roof and grass grew out of the roof. A stovepipe stuck up out of the roof.

For a long while he stared at the cabin, wondering who had built it and who lived in it. He saw no sign of life, and no smoke came from the stovepipe chimney. There was no road leading to it and no other buildings. A small stream ran in front of it and a bucket lay on its side beside the stream. An ax leaned against a small pile of dead tree limbs. It had to be home to someone.

He hurried back to the girl. "Josephine, there's a cabin over there. Maybe we can get something to eat."

When she didn't move, he knelt beside her and touched her shoulder. "Josephine," he said softly. "Maybe we can find something to eat in that cabin over there."

"Huh?" She raised her head. "Where?"

"Over there." He pointed. "Come on."

She got to her hands and knees and, with his help,

to her feet. He pulled her along. "Come on. It's home to somebody, and whoever lives there has to have some food."

Suddenly, she pulled back. "Could it be—them?"

"Who? Oh, the ruffians who tried to kill us? No, I don't think so. They're horsemen and I don't see any place to keep horses."

"Food," she said, stepping sorely ahead. "I can't remember what it's like."

They stopped before the door and Alexander hollered, "Hello? Hello? Anybody home?" The door was latched from the outside with a wire hook, and he raised the hook and slowly pushed the door open. "Hello? Anybody home?"

Leaving the door open, they stepped inside. The tiny, one-room cabin had a dirt floor and was furnished with only the barest necessities. No bunk, only a mattress and some blankets on the floor. The stove was only about two feet high and had no legs. It sat flat on the dirt floor with the tin pipe sticking up from it through the roof. But there was a table made of small tree trunks and the table held more than a dozen tins of food.

"Whoever owns this cabin will be well paid for this," Alexander said as he picked up the tins one at a time and examined them. There were three cans of peaches, one can of apricots, three cans of beans, two cans of corn, and five cans of Libby's Corned Meats.

"Not exactly gourmet food," he said, "but it's edible. What would you like Josephine?"

"Anything. Is there any silverware?"

He looked around and found a small box under the table, containing a tin plate, a knife, spoon, and fork.

With his bowie knife he opened a can of beans and a can of corned beef, dumped half into the tin plate and handed her the spoon.

"I'll eat out of the cans," he said.

"Excuse my manners," she said, taking the spoon and digging in. She chewed and swallowed two spoonfuls and said, "It's good. Not delicious, but good."

They ate the contents of four cans before their hunger was sated. Alexander searched his pockets for money and then remembered that he had been robbed by the two hoodlums back at the mine. "I don't suppose you have any money to leave," he said.

"Well," she answered hesitantly, "yes. If you will be so kind as to turn around." He did, and she unbuttoned her shirtwaist and took a small silk purse out of her bosom. "Here's a few dollars. How much do you think we should leave?"

"How much have you got?"

"Not very much. I—it took nearly all I had to get to El Tejon."

"Leave two or three dollars. That ought to more than pay for it."

"I don't have any single dollars. I'll have to leave a five-dollar bill."

"I'll repay you when we get back to town. I've got some money hidden in my luggage."

"O.K. then."

"Shall we go?"

"Do you think we're any closer to town than we were this morning?"

"We have to be. Listen, whoever lives here has to get to town now and then and there should be a path we can follow."

110

Outside, she was the first to spot a path. "Here. Here's one."

He came over and saw the faint skid marks on the ground. "It doesn't look like the kind of path one would make by traveling over it, but I'll see where it goes."

Where it went was back into the timber, to a spot where trees had been cut down and trimmed. Alexander knew then that the path was made by dragging logs to the cabin. When he rejoined her he was discouraged. "I walked all around the cabin and all I found was another deep hole in the ground. I think someone was looking for gold and dug it. It has a homemade ladder sticking out of it."

"Perhaps that's why he built the cabin. For shelter while he looked for gold around here."

"More than likely. But I didn't see any digging tools. He must have gone somewhere else to dig. I also saw some, uh—"

"What?"

"Uh, droppings from a, uh, burro, probably. It doesn't look like horse droppings. And it's not fresh."

"Could that mean that whoever lives here had a burro to carry supplies and hasn't been here for some time?"

"Looks that way. And those empty discarded cans over there, they're not new either."

"But he left groceries and blankets. He must be planning on coming back."

"Looks that way."

"What shall we do? Continue walking?"

"Tell you what, I'll climb to the top of that peak and see if I can see anything."

"I'll go with you."

"Why don't you stay here and rest? I feel stronger now that I've had something to eat."

"I don't want to stay here by myself. What if someone comes, the man who owns this cabin?"

"You're right. Do you think you can make it?"

"I'll have to."

He looked at the peak and guessed that it was a good hour and a half away, and he looked at the horizon and knew it would be dark in an hour and a half. Shaking his head sadly, he said, "It'll be dark by the time we get up there."

"Perhaps we should wait until tomorrow. I don't care much for walking around in the mountains in the dark."

"Good idea. We both need rest. Let's stay here tonight. There are blankets in the cabin, and if no one shows up we can use them."

"Suppose the owner comes back?"

"I hope he's sociable."

Alexander went to the stream, knelt, and splashed water over his face. He gingerly fingered the cut on his head. She came over and knelt beside him. "Let me see. Not that I know anything about treating wounds, but if necessary I can make a bandage out of my petticoat."

He let her touch his head, heard her cluck sympathetically. "It must have hurt terribly. It's not bleeding, though. Do you think I should bandage it?"

"No, I guess not. It would be hard to bandage, and apparently I'm not suffering a concussion or anything."

"It's not deep. Looks like the blow just broke the

skin."

Her breath on his cheek was sweet and pleasant. "I'm lucky," he said.

"I'm the lucky one, Mr. Alexander. If they had killed you, I would have died too."

"Call me James."

"James."

She splashed water on her face and washed her hands, then sat with her feet under her on the grassy bank beside the creek. "I want to apologize again for causing you so much trouble and danger."

Her eyes were dark blue again, though lines of fatigue showed around them. They reminded him of the first time he saw her, with her pretty smile and bright eyes, but with a barely discernible hardness around her eyes.

"Tell me something, Josephine, how long did you live in St. Louis?"

"A long time. Since I was about thirteen."

"You said your family lived somewhere near the town of Rosebud, when did you leave there?"

"When I was about thirteen. My mother became discouraged with the kind of life we were living, and she just packed a few of our belongings, said goodby to my dad, and put me and my sister in the one wagon we had behind the only team of horses we had, and left."

"And she took you to St. Louis?"

"Yes. By wagon, stage, and rail. We've lived there ever since."

"Were your mother and father ever divorced?"

"Oh, no. My mother thought divorce was disgraceful. She had no intention of ever living with him again, but she wouldn't even consider a divorce."

"Then you really were raised in the mountains." He said it as a fact, not a question.

"Yes." She lifted one shoulder in a small shrug. "It was a long time ago, and my mother didn't want to remember it, and she wouldn't allow my sister and me to talk about it. She taught us to talk like city people."

He tossed a twig into the stream and watched it float away. He remembered that she had said something about a destructive fire, and he asked about that.

She remained silent, staring into the water as if mesmerized. He apologized, "I'm sorry. It's none of my business."

"It's—my mother and sister died in the fire. A lot of people died. I wasn't at home when it started, and I'm one of the few survivors."

"I'm sorry, Josephine. Forgive me for prying."

"It's all right. I have to accept that it happened. Nothing can—make it . . ." She stopped talking, and he realized she was trying to control her emotions. He scooted over beside her and put an arm around her shoulders. "Try to forget it. You have to forget it, Josephine."

"Yes." She sniffed her nose and wiped her eyes with the palms of her hands. "Do you think, Mr. Alexander—James—do you think we will get back to town alive?"

"I'm sure of it. I don't know when. Maybe tomorrow, maybe the next day. But we have food and blankets now, and we will survive. You have to believe that."

She stood slowly and tried a weak smile. "I wonder

what it will be like to sleep on a dirt floor?"

He grinned. "It'll be better than where we slept last night. We'll be warm. With a night's rest and some food we'll find our way back to town. You can bet on that."

But back inside the cabin, Alexander felt uncomfortable. Not because of the hard floor, but because he knew they were intruding on someone else's property. He wondered how they would be greeted if the owner suddenly appeared in the door. What would he say? What would he do? What kind of person was he? Understanding and kind or violent?

"Miss, uh, Josephine, I've been thinking. The ground outside is no harder than this floor, and maybe we ought to sleep outside. If the owner comes back, I'd like to see him before he sees us. I'd feel safer that way."

"I understand. Thank God you have a strong sense of self-preservation."

They consumed two more cans of food and took the blankets and mattress back into the trees a short distance from the cabin. He spread the mattress under a tall spruce for her and found a grassy spot for himself. He untied his boots and pulled them off. She spurned his offer to untie her shoes for her and managed to do that herself.

Dark came quickly, and both man and woman were so weary they talked very little. The night wind whispered through the tops of the pines while on the ground the air was still.

He heard the mattress rustle and heard her say softly, "Good night, James."

"Good night, Josephine."

A full moon climbed slowly to the top of the trees to the east, and as it climbed higher the light it put out was surprisingly bright. Alexander could see the cabin clearly, could even see the mud chinks between the logs. Back in the woods where they were it was dark.

He lay on his back with his hands under his head for a long time. His mind was on Josephine Dobbs and a woman and her two daughters living in a shack in the mountains with a man who was probably considered a ne'er-do-well; a woman who became discouraged and took her daughters back to the city. And the man who continued wandering in the mountains, digging and hoping, living a lonely existence until finally he struck it rich. A man who then wanted to share his wealth with the family that he missed very much. The woman and one of her daughters dying in a fire. The man murdered.

A tragic story. A very tragic story.

Believing breakfast would be their last meal for many hours, they ate two cans of fruit and two cans of corned meat, and went to the creek and washed it down with cold, clear water.

She looked better and her voice and energy showed she felt better too. When she brushed her hair back with her fingers and allowed the long blond curls to fall back into place, he was reminded of what an attractive young woman she was.

For a moment, they stood beside the stream and looked up at the high peak. The morning was typical for August in the Colorado mountains, clear with a bright sun just showing itself in the east and casting

116

long shadows among the pine and spruce. A few white clouds sat on the western horizon. A raven cawed loudly, breaking the silence as it flew overhead.

"Well," Alexander said, "there's only one way to do it."

"Only one way," she said. "You lead and I'll follow."

They started out, heading into the woods, trying to keep to a northeasterly course. Alexander's toe was no longer sore, and he walked easily. The girl was having to hold her skirts up with both hands at times, but she appeared to be walking easily too. The farther they went the sharper the ground rose in front of them, and they had to stop and catch their breath.

"How much farther to the top?" she asked.

"I don't know. If we could get out of these woods we could see the top. Can't be too far, though."

Soon the ground became so steep they had to grab rocks, tree roots, grass, and anything they could find to pull themselves up. Breathing in the thin air was so difficult they had to stop every few yards. "It's farther than it looked," he panted. "Good thing we didn't try to climb it last night."

She didn't answer, only gasped for breath. Finally, they came out of the timber and found themselves surrounded by huge boulders.

"Good," he said between breaths. "We're getting there."

"It's cooler," she said. "We must be a lot higher."

He glanced at the sky. "Cloudy. The sun is behind a cloud."

The white clouds that had hung over the western horizon that morning had joined more clouds from the

117

south and they had turned dark.

The man and woman went on up the mountain, a few steps at a time. When they stopped to rest again, the clouds had grown ominous, and thunder was rumbling to the west.

"Do you feel anything?" she asked.

"Feel anything? Like what?"

"Like something raising your hair."

After thinking it over a moment, he answered, "No. Do you?"

"Yes. Like electricity in the air."

Chapter Eleven

"I don't see any lightning," Alexander said. "Looks like it could come, though. Let's get over there under that rock wall and see if we can see anything."

They had to skirt a half-dozen huge boulders to get to a spot where the mountain rose almost straight up. But there they could stand on a narrow ledge and see over the rest of the world to the east.

"See anything?" she asked.

"No." He squinted and strained his eyes, but could see nothing but more pine forests, a lower ridge, and the valley they had seen the day before. "No sign of a town or a road or anything."

She was silent for a long moment, then said, "It seems we're all alone in the world, doesn't it? It's scary."

Shaking his head sadly, Alexander said, "It makes me realize how small and insignificant we are."

Her shoulders slumped and her voice had a dejected tone. "What are we going to do? I don't see any sign of civilization down there. Are we going to be lost in the mountains forever?"

His answer came without enthusiasm. "No. I guess the best thing to do is go back to that cabin and stay the night, then start out again in the morning. Sooner or later we'll find our way back."

Leading the way, Alexander half-walked and half-climbed around the boulders and started across a wide expanse of granite floor. The thunder was louder and a bolt of lightning hit a boulder three hundred yards below them.

"Oh," she yelled, "my hair is standing on end."

He felt it too, a feeling he had never experienced before. His hair felt as though something were pulling on it. The pull was so strong his scalp stung.

Another bolt cracked into the rock wall five hundred yards above them, and the accompanying boom of thunder was deafening.

"James," she yelled. "What shall we do?"

"Hurry. Let's get downhill."

He was slipping and sliding across the expanse of granite floor when a bolt of lightning blasted one of the boulders they had just left. At the same instant thunder boomed and reverberated so loudly it seemed to shake the world.

Static electricity hissed out of the rocks around them.

Terrified, the girl covered her ears with both hands and screamed. Alexander put his hand on a small boulder for support as he moved his feet faster, trying to get off the granite and farther down the slope.

Another bolt of lightning hit the peak and another explosion of thunder pounded their ears. Still another brilliant flash of white light sprang up, and an awesome explosion of thunder left him shaking in his

120

boots.

A jolt of electricity traveled along the granite and entered his right hand, the hand that was grasping the top of the small boulder.

He could feel the electricity trace a path up his right arm, into his shoulder, and down his back. Instantly, he jerked his hand away from the rock and discovered that his hand had curled into a claw. He felt no pain, but he couldn't straighten his fingers.

Looking back at the girl, he saw her squatting on her heels on bare ground at the edge of the granite floor, holding her hands over her ears.

Then the hail started. It pounded their heads and shoulders and small pellets of it bounced off the rocks and gathered in the low places.

He glanced around and had a powerful urge to get under one of the boulders, to get out of the storm. But another bolt of lightning and another explosion of thunder made him change his mind. The rocks, he knew then, conducted electricity, and the girl, squatting on the dirt, making herself as small as possible, was doing the right thing.

Yelling at her to stay where she was, Alexander made his way across the granite to a small brushy ravine, jumped into it and sat on his heels, wishing he could draw into himself.

Hail pounded down, bouncing off the boulders until the ground was covered with small white hailstones. Alexander tried to straighten the fingers of his right hand and managed to move them, but only a little. He still felt no pain, only a strange tingling in his arm and shoulder.

Within a few minutes the hail turned to rain, a cold

high country rain, and both man and woman were soon soaked. The thunder appeared to be moving eastward, though, and Alexander stood up to where he could see out of the gully. Lightning was flashing to the east.

"Come on," he yelled at the girl. "Let's get off this damnable mountain."

At first she didn't move, and he felt a hollow sickness in his stomach at the possibility that she could be hurt. "Hey, are you O.K.?"

She stood then and took a tentative step toward him.

"Be careful, but come on."

Climbing out of the gully, he made his way cautiously onto the granite to help her. Hailstones had made the granite even more slippery and his feet slid out from under him. He got up immediately and then dropped onto his knees. He still couldn't straighten the fingers of his right hand, but he made his way across the slippery surface on his knees and one hand.

The girl took hold of his crooked hand and leaned against him while he crawled backward. When they were off the granite and onto the rocky ground, he stood up.

"Let's get back to that cabin."

She said nothing but managed to keep pace with him as he walked and slid downhill and into the timber. Once, when he looked back, he saw her sliding on the seat of her skirt, and the hem of the skirt was up to her knees. "Are you O.K.?"

She only grunted.

When they got to lower ground to where they could walk without slipping, he took her arm to help her.

The cold rain came down. She was shivering uncontrollably.

"It's not much farther," he said. "We're making better time going down than we did coming up." She wasn't talking, only shivering. He put his right arm around her waist, wishing he could straighten his fingers. He tried to be reassuring. "Not much farther," he said again. Rain continued to fall.

It took awhile, but eventually he could see the cabin through the trees. "We're almost there, Josephine." Still no sound from her. They went on, his right arm around her waist. Now she was leaning hard against him and walking with wobbly steps. He stopped then and looked into her face.

The girl was wet clear through. Her hair was plastered to her head, her face was white, and her eyes were half-closed. She was shaking violently.

"Oh, my God," Alexander said. He had read about what a cold rain in the mountains could do to people, and he knew it could kill. "My God," he said again. The girl had gone into the deadly grip of hypothermia.

"Come on. We've got to get to that cabin." Half-carrying her, he quickened his steps, grunting and straining, summoning every ounce of strength he had. "Not much farther," he said through clenched teeth. "Hang on, Josephine. We're almost there."

The cabin was still unoccupied, and the mattress and blankets were still on the dirt floor where they had left them. Water was dripping through the dirt roof in two places, but most of the cabin was dry.

He laid her on the mattress and started undressing her. "Excuse me, but we've got to get these wet clothes

123

off," he said. "Got to get you dry and warm. Got to hurry."

He discovered he could straighten his right-hand fingers now, but they were awkward. "How in the world—?" he muttered, picking at the dozens of buttons, straps, and hooks, and raising the yards of wool skirt and petticoat. The small silk purse hung from her neck on a strong silver cord. It was wet, and he removed it too. Next came the high-laced shoes.

The girl was helpless, just shaking violently.

"Stay awake, Josephine," he begged. "You've got to stay awake."

He peeled off her stockings and stopped suddenly. She was almost naked. What little she had on was surprising. In spite of the good quality of outer clothing, her underclothing consisted of a common, working woman's union suit.

She had cut off the legs just below the knees and had cut the arms off at the shoulders to make it cooler for the summer. The wet suit fit her figure tightly.

Alexander's breath caught in his throat as he looked at her. She was unbelievably beautiful. She was the most beautiful sight he had ever seen.

Suddenly, he realized that he was looking at a very sick and helpless young lady, and he was ashamed of himself. Should he take off the union suit? He hesitated. The clothing was wet.

He fumbled open the buttons down the front, then with his eyes tightly closed, he pulled the one-piece suit down off her shoulders, down over her hips and finally off her feet.

Still keeping his eyes closed, he wrapped her in a blanket, then he opened his eyes and wrapped her in another blanket until she looked like a mummy with only her face showing.

She was still shaking and her eyes were closed too. He had read that a person suffering from hypothermia should not be allowed to sleep. Sleep could be fatal. He shook her and spoke to her. "Wake up, Josephine. Stay awake. You have to wake up."

Her eyes flickered but opened only halfway. She groaned.

He had to get her warm quickly. With shaking knees and trembling fingers, he broke up some of the dead tree branches piled beside the stove and stuffed them into the firebox. Matches. He was grateful to the salesman in Chicago who had talked him into buying the tin matchbox. Water was dripping through the dirt roof onto his shoulders, but he ignored that as he struck a wooden match and touched it to the wood. It caught fire, then died. He struck another match and tried again, afraid to breathe. The flame caught, flickered, and grew. He let it grow, then blew on it gently, and watched it spread quickly over the dry sticks.

Soon it was crackling, and he could feel heat from it.

When he turned back to the girl, her eyes were closed again and she was still shivering. He took her by the shoulders and shook her. "Wake up. Come on, Josephine. Fight it. Stay awake. Please, Josephine." He shook her again.

Her mouth opened and she tried to speak, but no words came out.

What to do? Something hot to drink. What? Water. He jumped up a grabbed a pot that was hanging on the wall and hurried outside to the creek. When he returned with a pot half-full of water, he set it on the stove and put more wood in the firebox. Moving quickly, he turned back to the girl, grabbed her by the shoulders, and shook her again.

"Come on, Josephine. Fight. Come on. Live."

The fire was crackling merrily in the stove. He turned around and put his finger in the water. Still cool. "Come on, Josephine. Stay awake."

Now her eyes were open and her teeth were chattering. The only sounds from her throat were groans.

"You're a fighter, Josephine. I know you are. Don't give up now. Stay awake."

Another test of the water. It was warm, but not hot. He found a tin cup in the box under the table and half filled it. Then with one arm under her shoulders he raised her to a sitting position. "Here. Drink."

He held the cup to her lips. "Drink, Josephine. Try."

Her lips parted, and he managed to pour some of the liquid into her mouth. She swallowed.

"Atta girl. Come on, Josie. You can do it. Come on, take another swallow."

Her lips parted again and she swallowed again. She groaned and tried to talk. He continued feeding the warm water to her until the cup was empty. He refilled the cup this time with warmer water, and she drank it a swallow at a time.

The next time she tried to talk, three words came out. "Thank—thank you."

A wide smile spread across his face. "Atta girl. You're a fighter, Josie. You're going to be all right. How do you feel now?"

"C—cold, but—better."

His smile widened even more when he noticed that she was no longer shivering. "You're going to be all right. You can sleep now." He laid her down again, made sure she was still wrapped tightly in the blankets, and stood up.

The heat from the stove felt good, but the fuel piled beside the stove consisted of small sticks, and he knew it wouldn't last long. He made another dash outside to the pile of tree branches and broke some up by stomping on them. When he had a double armload, he carried it inside the cabin and dumped it on the floor beside the stove. He hoped it would dry before the rest of the fuel was burned up. To be sure he had enough, he hurried outside and carried in another load. The rain, he saw, had slackened but was still falling gently.

Chores done, he was reminded that he too was soaked to the skin. He wanted to take off his clothes, but not before her. He looked back. Her eyes were closed and she was breathing evenly. Asleep? Yes.

With an eye on the sleeping girl, Alexander stripped off his wet clothes until he stood beside the stove wearing his thigh-length Munsingwear shorts and nothing else. The heat felt wonderful. He hung his clothes on the side of the table and moved the table closer to the stove. He hung the girl's clothes on nails protruding from the wall behind the stove.

Now he wished he could sleep, but there was no place to lie down except on the dirt floor, which was turning to mud in places. All he could do was stand there in his shorts and envy the girl sleeping soundly on the mattress.

Outside, the rain had quit altogether, but inside the dirt ceiling was still leaking. Alexander could see why. The ceiling was made simply of poles nailed tightly together across the top of the cabin, and the roof was nothing more than dirt piled on the poles. Water would continue to drip between the poles as long as the dirt was wet.

Wearily, he sat on the dirt floor in his shorts, wishing he had a chair or something to sit on. Or a bed. Wouldn't a bed be wonderful? But there was only one mattress. Too bad.

He sat with his knees drawn up, arms folded on top of them and his head on his arms. Once, he caught himself as he started to doze off and fall over. He couldn't stop thinking about that mattress.

"Josie?" he called softly. No answer. Standing, he put more wood in the stove, rearranged the clothes so that all sides would absorb the heat, then stealthily lay down beside her, between her and the stove. She was breathing evenly and didn't move.

"Aaah," he sighed as he turned over on his side, his back to her. He didn't know how comfortable a grass-filled mattress on a dirt floor could be. "Aaah."

His dreams were pleasant: his comfortable bed in his own room at home. The cook, old Mrs. O'Brian, humming an Irish ballad as she fried bacon in the kitchen downstairs. His father, James J. Alexander the Second, splashing water as he shaved in the water closet next door. How pleasant.

All that ended abruptly.

"What in the blue-eyed world?"

He awoke with a start. What was happening?

"Just what do you think you're doing?"

"Huh?" He sat up, his mind still foggy with sleep. She was sitting up too with the blankets wrapped loosely around her.

"Would you mind getting the hell out of my bed?"

Josephine Dobbs looked again at herself inside the blankets, then looked at him sitting beside her in his shorts.

"Well?"

He jumped up, embarrassed. "I, uh, I—"

"You what? What have you been doing?"

Not knowing what to say, Alexander took two long steps to his clothes, yanked on his pants and shirt, then hopped on one foot at a time as he pulled on the lace boots. Glancing back at her, he saw she was holding the blankets up to her throat, and her green eyes were shooting sparks at him.

"I'm, uh, I didn't—I mean, I'm sorry, I—" Hastily, he yanked open the door and hobbled out. The tops of his boots, not laced up, flopped awkwardly around his ankles.

He walked spraddle-legged to a nearby stump and sat down. What was she so angry about? All he did was—well, he didn't touch her. Sure, he saw her nearly naked, but that was unavoidable. Wasn't it?

Women. No man would ever understand them.

Chapter Twelve

With his boots laced now, Alexander walked around outside the cabin, wondering what to do. He had an urge to leave, just walk away without looking back. But it would be dark soon and he had had enough of wandering around in the woods in the dark. Even with a full moon it was dark back in the woods. Besides, he couldn't just leave her. He noticed with some satisfaction that the sun, though it was close to the western horizon, was shining brightly. The storm was over.

His stomach grumbled, reminding him that it hadn't been properly fed lately. He repeatedly looked back at the cabin, wondering what she was doing, wonder if she was still angry. Then the cabin door opened and she was standing in the doorway smiling sweetly.

"Oh, James. J.J." She was fully dressed and her long, blond hair was tied behind her neck with a rag she had found somewhere. "I'm sorry, J.J."

He didn't know whether to approach her or not. She was lovely.

"I'm sorry, James. I didn't realize at first that you

probably saved my life. Can you forgive me?"

"Uh, yeah. Yes. Sure." He grinned crookedly. "I guess I would have been shocked too if I were in your place."

She smiled and her blue eyes shone. "It was quite a shock, all right, waking up like that."

"I didn't mean to scare you or anything."

"I know that, now that I've had time to think about it. Won't you come in?"

Alexander walked toward her. "Yeah. Yes. Sure."

She stood aside as he entered the cabin, but not so far aside that he could get past her without brushing against her. She put one hand on his shoulder. He noticed, when he turned to face her, that her eyes were only two or three inches below his. Bright blue. Her lips were slightly parted, smiling a half-smile. With a hungry groan, he wrapped his arms around her and pulled her tightly to him. His mouth found hers, and her lips were willing. The kiss was the sweetest thing he had ever experienced.

Finally, she got her hands between them, against his chest, and pushed away. "Easy there, J.J."

He didn't want to stop and tried to pull her to him again, but she put her fingers against his lips and held back. "Not now. Please, J.J. Don't."

"Why?" His voice was husky with passion.

"It's just—just not right. I mean, we can't. Not here. Not now." She twisted away from him, walked across the small room, and stopped when the table was between them. "I know I owe you, but . . ."

Alexander let his breath out slowly, trying to force down the passion he felt. She was right. This wasn't the time or place. My God, they were lost in the mountains Out West. They were faced with the problem of survival.

"Anyway," she said, "we have food for tonight and tomorrow morning. What do you think we should do?"

There were four cans of food left on the table. It would keep them from starving for a little while. Then what?

It took some time, but he finally forced his voice back to normal. "We'll have to go on. I suggest we walk in an easterly direction and downhill. All we can do is hope we come to a road or a trail or something."

"Yes," she said. "If we keep walking in a straight line, we're bound to come to something." She sighed. "That's all we can do."

"We're alive, Josie. As long as we're alive and not crippled we have a good chance of surviving."

"Yes, we have to believe that." Her lips parted in a small, forced smile. "I do believe that. We'll survive, J.J."

The fire was nearly out, but Alexander revived it by putting some dry twigs in the stove and blowing on the coals until flames surrounded the twigs. They carefully divided a can of dried apricots and a can of beans. By that time it was almost dark inside the cabin.

"Do you think we should sleep outside again?" she asked.

"No, the ground is wet and we both need sleep. With a good night's sleep and the rest of the food, we can start out fresh and strong in the morning."

"Yes. We're lucky we found this cabin."

"It has been a lifesaver. I regret having to eat all the

132

food we found in it, but we had no choice. It was a matter of life and death. I hope whoever owns this cabin realizes that."

"Surely, he will."

"If I ever find the man who owns it, I'll pay him well, you can bet on that."

They sat side by side on the mattress, hugging their knees but not touching each other. "Tell me about yourself, J.J. You obviously have an education. Where did you go to school?"

In the darkness, warm and with their hunger at least partially sated, they talked. Alexander told about dropping out of Harvard law school. He told about how his parents were so disappointed that his mother cried and his father stomped out of the house in anger. About joining the Pinkertons because he wanted to do something different. About volunteering to come Out West because he wanted adventure. Then he asked about her.

She shifted positions and rested her chin on her knees. "I told you about my mother taking my sister and me to St. Louis. My mother saw that Ettie and I got an education. Oh, not like yours of course, but we went to the eleventh grade. Ettie got a job in a business office keeping books and I took an interest in the theater."

"The theater? Really?"

"Yes. I started performing in the theater arts in school, and later I joined a touring theater company."

"You were an actress."

"A tragedienne. I didn't care much for Shakespeare, but I like the melodramas. I was a natural for the Poor Pauline roles. I noodled a little bit on the

133

baby grand too and sang. We played the Top Hat trade. I—oh, it was grand. We could have everybody laughing one minute and crying the next. And afterward we sang for the audience. We sang 'Wait for the Wagon,' and 'Nelly Bly,' and the audience loved it."

She paused and chuckled. "It was funny. In Boston, those Irish politicians who were stealing the state blind, they would cry like babies when we sang 'Rose of Killarney.' Oh, it was grand."

"You really were an actress?"

"I tried to be. We didn't make much money. Barely a living. Sometimes the big muckamucks thought we ought to . . . well, we didn't. We had to pay so much to the money grubbers to allow us to use the municipal theaters that we sometimes didn't get to eat as much as we wanted. But, oh, it was grand."

Alexander was no longer listening. An actress indeed. Had she been putting on an act all this time? It would be easy for a professional actress. Particularly if she happened to know the real Josephine Dobbs. Suddenly, he felt sick with disappointment. He had been sure that she was the real article, and now he found out that she was an actress.

"Once," she went on happily, "after we went to Boston in the caboose of a rattler, we practiced doing the French cancan, you know what I mean? We didn't really show anything, but I'll tell you we had their eyes out on stems."

An actress. And if she was putting on an act, what had become of the real Josephine Dobbs? A horrible thought popped into Alexander's mind, but he immediately rejected it. No, it couldn't be. She just couldn't. No. Absolutely not.

But he was troubled.

"We were in Boston when our manager did the skip on us. He skiddaddled with all the money, and we were stranded with nothing but our grouch bags, you know, the little purses we carried around our necks? I had just enough money to get back home with nothing but the clothes I was wearing. I was looking for a job when—" Suddenly she stopped talking for a moment, then, "You're awfully quiet, James."

When he didn't answer, she added, "Compared to you a clam is a chatterbox. Are you awake?"

"Huh? Oh. Yes, I'm awake. That's a fascinating story. What were you about to say?"

"Oh, nothing much." She yawned and stretched with her arms over her head. "I'll share the mattress with you, James. You're a gentleman, I know."

Without another word, she unlaced her shoes, took them off, and settled back for the night. He unlaced his boots, pulled them off, and lay on his side with his back to her. In spite of the weariness, sleep was a long time coming. All he could think about was a beautiful blonde actress, broke, looking for a job, acquainted with a young woman named Josephine Dobbs, seizing an opportunity.

He got up when he felt chilled and, working by feel, put more fuel in the stove. When he lay beside her again, he was careful not to touch her. Finally, he dozed off into a fitful sleep.

He was awakened by a scream.

At first, when he saw what she was staring at, his eyes were so sleep-blurred he couldn't make out what it was. It stood in the open door with the early morning light behind it. After he blinked a dozen times, he saw that it was a man. Or something that resembled a man.

It was short and squat with a round, brown face and black hair that hung straight to its shoulders. A bowler hat sat on top of its head. It wore a blanket draped over its shoulders, exposing a bare hairless chest, and filthy black pants four inches too long and rolled up over ragged high-topped moccasins.

After blinking his eyes a few more times, Alexander determined that what it held in its left hand was a knife with a long, shiny blade, and what it held in its right hand was a long-barreled Civil War revolver.

The girl tried to scream again but was so terrified that all she got out was a gurgling sound. Alexander let out a squawk and jumped to his feet. Two more figures appeared in the door, both with the same long, black hair and the same round, brown faces. One of them carried a bolt-action rifle.

"Who—who are you?" Alexander stammered.

They came into the room, nearly filling it. He saw then that there were four. Two of them had eagle feathers tied to their hair and hanging down below their shoulders.

"What—what do you want?" He wished he had his boots on.

The one with the pistol and knife pointed the knife at him. "You fella," he grumbled in a deep voice. "Who you fella?"

"Who am I? I'm James J. Alexander the Third. We're, uh, we're lost. If this is your cabin, we're sorry we had to use it, but—"

"Food," the Thing grumbled, pointing to the two cans on the table.

"Yes, I'm afraid that's all that's left. We would have starved without your food. I'm sorry. I'll be happy to pay you for it."

The Thing took a long step up to the table and jabbed the point of his knife into the top of a can. The others surrounded the table, ignoring Alexander and the girl. The Thing quickly sawed the can open with his long knife, reached in with his fingers and extracted a dried peach. He popped it into his mouth and grinned. Others reached in with their fingers and smacked their lips loudly as they ate.

Alexander took that opportunity to put on his boots. "I, we're grateful for the use of your cabin and food. It saved our lives. We'll always be very grateful." With his eyes, he motioned for the girl to put her shoes on. She did and stood up.

Alexander took her by the hand and began moving slowly toward the door, hoping that the creatures wouldn't notice. They almost made it.

With lip-smacking and grunting, the creatures emptied the can, then turned their attention to Alexander and the girl. "You fella," said the one with the knife and pistol. Alexander and the girl were almost to the door. They stopped, fearful of what might happen next.

The Thing placed his pistol and knife on the table, then rubbed one hand across the other, looking expectantly at Alexander.

"What?" Alexander asked. "I don't understand."

The Thing scratched the palm of its hand with a forefinger, and grunted, "Fire."

"Fire? What to you mean?"

"Make-um. Fire."

"I don't understand. The fire in the stove went out last night, I don't, uh, oh, do you mean matches?"

The creatures were all keeping their black squinty eyes on them. "Matches," the Thing uttered. "Make-um fire."

"Oh, sure, I've got matches." Alexander unbuttoned his shirt pocket and took out the tin box. "Here."

The Thing grabbed the box out of his hand, opened it, and shook out the half-dozen wooden matches. The others gathered around.

Motioning with his eyes again, Alexander made the girl understand that she was to quietly, unobtrusively, go to the door. They both started in that direction again. And again they almost made it.

"You fella." It was the Thing talking. It pointed with a short stubby finger to the mattress and blankets on the floor. "You. Stay."

"You want us to stay?" Alexander tried to smile, but his face felt frozen.

"You fella," The Thing pointed next at the girl. "You fella. Stay. There." He pointed again at the mattress.

Alexander, leading the girl by the hand, went back to the mattress and sat, pulling her down with him. They sat cross-legged. She whispered, "What are they going to do? Are they Indians?"

"I don't know," he whispered. "Must be. They don't look like the Indians I've seen pictures of in the magazines." In his mind, he could see sketches in the Wild West magazines of Indian braves, beautifully proportioned, wearing only breech clouts and decorative eagle feather headdresses.

138

"They look like savages," she whispered. "I'm afraid."

"The Indians are supposed to be civilized now. Don't be afraid." He didn't believe his own words, but he wanted to make her feel better.

Two of the creatures left, and the other two tried to pry the top off the small stove with their fingers. When they failed to do that, one went out and got the ax. It took them only a couple of minutes to chop a large hole in the top of the stove. That done, they went to work building a fire.

Alexander and the girl were ignored again. He whispered, "I always thought Indians could build a fire without matches."

"Perhaps they're too civilized." she whispered.

"I hope so."

Soon they had a fire burning wildly, with the flames reaching a foot above the stove. The two creatures grunted with satisfaction and stood back. The other two returned, carrying raw meat.

"Ugh," the girl whispered. "What is that?"

"Looks like part of a deer or something. They're going to cook it over the open fire."

A large piece of the meat, a piece with bone sticking out of one end, was laid across the top of the stove. The creatures grunted as the flames wrapped around it.

Smoke filled the cabin, but the creatures didn't seem to notice, though it was burning the eyes and noses of Alexander and the girl. She coughed.

"I've got to get to the door," she whispered.

"Me too."

"You go first and I'll follow."

"Right."

Slowly, he stood up. When none of the creatures paid any attention to him, he took a step toward the door. Then another step. The creatures were gathered around the stove, watching the meat cook. In a few more steps, Alexander was at the door. He looked back at the girl and motioned for her to follow. She stood up.

"You fella." The Thing was watching him.

Alexander froze. The girl froze.

"Now listen, gentlemen," Alexander pleaded, "we're only trying to find our way back to El Tejon." He tried another smile to show he was friendly. "If you would be so kind as to tell us how to get there, we'll be on our way."

The Thing went to him, got between him and the door, and pushed him toward the table. Alexander went obediently to the center of the room, not knowing what else to do. The Thing turned back to the cooking meat.

Smoke and the odor of burning meat filled the room, and the girl was coughing again. Alexander was desperate to get her and himself out of there, but he was trapped. He believed he could bolt for the door and get outside before the creatures realized what he was doing, but that would leave the girl to their mercy. He couldn't leave her, even though she was an imposter. What to do?

It was the girl who did something. While the creatures were watching the cooking meat, she reached for the big army pistol lying on the table. It was a heavy gun and she had to use both hands to pick it up and hold it pointed in the direction of the creatures.

Oh, my God, thought Alexander. She doesn't know how to shoot. The gun has to be cocked. She doesn't know how to do that. They'll just take it away from her and maybe beat her.

One of the creatures touched the meat with a finger, drew back suddenly, and jabbered something unintelligible. Another grabbed the bony part and quickly turned the meat over.

While that was going on, Alexander got the girl's attention and, using sign language with his hands, tried to tell her to cock the hammer back. She understood and, using her right hand, tried to force the hammer. She struggled with her fingers and the palm of her hand. She turned the gun down, sideways, and up and finally got it cocked.

The creatures heard the loud "click" as the hammer stopped in the cocked position, and they turned immediately to the girl. She pointed it in their direction and yelled:

"S—S—Stick 'em up."

She held the gun in both hands and her hands were unsteady. But the creatures stood motionless.

"O.K.," Alexander yelled, "Let's go. Keep the gun pointed at them and let's get out of here."

She started moving in his direction, still holding the pistol out in front of her with both hands.

"You fella." The Thing took a step toward her.

She squeezed her eyes tight and jerked the trigger.

The explosion from the big army pistol sent shock waves over everyone in the small room, and a second later Alexander was knocked aside as the creatures stampeded through the door.

The girl dropped the pistol as if it were hot and ran to him. He grabbed her by the hand and bolted for the door and out into the clean morning air.

They started to run straight ahead, then saw that the creatures, all four of them, had stopped in front of the cabin and were watching them. "This way," he shouted, pulling her in an easterly direction. They ran, splashed across the creek, stopped for breath, and looked back. The creatures were running after them.

"Come on, run," he shouted. They ran, but her long skirt was a handicap. The creatures were gaining. "Oh, they're going to catch us," she cried. "Run on, James. Go on."

"No. Keep running."

A shot.

Alexander remembered the rifle one of the creatures had, and he thought they were done for. He thought it miraculous that they were not hit. He glanced back over his shoulder—and was surprised.

The creatures had stopped. They were standing, staring at something beyond Alexander and the girl.

Another shot, and a bullet hit the ground near their feet. The creatures turned and ran back to the cabin.

The only sound for a long while was the ragged breathing from the young man and young woman. Then, "Halloo," a man yelled from somewhere in the timber.

"Hey," Alexander answered, hopes rising. "Hey. We're friends."

The man appeared about two hundred yards ahead of them, carrying a rifle in the crook of his arm. He was a tall, thin man wearing a slouch hat.

Alexander and the girl stood still as he approached. They saw a burro tied to a tree behind him.

"Danged Injuns," the man said when he got closer. "Alus breakin' in a man's cabin and stealin' ever'thing in sight."

"Indians?" Alexander asked. "Is that what they are?"

"Yup. Prob'ly Utes. Alus sneakin' away from the reservation. Most of the time harmless but alus stealin'."

"But they were chasing us."

"Must of riled 'em." The man wore baggy denim pants held up with suspenders. The legs were stuffed into worn-at-the-heel jackboots. The boots were the largest Alexander had ever seen. Had to have been a size sixteen. The man's gray flannel shirt was buttoned up to the throat. He had a week's growth of salt-and-pepper whiskers and sad, brown eyes with droopy lids.

But what was important was that the man grinned a friendly grin. "Whar'd you two come from, anyhow? You must be the pair they're lookin' fer back 'er at El Teejon."

"We're lost, I must admit," Alexander said. "We spent two nights in that cabin, and then the Indians came this morning. We didn't know what they planned to do with us, but they tried to keep us from leaving."

"Prob'ly wouldn't of hurt you none, but there ain't no aces in traffickin' with Injuns."

Alexander held out his hand. "I'm James J. Alexander, and this is, uh, Miss Josephine Dobbs."

The man shook with a callused hand. "Names

Henshaw. Clarence Henshaw."

"Why, you're the gentleman who wrote to Mrs. Dobbs, aren't you?"

"Yup." He turned sad eyes to the girl. "I guess you got my letter. The shurf said you did."

"Yes, I did, Mr. Henshaw, and I am grateful to you. I understand you knew my father quite well."

"I knowed 'im. I knowed 'im ever' since you was a papoose. There was long spells when I didn't see 'im, but our trails crossed ever' onct in a while." He squinted at the girl. "You could be one a his little girls. I dunno. There's folks that thinks you ain't."

"Is that so?" she asked. "Who would that be?"

"That dandy that runs the bank in El Teejon is one. I heered 'im tellin the shurf he's gonna havta have proof."

The girl looked at Alexander. He looked away.

"Wa-al anyways, I don't reckon I'll go over there and try to pry them Injuns out'n my shack," Henshaw said. "They'd be meaner'n a jackass's kick if I was to do that."

"Is that your cabin?"

"Yup. Ain't lived in 'er fer a spell, but I like havin' 'er there when I need 'er."

"I want to apologize for eating your food," Alexander said. "I'll pay you for it when we get back to town. By the way, how far is it to town?"

" 'Bout six, eight miles is my best guess."

"Which way?"

"The way you was headin', then to the north when you get around Old Thunder Butte up thar."

"The town is north of that peak?"

"North and east. If you'd a kept goin' in the

direction you was headin', you'd a come to the Josey Road."

"Well, I'll be darned," Alexander said. "We climbed up there and looked and didn't see any sign of civilization. But we didn't get to the north side. If we had, we would have seen the town." He turned to the girl. "Can you walk another six or eight miles?"

"Certainly. I'm just happy to learn that it isn't any farther. And," she smiled at Henshaw, "I'm happy that you came along when you did. Those Indians scared me."

"Wa-al, there's folks lookin' fer you-uns. I'll git my jackass and let's skin out'n here."

The burro carried a crossbuck saddle with a canvas-wrapped bedroll on top and small canvas panniers on each side. "I fried up some boar belly a couple miles down," Henshaw said. "That's whar I spent the night. I'd cook you some grub but I reckon we'd best git away from those Injuns."

He reached into the pockets of his baggy pants. "Here, this's better'n nothin." He held out a biscuit to the girl, then reached into his pants again and pulled out another, which he handed to Alexander.

Alexander turned the biscuit over in his hand and studied it. It wasn't the cleanest food he had ever handled and it was hard from age. Tentatively, he took a small bite, then another.

The girl watched his face for a reaction. When he took a third bite, she pinched off a small piece of her biscuit and put it in her mouth. Within a minute, both biscuits had been devoured.

"Ain't much," Henshaw said, picking up the burro's lead rope, "but it'll keep yu goin'." The burro

145

waggled its long ears. It had sad brown eyes like its master. Henshaw led the way and they followed.

It was a long six or eight miles, but it was downhill most of the way and walking wasn't difficult. They came out of the timber on top of a hill and looked across a narrow valley full of aspens, tall grass, wild flowers of every color, and a string of willows. It occurred to Alexander that he was seeing the mountains as they were described in the books and magazines he had read, and the scenery was every bit as beautiful as described. In fact, the magazines didn't begin to portray the color and beauty of the land.

Now that they were safe and on their way back to civilization, he took time to enjoy it all.

When they got to the willows, he could see a small stream running through the middle of them. At places, the willows grew so dense that only the cottontail rabbits and small striped chipmunks could get into them. Henshaw turned and, leading the burro, followed the line of willows downhill.

They were walking on a dim game trail and the footing was good. The girl was between them, and Alexander brought up the rear. He could see that she was weary, and he felt sorry for her, wishing he could help. Then he remembered that she was a phony, and he felt a small surge of anger.

Or was he angry at himself?

For a time there she had had him completely fooled. She obviously knew something about the Dobbs family, and she was an excellent actress. Still, he had let his admiration for her blind him to the fact that she had actually proven nothing. Admiration?

Yes. She was a very admirable young woman. He

had to admit that. If a man had to dig his way out of a mine with his bare hands, be lost in the mountains, go hungry, suffer the cold, and fight off Indians, he couldn't find a better person to do it with. She hadn't complained one time. Not once. Instead, she had apologized to him. And she was the one who had fought off the Indians.

Alexander had to smile a small private smile when he thought about it. Did they really do all that? Wouldn't the people back home be shocked when they heard about it. But—the smile faded—a man hates to be fooled. And she was the enemy. He would have to expose her.

Once, when she looked back at him, he frowned at her. A puzzled expression came over her face, but she turned back and kept walking.

Henshaw didn't look back, just took it for granted that the two young people would keep up. The burro followed obediently, never letting the slack come out of its lead rope. When they crossed the creek and Alexander saw Henshaw's footprint in the wet earth, he understood why the man was nicknamed "Bear Tracks." Those size-sixteen boots left a track that he could almost put both feet in.

They followed the creek as it wound its way through the willows and aspens. At times they had to step over fallen aspens and walk around huge granite boulders. The burro had no trouble getting over the downed trees and its hooves seemed to grip the rocky surface like rubber pads.

Then they were back among the tall spruce and pines again and had to go uphill a ways, and when they topped a ridge they could look down and see a road below them.

Henshaw walked on and they continued to follow. Again the girl looked back at Alexander and again he frowned at her. She started to say something, changed her mind, and went on.

The next time they broke out into a clearing, they saw a cabin sitting in the midst of a field of tree stumps. Here, Henshaw paused, glanced back, and said, "Ol' Buckshot's wickiup." They knew then that they were close to El Tejon.

Next they were down on the road, and the girl looked back again. "Won't it be grand to have a bath and some clean clothes?"

Alexander only grunted. She dropped back to walk side by side with him. "What is the first thing you are going to do, James?"

"I don't know. Eat, I guess."

"Where?"

"There's a cafe run by a woman named Ma Blessing. Guess I'll go there." He couldn't keep the gruffness out of his voice.

She stared at him, puzzled, for a moment, then said, "Are you mad at me, James?"

"Naw."

"Are you sure?"

He met her gaze. "Well, maybe I am a little."

"Why?"

"This is not the place to talk about it."

She stared at him another moment with blue-gray eyes and shrugged and looked away.

They walked on in silence. Then, just as they walked around a curve and the town came into sight, she turned to him again. "Do you know what you are,

Mr. James J. Alexander the Third?"

"What?"

"You're squirrel food, that's what you are."

A half-dozen people gathered around them soon after they entered the town, and, by the time they got to the New Windsor Hotel, the crowd had grown to a dozen, all asking questions. Sheriff Boyd Hutchins joined them and took over the questioning.

"I can tell you've been through a lot," he said, "but it's my business to know what's goin' on in this county, and I'll have to get a statement from you."

"Yes, Sheriff," Alexander said, "I have things to tell you. But can I get something to eat first? And Miss, uh, Dobbs needs rest badly."

"Sure. Miss Dobbs, you go on up to your room. They've kept it for you. And you, young feller, you can tell me about it whilst you're feedin' your face over at Ma Blessing's."

The cafe was empty at mid-morning, and Ma Blessing hurried to their table in a corner of the room. "I'm happy to see you back, young man," she said, wiping her hands on her apron. Her plain face was divided into a wide smile. "Is that young lady all right?"

"Yes, Mrs. Blessing, we're both all right. We've had a hard time but we're O.K. now. Or at least I will be as soon as I get some of your good food under my belt."

"You betcha. And I'll send a covered plate over to the hotel for her, if you want."

"That would be nice. I'm sure she would appreciate that."

He ordered hot cakes and bacon and strong black

coffee, then told the sheriff everything that had happened. The food arrived by the time he finished his tale, and he dug into it with a bent fork. It was delicious.

"Yeah, I've seen them two around town," the sheriff drawled. "One of 'em, the big feller, was a powder monkey at the Josey Mine before they shut 'er down. I thought he'd left the country. I didn't have no call to lock 'em up. Come to think of it, I ain't seen 'em for a few days. They must have quit the country when they saw you and the young lady got away from 'em."

"What I'd like to know," Alexander said between mouthfuls, "is who they were taking orders from. They tried to make it look like an accident, like the entrance to the tunnel caved in of its own volition."

"Yeah, it does seem like somebody put 'em up to it. If all they wanted to do was rob and kill you, they coulda just dumped your bodies down the old shaft instead a puttin' you in that drift."

"There's another shaft?"

"Oh, yeah. They sunk a shaft straight down and blasted some stopes and drifts out from it down there about three hundred feet. Then they decided to tunnel under that hill and look for another vein."

"They had two separate mine shafts, then?"

"Yep. They figgered to cut into that rich Josey vein down there under that hill."

"Who could they have been taking orders from?"

"The first thing that come to my mind when you mentioned it was that other young feller, the one that calls hisself Charles Dobbs."

"Is he still in town?"

"Ain't seen 'im for a few days either, but I got a feelin' he's still around somewhere."

"He's an imposter."

Sheriff Boyd Hutchins pulled on one end of his walrus mustache and asked, "What makes you say that?"

"The young woman tricked him. She got him to say his father's real name was John Dobbs when all the time she knew it was Fred."

"Fred? How did you find that out?"

"Papers in his desk at the mine, and some papers I found in his cabin."

"Now, just hold your hosses, young feller, we hunted through that cabin and didn't find nothin', no names nor nothin'."

"It was on a piece of paper folded inside a Montgomery Ward catalog. He had been practicing writing the names of his family and his own name. And his name was on some of the bills of lading we found in a desk at the mine."

"We went through his stuff at the mine too and didn't find anything."

"We?"

"Yeah, me and Joe Webber after he was appointed administrator of the estate."

"And you didn't see those bills of lading?"

"Nope. Reckon we overlooked that."

Alexander chewed rapidly and swallowed so he could say more. "Did you know he was illiterate and had a man named Bertrum Wingate handling his business papers for him?"

"Sure, we all knew that."

"Don't you think it's strange that both he and Mr.

Wingate were killed at the same time?"

"No, not so strange. They was together all the time out at the Josey Mine. They coulda taken a look-see in one of them drifts and done it without tellin' anybody and got blasted. It was Jeb Harlen, the gent you just described, that done the blastin'. He said he didn't know there was anybody in there. Says nobody told him they was goin' in there."

"You say he left after that?"

"He got to broodin' over what happened and took to the bottle and finally quit town. Somebody told me he went over to Cripple Creek. I was kinder surprised to see 'im back in town, but not much."

"I see." Alexander drained his coffee cup and noticed that Ma Blessing was standing behind the counter listening to all that was said. When she saw his cup was empty, she hurried over with a large galvanized coffee pot and refilled it.

The sheriff frowned into his cup and waved away the woman's offer to refill it too. "I'll have to have a man-to-man talk with that other young feller," he said. Suddenly, his face brightened into a smile. "Did she really do that?"

"Do what?"

"Trick that feller into callin' Old Buckshot 'John,' knowin' his real name was Fred?"

Alexander had to chuckle. "She surely did, Sheriff. And she made certain I heard him say it. In fact," he chuckled again, "she got him to repeat it several times."

"Wal, then all I have to do is get him to say it to me, then have a look at those papers, and catch him in the iie."

152

"I have a hunch, Sheriff, that if you can get him and that young lady face to face again, with you in the middle, she'll make a fool of him."

The sheriff reached for his hat, which he had placed on the floor, clamped it on his head, and stood up. "I'll do that." He chuckled and hitched up his gunbelt. "That'll be some event." He went to the door and paused. "You figgerin' on stayin' around?"

"Yes. For a few days, at least."

Two miners in their baggy wool pants came in and sat at the counter, and Ma Blessing stood in front of them, waiting for their orders. Alexander finished his second cup of coffee and reached into his hip pocket for his wallet. "Uh, oh," he said.

He waited until the proprietress returned from the kitchen and motioned her over. "I'm sorry, but I forgot about being robbed. I have no money with me. If you'll be so kind as to trust me, I'll go to my room at the hotel and return immediately with the necessary funds."

"Pay me next time, young man. How was the flapjacks?"

"Delicious. Simply delicious."

"You and that young lady had a purty tough time of it, didn't you? I sent my swamper over to the hotel with a plate of bacon and eggs, the last eggs I've got, and he said she was powerful glad to get it. Did somebody really try to blast up that mine with you and her in it?"

"Yes, Mrs. Blessing."

"And you had to claw your way out like a couple a gophers?"

Alexander grinned. "It was almost like that, except

153

we dug as high as we could get."

She shook her head, eyes sad. "It's a miracle, that's all, a miracle."

Back at the New Windsor Hotel, Alexander found some clean clothes in his suitcases, went downstairs to the men's water closet and took a long lukewarm bath. By the time he had toweled himself dry, he had a plan. He would take the stage to Rosebud next day and send off a telegram to his superintendent in Chicago. And tonight he would write a long letter home.

Wouldn't everyone's eyes pop out when they read it.

Chapter Thirteen

The ride on the Concord stagecoach was no smoother leaving El Tejon than it had been going there, and Alexander was glad he was going only a short distance. Two of the other passengers looked to be loggers with their Scotch caps and overalls, and the other, a well-dressed, short, fat man, was apparently a drummer.

Alexander was the last to board the stage and he found himself sitting between one on the timberjacks and the window. That was a situation that had to change. The man was chewing tobacco, and the stage hadn't gotten clear of town when he began nervously looking for a place to spit.

" 'Scuse me, mister, he said, leaning over Alexander's lap so he could spit out the window.

"Sir, would you mind trading places with me?" Alexander asked. "You see, I, uh, don't chew."

"Shore. Glad to oblige."

The coach bounced over a rock as Alexander raised up to trade places, and he bumped his head on the ceiling. "Thank you," he said to the man, resettling his hat.

The short, fat drummer held out his hand to shake with Alexander. "Allow me to introduce myself. I am Thomas C. Spitzweiler and I represent the manufacturing firm of Johnson and Hayward." Alexander shook hands with him.

"I came to El Tejon with the best line of men's underwear the world has ever seen," Thomas C. Spitzweiler said. "Here, let me show you." He opened the suitcase he held on his lap. "Just look at this. Genuine wool. And look at the crotch. Cut full with a pouch. No more bunching up and pinching the—" He winked. "You know what I mean. And the seat. Two, big, imitation-mother-of-pearl buttons, the kind you can handle by feel. Notice that the seat drops down out of harm's way." The drummer glanced around and grinned a lascivious grin. "I'm glad there are no ladies aboard. This article allows a man to answer the call of nature with a minimum of trouble. And it's warm. Feel of this material. Did you know that wool absorbs the body's perspiration better than cotton? Yessir, you can work up a sweat in this suit and never feel any wetness."

Alexander lost interest. His mind was back at the New Windsor Hotel and the girl who called herself Josephine Dobbs. He hadn't seen her since they got back to El Tejon, and he wondered what she was doing. He wanted to see her and yet he didn't. He had considered knocking on her hotel-room door, but he couldn't think of anything to say to her. Eventually

156

he would have to see her again, but first he wanted to find out everything he could about the Dobbs family.

What would he do if his suspicions were confirmed? Alexander slumped in his seat. He didn't want to think about that.

"I'd say you're a size forty," the drummer was saying as he held a pair of briefs up to one of the timberjacks. "Yep. A size forty for sure. I'll tell you, gentlemen, your underclothes are the most important garments you wear. If you're not comfortable with your underwear, you're not comfortable period. Here. Only six bits. O.K., since we're traveling partners, make it four bits."

By changing teams midway on the road to Rosebud, the stage made good time and arrived at a high trot at the stage office on the city's main street shortly after noon. Alexander climbed out stiffly and stretched his legs.

The town was alive. There was heavy horse-and-wagon traffic on the street and pedestrians were shoulder to shoulder on the sidewalks. There was even a motorcar chugging down the street, something that Alexander hadn't seen since he came through Denver on his way to El Tejon.

Most of the Main Street buildings were of brick and stone and were two story. A brick-and-stone bank building with a large clock hanging over the sidewalk stood on the corner next to the stage depot. Alexander stopped a pedestrian and asked directions to the telegraph office. He was directed to the railroad depot two blocks north and a block east.

It was cool inside the depot. Alexander approached a counter with a telegraph sign hanging over it. A

157

small, wrinkled, bald man wearing a green eyeshade and garters on his sleeves wrote down his message as he dictated it.

Believe Dobbs widow Margaret. Family live St. Louis. May have been in fire. Advise soonest. Will await reply.

It would take time for the superintendent in Chicago to wire the agency in St. Louis, and for the St. Louis agent to check out the recent fires that could have wiped out a family. Alexander had time to kill.

He checked into the Bedford Hotel, washed his face in the men's room, and went to a restaurant for a sandwich and a glass of milk. Feeling restless, he walked down the street, idly looking into the windows of the mercantile stores. When he heard the approaching train whistle, he decided to walk over to the depot and watch the train come in.

To the local citizens, the arrival of a locomotive was exciting, and thirty or more people were on hand to greet it. The train consisted of a ten-wheeler engine, a string of freight cars, and two Pullman chair cars. Some of the passengers who disembarked appeared to be getting their first look at the Wild West. They were all eyes. Others were greeted with hugs and kisses by relatives. Alexander smiled to himself, knowing that the newcomers hadn't seen anything of the Wild West yet. Boy, could he tell them a thing or two.

On an impulse, he went back inside the depot and sent another telegram, this one to his mother. It said: "Am fine. Do not worry. Love James."

He knew his mother was worrying about him. She

always worried when her sons were away from home.

Alexander walked around town for awhile and had supper in the same restaurant. He went to his hotel, read the latest edition of the *Rosebud Gazette*, then finished reading the Charles Dickens book he had brought.

When he blew out the lamp and settled into bed, he tried to think about his family back home in Chicago, but all he could think about was the young woman who called herself Josephine Dobbs.

There was no reply to his telegram when he checked the next morning, and he idly stood in front of the depot watching people come and go. A rail handcar caught his attention, and he watched the two men on it pump up and down on the teeter-totter handles to keep it going down the track. They pumped it to the nearby switching yards where the train engines could turn around and stopped beside a large pile of railroad ties and rail sections.

Alexander, with nothing better to do, walked to the switching yard and saw that that was as far as the railroad went. When he got there, he noticed four more piles of ties and rails. It looked, he noted with satisfaction, as though the railroad company was planning to extend the line in the direction of El Tejon.

It was a pleasant August morning, and he watched the two men count the number of ties in a pile, watched one write something on a clipboard he carried and go on to the next pile.

"Good morning," he said pleasantly as he approached.

Both men glanced at him, but only one spoke. "Mornin'." The man wore bib overalls and a high-crowned bill cap.

"Looks like you're getting ready to lay more track."

"Was," the man replied, studying his clipboard.

"I understand you're going to El Tejon."

"Was." The man went to the next pile and stopped, pencil poised, waiting for the other man to finish counting.

"Excuse me," Alexander said, following, "but I was told the D&RG was planning to extend this line."

The man dropped his hands to his sides, pencil in one and clipboard in the other. "Mister, I'm tryin' to count these here timbers and I can't do it with you askin' questions."

"I'm very sorry. I didn't mean to bother you. But may I ask, do you know what the D&RG plans to do?"

Clearly exasperated, the man said, "All I know is we piled this stuff here and was ready to build some more railroad and the boss tole us to hold off."

"Oh? Then you're not a railroad superintendent?"

"Do I look like a big shot?"

"Excuse me. I meant no insult."

"I'm a labor foreman and I was told to lay off my men till I got word from Denver."

"I see. Then you have no immediate plans to extend the line?"

"Not right now. Maybe later, maybe not. I just work here."

"I see. Thank you very much." Alexander left, somewhat puzzled by what he had learned.

At eleven o'clock by the clock outside the bank, he went back to the telegraph office and asked again. He was handed a handwritten note on yellow paper.

Margaret Dobbs and two daughters among fourteen died in tenement fire July twenty three last. Still checking. Watch for next dispatch.

It was a crestfallen James J. Alexander III who walked with slow steps back to the Bedford Hotel. The telegram left no doubt. She was an imposter. She had known the Dobbs family, and, when they were all killed in a fire, she assumed the identity of Josephine Dobbs. The letter she carried from Bear Tracks Henshaw could be a forgery. It would be easy to forge the penmanship of a man who is barely literate. And the postmarked envelope? Well, there had to be an explanation.

The more he thought about it, the more the evidence stacked up against her in his mind. How did she know about the Indians, panthers, and rattlesnakes Out West? Easy. She had taken a buggy ride with the sheriff, and the sheriff could have told her. She had said she was not at home when the fire was discovered. Did she live in the same tenement house? Probably.

He walked on past the restaurant where he had taken his meals and didn't stop. Eating was the last thing he wanted to do. What he wanted to do right then was to get into one of those Pullman cars and go back home. He was sick about the whole thing. Just sick.

In his room, he pulled off his shoes and lay back on

the bed, his right arm over his eyes. He couldn't stop thinking about her. She was the most courageous and wonderful girl he had ever met. They had had adventures together that would make the pulp Western writers shake their heads in disbelief. He would never forget her. Why, oh, why did she have to be a crook?

And he would have to be the one to expose her. She would hate him. That was the worst part. He was her enemy.

Suddenly Alexander sat up.

O.K., so she was an imposter. At least she hadn't harmed anyone. So she was trying to take over property that didn't rightfully belong to her. So what? It didn't belong to anyone else either. No one living, that is. She wasn't cheating anyone. If she didn't claim it, it would go to the state.

After what she, they, had been through, she was entitled to some kind of reward.

"Dammit," he said aloud. "I'll be darned—no, I'll be damned—if I'm going to stand in her way."

Once that decision was reached, he put on his shoes, combed his hair, and went back to the telegraph office. There he wrote a brief message on a sheet of paper and handed it to the agent. It read:

Must resign. Sorry.

One day he would explain to his superintendent in full, but not now. Now he would . . . what was he going to do?

Work for her, that's what. She had a pretty good case for herself but no definite proof. Well, he was going to see that no one else got the property. If she couldn't get it, by George, no other imposter was going to.

He started to leave the depot when he heard someone calling his name. It was the agent, peering at him from under his green eyeshade.

"Yes?"

"A dispatch is just coming in with your name on it. From St. Louis."

Alexander went back to the counter. A man sitting at a desk listened to the clickety-click-clack-clack of the telegraph key and copied the message on a sheet of paper. When the key stopped its noise, he brought the sheet over to the agent who handed it to Alexander. It read:

Josephine Dobbs identified two days after fire. Believe alive and in Colorado.

At first his mouth dropped open, and then he let out a loud "Who-o-op."

"It's her. She's real." He was so happy he danced a jig and waved the message in the air. "She's the real thing."

"Mister, are you O.K.?" the agent asked.

"Am I O.K.? I am the happiest man in the world. She's no phony, she's the real article."

Back on the sidewalk, Alexander walked with springy steps toward his hotel. He had to get back to El Tejon and tell her. Wait. He slowed his steps, deep in thought. O.K., if I'm working for her, what should I do? Just go back to El Tejon and wait for something to happen? Absolutely not. Make something happen. What?

163

O.K., what does an heiress have to do to prove she is entitled to the deceased's estate? For the first time since he had dropped out of law school, he wished he had gone on. What to do? Let's see. File a petition with the probate court?

Of course. Petition the court.

"Oh, sir," he said to a pedestrian. "Would you kindly direct me to the county courthouse."

"Down the block, around the corner, and across the alley," the pedestrian said.

The courthouse was a three-story building of gray stone with a red-tile roof, high ceiling, and a tile floor. The court clerk's office had a large sign over the door. He went in and stepped up to the counter. When he told the clerk, a middle-aged plump woman, what he wanted, she advised him to consult a lawyer.

Of course. He should have known that. He remembered an old axiom he had heard many times at home: anyone who represents himself in a court of law has a fool for a client.

Just before he started to leave through the big front doors of the courthouse, another thought popped into his mind and he went back.

"I wonder," he said, smiling pleasantly, "could you tell me whether anyone named Dobbs has filed a petition for probate recently?"

The clerk said she would check. She went to a nearby desk and shuffled a stack of papers. When she came back, she handed him a paper with the word "petition" across the top. He scanned it, and the smile left his face.

It was a petition asking that the estate of one John Dobbs, who died intestate on June 21, 1899, be admitted to probate and that one Charles E. Dobbs be declared the sole heir. The petition had been filed four days earlier by Jonas B. Wiltheimer, attorney at law.

Chapter Fourteen

Charles E. Dobbs indeed. He was wasting no time. The petition was filed while Alexander and Josephine Dobbs were lost in the mountains. The petitioner thought he had no opposition.

With slow steps, Alexander left the courthouse and walked out onto the sidewalks of Rosebud, Colorado. Filed by Jonas B. Wiltheimer, attorney at law. That phony con man from Kansas City knew to engage a lawyer.

Well, Alexander's steps quickened, if that keister spieler could engage a lawyer, then so, by George, could he.

Alexander walked down the street, looking at the business and professional signs on the upstairs windows. There was a sign for a land surveyor, a doctor of dentistry, an attorney at law. Oops, it was the offices of Jonas B. Wiltheimer. He remembered another axiom his father had often mentioned: anyone who hires an unknown for a lawyer is a fool. He could wire his father and ask if the Chicago law firm of Alexander and Alexander could recommend anyone in Rosebud, Colorado, but that would be a waste of time. His father and grandfather knew no one in Colorado.

In the next block he saw more signs in the second-floor windows, but he didn't find another lawyer's shingle until he had walked another block and passed a door that opened into a stairwell. Painted on the door was the message: The Honorable Silas K. Cantwell.

Alexander climbed the stairs to the second floor, wondering what kind of person Silas K. Cantwell was. The wooden floor creaked under his feet when he got to the landing. He stopped before a frosted-glass door with the name painted on it in gold script. He opened it and went in.

Cantwell had an impressive collection of statute books lining a wall of his office and a collection of diplomas framed and hanging on another wall. He had more law books and papers scattered over a large oak desk. But Cantwell had his back to the room and was idly looking out the window, watching the street below. He spun around when Alexander entered the room.

The first thing that went through Alexander's mind was another of his father's axioms: an idle lawyer is an incompetent lawyer. He wished he hadn't come here.

"Yes?" said Silas K. Cantwell, his eyebrows raised above his rimless glasses.

"I, uh, may need the services of a barrister," said James J. Alexander. When he got a look at the lawyer, his apprehension was somewhat abated. Cantwell was middle-aged, with a bushy mustache and thick hair parted in the middle, average height and stocky. Even though he may have been an idle lawyer, he was a well-dressed one in his dark suit with a matching vest, gold watch chain, cravat, and high stiff collar. He looked to be successful.

He sat in a wooden chair behind his desk and motioned for Alexander to occupy another wooden chair across from him. "What sort of legal problem do you have, sir?"

"It's a matter of probate. I, uh, am inquiring for a friend who is the next of kin of the late Frederick Dobbs who died intestate. She is from St. Louis."

The lawyer leaned back in his chair, and Alexander noticed that it had a spring under the seat which allowed it to be tilted back. "Who, may I ask, was Frederick Dobbs?"

"Mr. Dobbs owned the rich Josey gold mine just west of the small city of El Tejon. When he died last June, no one there knew anything about him. Very few even knew his first name."

"Ah, yes," Cantwell put his hands together with the fingertips touching. "Seems I've heard of him, rather of his death. Was he the gentleman known as Buckshot Dobbs?"

"Why, yes. How is it that you have heard of him?"

"Why, uh, I believe it was the Honorable Judge Rutherford who mentioned it. We had dinner one day."

"You know the judge?"

Cantwell rested his chin on his fingertips. "Oh, yes. We are a small community here, Mr. uh—?"

"Alexander. James J. Alexander. I am related to the Chicago law firm of Alexander and Alexander."

The lawyer sat up straight and his hands came down to rest on top of his desk. "You are?"

"Yes. My father is James J. Alexander the Second."

"Are you a practicing attorney?"

"No, sir, I am not. I have not yet finished school."

"Umm." Cantwell rearranged some papers on his desk. "Did your father by any chance recommend me?"

"No, sir. I doubt very much if my father knows anyone in Colorado."

Cantwell's shoulders slumped slightly, and Alexander could see that he was disappointed. He was silent while he studied his fingernails, then said, "You mentioned that you are acting on behalf of a friend?"

"Yes. Miss Josephine Dobbs. I have reason to believe she is the daughter of Frederick Dobbs and the only living heir."

"Do you have proof?"

Alexander unfolded the telegrams and handed them to the lawyer. "Until I resigned this morning, I was an agent for the Pinkerton National Detective Agency. These are messages I received from an agent in St. Louis."

Cantwell frowned in concentration as he read the messages. Looking up, he said, "You resigned this morning? May I ask why?"

"Call it a conflict of interest, Mr. Cantwell. I have become a, uh, personal friend of Miss Dobbs, and I feel that, under the circumstances, I cannot do an honest job of investigating any case that she is involved in."

The lawyer studied Alexander's face a moment, and Alexander could guess what he was thinking. He was thinking that Josephine Dobbs was probably an attractive young woman and this young man sitting here had become infatuated with her. Well, he was right.

"Where is this Miss Dobbs?"

"I last saw her in El Tejon. She is no doubt there now. I'm afraid you'll have to go there. I understand Judge Rutherford conducts hearings there."

"Yes. The judge divides his time between here, El Tejon, and Fort Bliss, a city forty miles east of here."

"That's for the better, I believe, Mr. Cantwell. As I said, I am not an attorney, but I was brought up in a family of attorneys and it seems to me we would have a better chance in El Tejon."

"Why do you say that, Mr. Alexander?"

"An attempt was made on her life a few days ago. Everyone in El Tejon knows about it by now. I have a feeling that the town is sympathetic toward her."

"You're probably correct. Are you authorized to engage an attorney on the young lady's behalf?"

"No, only she can do that, but I'll be happy to pay your expenses if you care to journey to El Tejon and meet with her. Can you do that?"

"Why, yes, I believe I can."

"When can you leave?"

"Oh, let's see, uh, today is Friday, I can be there on the stage on the, uh, let's see, Tuesday. I do have other matters to clear up, but I can meet you there next Tuesday."

"Fine." Alexander stood up and offered his hand. "I'm at the New Windsor Hotel, Mr. Cantwell. I'll be expecting you next Tuesday."

The lawyer shook hands with him but appeared to have more to say. "I, uh—"

"Oh, forgive me, sir. Of course." Alexander reached

for the folding money he carried in his inside coat pocket. He counted out three ten-dollar bills and handed them to the lawyer. "This will pay your expenses, and if you decide to represent Miss Dobbs, I'm sure arrangements can be made to handle your fee."

With that, Alexander left and hurried to the stage depot to buy a ticket back to El Tejon.

Only one passenger shared the coach with him on the way back. It seemed that fewer people were going to El Tejon than were leaving. The other passenger, a dour little man in a stiff collar and a dark suit with the coat buttoned only at the top, appeared to be no more interested in conversation than Alexander was.

But they had to at least say their "How do you do's," remark about the weather, and inquire of each other's professions. The little man was a barber and intended to open a tonsorial parlor in El Tejon. He had heard that the town was on the verge of becoming another boom town, and he wanted to buy a lot and erect a building while the price was affordable.

Alexander asked whether he had heard that the D&RG was planning to build track to El Tejon.

"Oh, yes. That's common knowledge, Mr. Alexander. Rosebud is the end point now, but the El Tejon accommodation is coming, yessir."

Conversation was only sporadic after that, and Alexander's mind was busy wondering how Josephine Dobbs would react when he told her about his activities on her behalf, and wondering too about the town of El Tejon. Was it really on the verge of booming? It could be. If the Josey Mine got back into production, the town's economy would pick up. He wondered if Miss Dobbs would stay in town as owner of the mine or sell it. Probably sell it. She was a city girl.

He couldn't help noticing the difference between El Tejon and Rosebud as the stage team trotted down El Tejon's main street and stopped at the New Windsor Hotel. Rosebud was alive with activity while the smaller community was quiet and dull.

After washing his face out of the china bowl in his room, he knocked on the door of room 206. He got no answer. He was disappointed.

Back in his room, he started to change into his new denim pants, but decided they needed laundering and patching before they were worn again. That left only city clothes, and he decided to buy some new denims. First, he counted his money. Enough for a time and, when that was gone, he could go to Rosebud and wire home for more. Besides, he had a salary check coming from the Pinkertons. He wouldn't starve.

As soon as he entered the mercantile he wished he hadn't. The owner, John Bokhauser, saw him come in and hurried from behind a counter to greet him.

"Mr. Alexander, how good to see you again. I was afraid you had left our little city after what happened to you."

"No, Mr. Bokhauser, I'm still here. I need some new clothes, however."

"You just name it, sir. We have just about everything in stock." The merchant called to a clerk. "Show Mr. Alexander the latest styles from New York." Turning back to Alexander, he said, "When the mine reopens and the sawmill is enlarged, we will be ready to serve the clientele that surely will come to El Tejon. Everyone from miners to sawmill hands to railroad builders to bankers and businessmen."

Without waiting for a comment from Alexander, he talked on. "Yes, sir, El Tejon will soon become the fastest growing little city in the West, Mr. Alexander, and a wonderful place to do business. May I ask, have you found anything here that interests you?"

"No, not yet. I'm wondering about the mining ventures. Activity seems to be a little slow."

"Don't worry about that. The Josey Mine will reopen soon, and, Mr. Alexander, when it does, they will be taking twenty-five to thirty tons of ore out of there every day and it will bring more than one hundred and twenty dollars a ton, you can bet on that. The mine employs fifty-five men, and with that much payroll money circulating the town will boom. Add to that an addition to the sawmill that Mr. Stewart is planning. You know, Mr. Calvin Stewart, prominent rancher and businessman? Just as soon as rail is laid here from Rosebud, he will be shipping lumber by the carload and will employ a hundred or more men."

He was trying a super sales job, Alexander knew. According to papers he had seen at the mine, only forty-eight miners were on the payroll. But Alexander had learned that, when someone was selling something, complete honesty was scarce.

"Tell me, Mr. Bokhauser, perhaps I'm invading your privacy by asking, but what brought you to El Tejon? What prompted you to invest here?"

"Gold, Mr. Alexander. El Tejon is going to be another Cripple Creek, and you no doubt have heard

173

how men are getting fabuously rich there."

"Yes, I've heard. But, as I said, activity here seems to be dying."

Bokhauser winked a conspiratorial wink. "Don't believe what you see. There's still a lot of rich ore under the ground here. It seems that Mr. Dobbs filed on the richest vein and has exclusive rights to it. When his daughter is declared the rightful heir, the mine will be reopened and you'll see. And that's not all. The General Assembly has only this year divided Ute County and El Paso County. El Tejon is now the county seat of the new Webber County, and Cripple Creek is now the county seat of Teller County. We'll have a courthouse built by early next year and it will be a beauty."

Alexander bought a pair of heavy blue cotton pants and a mountain-man shirt of homespun muslin. He went back to his room and changed, then knocked on the door of room 206 again. Still no answer.

Out of curiosity, he knocked on the door of room 202 but got no answer there either.

Sheriff Boyd Hutchins wasn't in his office, but a wizened little man with a wrinkled face and a bald head told him the sheriff was out at the Josey Mine with "that young lady from the East."

"Why?"

"The sheriff wants to collect all the business papers and stuff, and the young lady wanted to go along. Said she was skeered to go out there by herself. I don't blame her none after what happened to her and you."

"Do you know whether the sheriff has arrested anyone?"

"No, but he's lookin' for 'em."

"Tell me, Mr. uh—?"

"Wilson. John P. Wilson."

"Mr. Wilson, where does the circuit judge hold court?"

"In there. We got a judge's high bench, a jury box, and everything." Wilson pointed to a door on the opposite side of the sheriff's office, and Alexander remembered the wooden-frame building attached to the sheriff's stone office building.

"I see. I assumed the jail was in there."

"The jail is through there." Wilson pointed to another door.

"Then who is the court clerk?"

"I am."

"Oh, I see."

"I'm the clerk, bailiff, town clerk, and deputy sheriff."

Alexander had to smile. "Excuse me for asking so many questions, but I am curious, is the town of El Tejon incorporated?"

"You bet. The triumvirate took care of that. We'll have some elections by and by."

"The triumvirate?"

The wrinkled little man grinned. "That's what some of us call 'em."

"Call who?"

"Those three, you know, the banker, Mr. Webber, Cal Stewart, and old Bokhauser over at the store. They're the ones that platted the town and done most of the building. They've got a lot of pull up in Denver and they get what they want."

"I see." Alexander wasn't surprised at that. "When will the judge hold court again?"

"Next Wednesday. Ain't much on the docket. Sheriff arrested a miner for shootin' his gun inside the town limits, and there's a man accused of butcherin' a pig that didn't belong to him."

"Does he empanel a jury very often?"

"Hasn't yet. Everybody pleads guilty. The sheriff won't arrest 'em unless he's got the goods on 'em. But we can round up a jury if need be."

Alexander was hungry, but he waited in his room until he heard her door open and close. He washed his face again and combed his hair and went next door and knocked.

She took her time answering, and Alexander wished he had waited and given her time to freshen up before he knocked. When finally she opened the door, her face had a fresh scrubbed look and her blond hair was brushed and shiny. The young man's heart picked up a beat when he saw her.

"Good evening, Miss Dobbs."

"The Honorable Mr. Alexander." She said it in a flat tone, without expression. "Are you still detecting?"

He grinned a wry grin. "Yes. I have something to tell you."

"I'll bet you have. Do you disappear often, or only when you're on the trail of a terrible imposter or something?"

"I went to Rosebud, Miss Dobbs, and I learned some things that concern you. I would like to talk to you about it." He wished he could put more authority into his voice.

"I don't give a busted fingernail what you learned." She started to close the door.

"Miss Dobbs, please." My God, was he begging? Had he hurt her feelings that badly? "I'm on your side. I'm trying to help you."

She paused. "What was it you said back there on the road to town? You said you were mad at me and you wouldn't talk about it. What kind of whiffler are you, anyway?"

"I apologize. I was confused. Now I know more about your situation."

She stared hard at him and finally shrugged. "O.K., I'm a little confused myself. I'll have to try to find an attorney. Perhaps you can advise me about that."

"May I come in?"

She gave him a condescending look. "Well, not likely. Not in my room. There must be someplace else we can talk."

Grinning, he suggested that they have dinner together in the hotel dining room, and she promised to meet him there in half an hour.

Chapter Fifteen

When again they met, she was wearing the white lacy dress, and he wondered if she had washed it herself by hand. Men's heads turned when she entered the dining room, and Alexander was again reminded that she was a very attractive young lady. Their wine glasses filled and their orders taken, he wasted no time getting into his subject.

"The first step is to file a petition for probate, and I have engaged a lawyer to do that for you. Now if I have acted hastily, I apologize, but I felt that we have to act quickly. You see your competitor, the man who calls himself Charles Dobbs, has filed for probate ahead of you. He had to go to Rosebud, the county seat, the old county seat rather, to file, and he has engaged an attorney there."

She paused with the wine glass halfway to her lips. "He did that?"

"Yes. It appears, Miss Dobbs, Josephine, that he is serious about pursuing the matter. I know, and of course you know that he is an imposter." Alexander chuckled, "He didn't even know the deceased's first name. You tricked him into revealing that much."

She was shaking her head negatively. "I can't believe he's still serious. He hasn't a legal leg to stand on, as you lawyers say. When was he in Rosebud?"

"While we were lost in the mountains. I'm betting he thought we would never be seen alive again, and he had a clear road with no opposition. Now that we're back, I can't believe he'll go on with it. But even if he doesn't, you'll still have to satisfy a probate judge that you are the only living heir at law of Frederick Dobbs."

"I know that, but I have a problem. I have no funds for a lawyer. In fact, I am rapidly running out of money."

"Don't worry about that. I'll make you a loan. Now, the lawyer I have engaged is Silas Cantwell. I know nothing about him, and, if he doesn't please you, we can find another. He'll be here on Tuesday."

Their meal came and he was hungry. She picked at her food, chewing daintily, seemingly deep in thought. "Did you say you learned more about me? What and how?"

Wiping his mouth with a linen napkin, Alexander swallowed and said, "I wired the Pinkerton office in Chicago and they wired an operative in St. Louis. I mentioned what you told me about a fire, and the St. Louis operative checked on it. I can understand why you were reluctant to talk about it, Josephine. Apparently the authorities thought you had perished in the fire too but located you later." Alexander reached into his coat pocket and handed her the telegrams.

179

She read the messages slowly and looked down at her plate. "I guess you know all about it then."

"Yes. We should be able to convince the probate court that you are Josephine Dobbs and the only living heir of the late Frederick Dobbs."

"You keep saying 'we.' Why are you doing this?"

"Because I want to help. I misjudged you once and I'm sorry. We had some adventures together, and I—I want to help, that's all."

After dinner they went out and walked on the plank sidewalks from one end of the main street to the other, then went back to the hotel and sat in the lobby.

"What was it like growing up in a mountain cabin, Josephine?" She sat beside him on an overstuffed sofa and crossed her legs. "It wasn't as bad for Ettie and me as it was for Mother. She worked constantly and was taking on the characteristics of other mountain women, you know, kind of sinewy, with lips always compressed. Let me back up a step, my mother was a lady and she cared about her appearance. Why she married my father, I'm not sure. She wouldn't talk about it. But Ettie and I figured that he was once a handsome adventurer with dreams about the future, and she fell for him.

"After about ten years of the frontier life, she decided he wasn't so dashing anymore and was nothing but a failure vainly looking for a chance to get rich quick.

"Ettie and I remembered Dad well, though. He was good to us, always making us toys and things. We lived a rugged existence, but we never went hungry or cold. Dad saw to that. I—" she hesitated a second, then went on "—believe he loved us. But we were

180

poor."

"Did you have relatives in St. Louis?"

"Yes, my mother's family lived there and Mother was raised there. My grandparents helped us when we went back, then they died one at a time. They didn't leave much, but it was enough that we were able to keep a small flat in a tenement house. Not in the best part of town, but not in the worst either."

They were silent a moment, and she added with a smile, "We had a hard time getting used to the city, Ettie and I. Mother warned us ten times a day about the traffic in the streets. We were strong, though, brought up the way we were, and when other kids hoo-rawed us too much we just socked them on their noses."

Alexander chuckled. "I'll bet they thought you talked funny. When I first came out here, I thought everyone here talked funny, then I realized that I was the strange one."

"Oh, I had a terrible time learning to talk like a city kid. The hardest was learning to pronounce the 'g' endings, you know, putting the 'g' at the end of everything, like 'going' instead of 'goin'.' But Mother insisted that we learn, and she made us practice every day."

They talked until it was late. Alexander was enjoying himself. The more he got to know her the more attractive she became. When he walked her to her room, he tried to find a way to extend the evening, but all he could do was stammer, "I, uh, would you care to, uh, may I come in? Just for a second?"

Smiling sweetly, she stood on tiptoe, kissed him quickly on the lips and stepped back.

181

"No way, J.J." She closed the door.

Alexander was impatient to get the legal proceedings underway, but he had learned in a lifetime of hearing lawyers talk that the wheels of justice turned slowly. Not always because of overcrowded dockets, but often because the lawyers wanted it that way. They got bigger fees that way.

Miss Josephine Dobbs was staying in her room most of the time now and he saw her only at dinner. He went for short walks in the mountains, being careful to look behind him now and then and pick out landmarks. He wasn't about to get lost again.

He liked the mountains, the tall trees sighing in the breeze, the friendly little chipmunks, the squirrels and birds. He was held spellbound one afternoon when he heard a racket in the sky, looked up, and saw two ravens and a bald eagle playing a game with one another.

First the ravens would chase the eagle, cawing wildly, and then the eagle would chase the ravens, screeching at the top of its voice. They soared so gracefully in the blue sky that he smiled with the pleasure of watching them. The eagle was bigger and stronger, but the ravens could outmaneuver it. They played tag for several minutes, cawing and screeching, then finally went their separate ways.

The same day, he was sitting at the base of a large boulder, contemplating the world, a law career, Harvard, when he was startled to see a tawny coyote contemplating him.

The animal was sitting on its haunches not more

than seventy-five feet away. Its head was cocked to one side as it tried to figure out what kind of animal he was. Alexander stayed still, not knowing whether to run or stay. He had read about the wild coyotes and wolves out West and was made to believe they were man-eaters. But this one didn't seem to be dangerous at all. It just sat there and studied him.

Alexander stiffened when the coyote stood up and took a few steps toward him but relaxed when it stopped and sat on its haunches again. Now they were studying each other, each trying to understand the other.

When the four-legged animal took a few more steps toward him, Alexander tried talking to it. "I mean you no harm. I won't hurt you. Besides, you've got better weapons than I have." The coyote came a little closer.

"Come on. If I'm not afraid, you shouldn't be." Finally, the coyote was only thirty feet away, sitting on its haunches, ears pricked up, head cocked to one side, listening. It looked just like a friendly dog trying to decide whether the man-animal was also friendly. Man and beast watched each other for several minutes.

Then the coyote, deciding it had seen, smelled, and listened to enough, got up and trotted away. It stopped and looked back before it disappeared into the timber.

How human it was, Alexander thought. The birds too. The main difference between humans and wild life, he thought, was hands with fingers. And intelligence. Man has the intelligence to organize and enact laws to live by rather than to live by the law of the jungle. And that reminded him of what he was thinking about before he saw the coyote. Where there are laws there are disputes over the law, and that's where the courts come in. Arguing in a court of law is better than any alternative. Anything else is a jungle existence. Lawyers were a necessary part of civilization. They served a vital function.

And Alexander had given up a career in law. Would Harvard take him back? He couldn't help thinking about how foolish he had been.

On Tuesday, the stage from Rosebud rattled into town, and the lawyer, Silas K. Cantwell, stepped out.

The dapper lawyer wasted no time. He checked into the hotel, carried his Gladstone bag and briefcase to his room, washed his face, and met Alexander in the plush hotel lobby. Alexander had knocked on Miss Dobb's door and advised her to meet with them.

"Nice place here," the lawyer said, looking around. "One wouldn't expect to find such luxurious accommodations in such a tiny town."

"They've got plans for El Tejon," Alexander said. "They expect the town to become another Cripple Creek."

"And well it might. Now then," the lawyer opened his briefcase, "I checked with the court clerk of Ute County and learned that a Mr. Charles Dobbs has also filed a petition for probate, claiming to be the heir at law of John Dobbs."

Chuckling, Alexander said, "I don't think we have to worry about him. He doesn't even know the deceased's real first name. I happen to know his name was Frederick."

"Umm. You're sure about that?"

"I'm sure, and I'll bet the sheriff is also sure by

now. He'll be able to testify."

Silas K. Cantwell digested that bit of information, then stretched his arms out in front of him, freeing his shirt cuffs from under the short, dark coat he was wearing. "I consulted with his attorney, the Honorable Jonas B. Wiltheimer, and told him of the telegrams you received from the Pinkerton National Detective Agency. He was impressed and admitted his client has a weak case."

"Is he going to pursue the matter further?"

"He appeared to be undecided. But we're not out of the woods, so to speak. The attorney general's office is interested and has announced that it will contest our petition on behalf of the state of Colorado."

"I suppose someone has to contest it."

"I'm sure the judge would insist that the A.G. do some investigating."

"What do you think they'll do?"

"They will no doubt contact the Pinkertons and the authorities in St. Louis, and no matter who we call as witnesses, they'll no doubt cross-examine them relentlessly. By the way, do you know anyone we can get to testify on our behalf? You know enough about law to know what kind of witnesses we need."

"There's the sheriff and Clarence Henshaw, also known as Bear Tracks Henshaw." Alexander explained who Henshaw was, and it was then that Miss Josephine Dobbs descended the curving stairs, holding her long skirt above her shoes with one hand and smiling sweetly. Her blond curly hair shone from a recent brushing and her clothes were neat and fresh.

Both men stood up, and Alexander introduced the lawyer to her. Silas K. Cantwell was immediately

185

taken by her. He bowed and kissed her hand and gushed something about how nice it was to meet her and how he hoped he could represent her in her petition for probate.

She smiled and her blue eyes were lively. "Of course, Mr. Cantwell. If Mr. Alexander recommends you, I am certain you'll be an excellent legal counsel."

Alexander moved a chair closer for her, and she sat in it with her ankles crossed, facing the two men as they sat on a divan.

The lawyer cleared his throat, shot his cuffs, and spoke again, "Miss Dobbs, as your counsel, I need to know all about you. I wonder, do you suppose we could have dinner?"

"Why, yes," she glanced at Alexander, "that would be nice. We do need to include Mr. Alexander as he has done some investigating into this affair."

"Very well." The lawyer's voice showed he was disappointed over including Alexander. "Now, tell me about yourself and your family."

She talked in a clear voice, with just enough volume that the two men could hear but no one else in the lobby could. She told about the letters, the first two from her father informing his family that he had struck it rich, and the sad one from Bear Tracks Henshaw. When she mentioned the fire, her voice dropped so low that the men could barely understand her, and she seemed to be fighting hard to control her emotions.

They talked for more than two hours, then went to their respective rooms to dress for dinner. At dinner in the hotel dining room, they continued their conversation, and Alexander noticed the lawyer never passed

186

up a chance to put his hand over hers, to touch her.

A pang of jealousy started in Alexander's stomach and crept into his throat, causing him to swallow hard. When she smiled sweetly at the lawyer, and he half-turned his chair toward her, putting his back to him, Alexander couldn't stand it.

"Uh," Alexander cleared his throat, "as I said in your office, Mr. Cantwell, I believe the town is sympathetic to Miss Dobbs and is eager to get the estate settled and the Josey Mine reopened. May I ask, is it possible under Colorado law to have the hearing before a jury?"

"Yes." Silas K. Cantwell reluctantly turned back to Alexander. "It is our prerogative. The only problem might be in finding six jurors who can read and write. I have had enough experience in Judge Rutherford's court to know that he insists on literacy."

"There seems to be considerable unemployment in El Tejon. Surely we can find six idle literate men to sit on a jury."

"They don't have to be idle, you know. If the judge says they sit on a jury, they sit on a jury no matter what else they have to do. The judge accepts no excuses."

When they finally retired to their rooms, Alexander listened carefully to activity in the hall, fearing that Silas K. Cantwell would try to talk his way into Miss Dobbs's room, and, sure enough, an hour after she had closed her door someone was knocking lightly on it.

Walking softly in his sock feet, Alexander went to his door and listened. He couldn't hear much of what was said, but he smiled to himself when he heard her door close again and heard someone walking away. Miss Dobbs had been sweet-talked before and she wasn't having any.

The first thing Alexander did next morning was to go looking for Bear Tracks Henshaw. He looked in the Top Hat saloon, on the streets, and at the livery barn. He went to the sheriff's office and told Sheriff Boyd Hutchins that he and Henshaw were necessary witnesses in a legal hearing. Hutchings promised to be available and to try to locate Henshaw.

Finally, Alexander went to Ma Blessing's cafe, ordered pancakes, bacon, and coffee and asked her.

"Old Bear Tracks? You're in luck, young man. He's back there in my kitchen right now warshin' dishes to pay for his meals."

Henshaw was up to his elbows in a tubful of soapy water and still had a week's growth of salt-and-pepper whiskers. Without his hat and with his black hair combed straight back, he looked younger. He looked at Alexander with his sad eyes and said, "I allow I c'n be thar. I done gambled away the stake you paid me, an' I'm havin' to do this here woman's work to get another'n."

"Mr. Henshaw, the money I gave you paid for the food we ate at your cabin, but it doesn't pay for the damage. Here," Alexander reached for the folding money he carried in his inside coat pocket, "let me pay you something now."

"I shore am obliged," Henshaw said, stuffing a bill into his pants pocket.

Alexander almost did a double take when he first

saw the Honorable Judge Rutherford. He was stout with a brown mustache and pince-nez spectacles, and he could have been mistaken for Theodore Roosevelt.

"That's bully," the judge said when he read the petition for probate. He sat behind his high bench and looked over the courtroom with its plain-board jury box and plank benches. "I was contacted by an assistant attorney general just yesterday, and he informed me that he has some questions about the matter. I understand too, that a Mr. Charles Dobbs has also petitioned the court."

"Yes, Your Honor," Silas K. Cantwell said, standing humbly before the judge's bench. "We are prepared to argue our case anytime."

"Very well." The judge took off his pince-nez spectacles and squinted at the lawyer. "I will set a hearing for one week from today."

The lawyer had just closed his briefcase and was ready to leave the courtroom when the connecting door between the courtroom and the sheriff's office swung open. A well-dressed but dust-covered man entered, carrying an almost identical briefcase. "Your Honor," the newcomer said, approaching the bench, "may I have the privilege of addressing the court?"

"You may, Mr. Birdsell."

The man opened his briefcase and brought out a sheaf of papers, including two yellow papers that looked exactly like the telegrams that Alexander had received in Rosebud.

"Who is he?" Alexander whispered.

"That," whispered Silas K. Cantwell, "is Deputy Attorney General John Birdsell."

"I wish to inform the court, Your Honor, that the

attorney general's office opposes the petition filed on behalf of Miss Josephine Dobbs. We have reason to believe that she is an imposter."

Alexander glanced at the young woman. Her face showed no expression, but her eyes were green.

"Very well, Mr. Birdsell," the judge said. "I have just scheduled a hearing for next Wednesday. Is that satisfactory?"

The man hesitated, seemingly going over time schedules in his mind. He was young, clean-shaven, and athletic-looking. Alexander had seen young lawyers like him before and knew that they could be so full of self-importance and arrogance that they were insufferable.

"Why, yes," he said finally. "My witness should be here on Monday, and we can be ready for trial, Your Honor."

"I will brook no delays, Mr. Birdsell," the judge said. "I have a busy schedule. Can you be ready for trial next Wednesday, Mr. Cantwell?"

"We have only two witnesses besides Miss Dobbs, Your Honor, and we have already informed them that they are to be ready to testify."

"Bully." With that, Judge Rutherford banged his gavel, gathered his black robe about him, stepped down from behind the bench, and walked rapidly through the door to the sheriff's office.

"John," Silas K. Cantwell said, approaching the deputy A.G., "you're making a serious accusation. May I ask on what evidence you base your accusation?"

The young lawyer slapped dust from his pants legs with both hands and straightened the silk cravat at his throat. "I had no time to wait for the next stage and had to hurry here in a buggy." He reached into his briefcase and again extracted the yellow sheets of paper. "These are telegrams from police authorities in St. Louis. We—" he looked around to be sure he had everyone's attention "—have reason to believe that this young lady is not Josephine Dobbs and is instead Miss Betty Blakely who lived across the hall from the Dobbs family in St. Louis."

Chapter Sixteen

All the pretty young lady from St. Louis could do was deny it. Silas K. Cantwell waited until they were seated in their favorite place in the hotel lobby before asking her to explain.

"Betty, that is Betty Blakely, and I were acquainted, of course," she said, looking at her hands folded in her lap. "After all, we lived across the hall from each other on the second floor of a three-story tenement building."

"How close were you?" asked the lawyer.

"Close. What else can I say? We were both interested in the theater and we visited often."

"Is she alive?"

"No. She was one of those who died in the fire."

"What did she look like?"

"She was pretty. And blond."

"It appears," said the lawyer, "that we have a legal fight on our hands."

They adjourned for dinner, which they ate in silence. The young woman picked at her food and ate very little. Alexander wanted to say something to cheer her up.

"Josephine," he said softly. She looked up at him. Her eyes were a blue-green. "Whatever happens, I'm still on your side."

A weak smile turned up the corners of her mouth. "I'm happy to know that, James. There's nobody in the whole world I would rather have on my side."

"Together we can lick anything."

Her smile widened. "We've proved that, haven't we, James?"

The lawyer excused himself, saying he wanted to read the law and retire early. They stayed and lingered over their coffee.

"Remember when they thought they had us sealed inside a mine, Josie, and we scratched and clawed our way out."

The smile that appeared on her face was real, and her eyes were a bright blue again. "We did that, didn't we?"

"And those Indians? The way you fired a gun and sent them dashing for cover?"

"I was so scared. When the gun went off, I thought the whole world had exploded."

Alexander chuckled. "What was it you said, 'Stick 'em up'?"

"Isn't that what one is supposed to say?" She was chuckling too now.

"You certainly made a believer out of old You Fella. Those Indians tore out of there like a bunch of rats through a hole in the wall." Alexander was laughing.

"It's a miracle I didn't shoot myself. Where did you learn how to cock a gun?"

"A friend and I visited a gunsmith once, just out of

193

curiosity. That gun was an old Civil War model. It was what they call a single-action army revolver."

She was laughing now. "At first, when you tried to tell me in sign language to pull the hammer back, I thought you were going into the first stages of the Saint Vitus's dance."

"I—" Alexander was laughing so hard he could barely talk. "—very nearly did. It was the Indians versus the palefaces until you got your hands on that gun and then it was palefaces versus the Indians."

Restaurant patrons at the other tables were staring at the laughing couple.

"If I ever hear of a ladies' shooting contest someplace, Josie, I'm going to sponsor you."

"If I ever shoot a gun again, I'll try to keep my eyes open."

They laughed and joked until finally they could think of no more funny remarks, and their laughter subsided. She put her hand on top of his and said, "Seriously, James, do you believe me?"

He tried to find the words to say what he wanted to say, but she spared him that.

"Don't answer. That wasn't a fair question."

He started to answer anyway, but she placed a forefinger across his lips. "Don't. That wasn't fair. Please don't."

He paid the check and she went to her room. He went out onto the sidewalk. The air was chilly and he shivered. It made him wonder what winter was like in the high country of Colorado. After a short walk, he went up to his room, took off his shoes, picked up a book of Shakespeare's plays, and settled down to read. A light tapping on his door brought him to his feet, and he went to the door and opened it. She stood there.

"May I come in, James?"

"Of course." He stepped back, allowing her to enter.

She walked to the center of the room and turned to face him. "I don't want to stay long, James. I—just wanted to talk, or something. I . . . please don't get the wrong impression."

He put his hands on her shoulders, pulled her to him and kissed her. She was pliant, but only for a second.

"This is not what I—oh, I don't know why I came here. Forgive me." She hurried to the door and opened it. "I didn't mean to—I'm sorry." She was gone.

Alexander wanted to rush after her and take her in his arms again, but he knew she wouldn't allow it. Not yet. One day, if he was lucky. One day.

The news was all over town, but Alexander didn't hear it until he was eating breakfast in Ma Blessing's cafe.

"They arrested the man that tried to have you and that young lady killed," Ma Blessing said.

Alexander had a forkful of pancakes halfway to his mouth, and he paused. "They did? Who was it?"

"That other Eastern feller, the one that says he's Ol' Buckshot's boy."

"The man who calls himself Charles Dobbs?"

"Yep. Ol' Hutchins went over to Rosebud yesterday and collered 'im there. Brought 'im back in a buggy."

Alexander chewed slowly, thoughtfully. He wasn't

surprised. After all, the con man appeared to be the only one who could profit from the death of Josephine Dobbs. He could have hired two killers to do his dirty work.

And yet—Alexander stopped eating and sat in deep thought—he could be innocent. The two cutthroats said something about arranging the deaths of Buckshot Dobbs and his business manager Bertrum Wingate. If they did that, then the whole conspiracy started before that keister spieler ever arrived in El Tejon.

But Alexander couldn't waste his time feeling sorry for a con man from Kansas City. The problem now was to keep Miss Dobbs out of trouble. If she couldn't prove that she was Josephine Dobbs, she could be charged with the crime of fraud or attempted fraud. She could end up in jail. What kind of evidence did that assistant A.G. have?

Alexander finished his meal, paid, and left Ma Blessing's cafe. The first problem was the upcoming trial, and, if that turned out in her favor, he could turn his attention to other matters. There were other matters that ought to be attended to.

There were, for instance, two murders and two attempted murders. Something in El Tejon wasn't what it appeared to be.

Chapter Seventeen

The lawyer Silas K. Cantwell was busy for a time interviewing Sheriff Boyd Hutchins and Clarence "Bear Tracks" Henshaw. That done, he took a stage back to Rosebud, promising to return on Monday. Judge Rutherford left town too, saying he had to preside over a trial in Fort Bliss. His clerk, John P. Wilson, went to work, trying to find enough literate men to make up a jury panel. He started at the Top Hat saloon, then began buttonholing people on the sidewalks. It took two days, but he finally had the names and signatures of eleven men who could read and write and were residents of the new Webber County.

The subject of the upcoming trial was on the lips of everyone, and Ma Blessing asked Alexander one day if the young woman was really the rightful heir.

"I hear she's an actress that's tryin' to take over the life of a dead friend of her'n," Ma Blessing said.

"Don't believe rumors, Mrs. Blessing." Alexander grinned. "I understand women are allowed to vote in Colorado now, and that means women can probably sit on a jury too. Don't convict her yet, Mrs. Bless-

197

ing."

On Monday, Silas K. Cantwell arrived on the stage from Rosebud, and so did the assistant attorney general and an officious-looking man in a fedora hat and a travel-wrinkled suit.

Alexander was waiting for the lawyer, and they agreed to meet in the hotel lobby in half an hour with Miss Dobbs.

"How does it look?" was the first thing Alexander wanted to know when they were seated in the lobby.

"Bad and good too," the lawyer said. "Let me explain. Did you see the gentleman who arrived with us? Well, he is a police detective from St. Louis and he is prepared to testify that Josephine Dobbs died in that tenement fire, and her identity was taken over by Betty Blakely."

"Can he prove it?"

"I don't know. And that's the good news. It's obvious that if anyone wanted to prove the petitioner's identity, all he would have to do is bring someone from St. Louis who knows her."

Miss Dobbs shifted positions, uncrossed and recrossed her ankles. Alexander kept quiet, waiting to hear what else the lawyer had to say.

"But that would be easy to counter. All it would take is money. And time. Regardless of whether Miss Dobbs is the actual heir, we could, with enough money, get someone to say she is. That would take an awful lot of time, sending back and forth for witnesses, and an awful lot of money."

"You mean, if necessary, we could hire someone to perjure himself? Or herself?"

"Certainly." The lawyer leaned toward Alexander

and talked in a lower tone. "You know, don't you, that for enough money you can import witnesses who will say anything you want them to say?"

"Well, yes, but—"

"Now," the lawyer smiled briefly at Miss Dobbs, "the real question here is not who is who, but whether we can make the jurors believe what we want them to believe."

Both Alexander and the young woman started to protest, but Silas K. Cantwell shushed them. "Listen to me now, don't even think it." Turning to Alexander, he said, "You've associated with lawyers all your life and you've studied law. What was one of the first things you learned?"

Alexander had the answer immediately. "I remember one of the first lectures on the subject I ever heard. The professor said we were not there to study justice but to study law."

"And he was perfectly right. Now, you know as well as I do that my duty as legal counsel is not to determine whether my clients are guilty or innocent, but to see that they have every opportunity to prove they are what they say they are."

"I see," said Alexander. Miss Dobbs was quiet, but her blue eyes were studying the lawyer's face.

"Now, I have struck a deal with Mr. Birdsell. After talking it over, we agreed that it would be costly and futile to engage in a battle of character witnesses. The state can afford the money but not the time, and I assured him that with a gold mine at stake we would lay out whatever amount of money and use whatever amount of time it takes. So we are ready to stipulate that we will not get into that arena."

"What you are saying then is that for enough money you can prove anything."

"Not anything, Mr. Alexander, but money helps, you can bet on that."

Alexander was suddenly pensive and quiet.

"I have talked extensively with your Mr. Henshaw, and he and you, Miss Dobbs, will be our main witnesses. The sheriff will testify that there was an attempt on your lives. You, Miss Dobbs, will be on the witness stand to tell your story, and I must warn you, the assistant A.G. will cross-examine you relentlessly. You must be prepared. We must anticipate his questions and prepare logical answers, and you must be both physically and emotionally prepared."

"How about me?" Alexander asked. "I can testify as to the attempts on our lives."

"I'll try to let Miss Dobbs and the sheriff establish that fact, but you may be called on by Mr. Birdsell. Can you deal with that?"

"I think so."

"There is one other point that I must make. The deputy, or assistant, A.G. is a young man from Denver with a brand-new diploma and he is eager to establish a reputation for himself. He is smart and he is dangerous. Give him half a chance and he'll eat you up alive."

"How about the judge?" Alexander asked.

"He's from Denver too. He was appointed only last spring and sent here from the big city, but he's no greenhorn."

Outside, a mountain rain squall had moved over El Tejon with booming thunder, flashes of lightning, and hail. Alexander went to the open hotel door and looked out. Small white hailstones peppered the street, turning it into mud.

He was reminded of another electric storm that had almost cost him and the girl their lives on a high peak not more than—how long ago was it?—not long ago. He could remember clearly how his right hand had curled into a claw and how the girl had squatted in the dirt, holding her hands over her ears.

Whether she realized it or not, she had done exactly the right thing, making herself a small target and sitting in the dirt, which didn't conduct electricity the way the granite boulders did. She was no dumb blonde. But could she take care of herself on the witness stand under the questioning of a cannibal lawyer? Alexander remembered the way she had finessed one Charles Dobbs into revealing the fact that he didn't even know Buckshot Dobbs's real name. He grinned to himself. That gentleman was now wishing he had never heard of Buckshot Dobbs and El Tejon, Colorado.

The girl moved quietly up beside him. "Remind you of anything, James?"

"Yeah, it sure does. It reminds me of how we battled the elements and won."

"And now we, I, am facing another battle. May I ask you something, James? May I ask again why you're so involved in this? You said you resigned your position with the Pinkertons, so why should you care what happens now?"

"I asked myself that question just this morning, and know what?"

"What?"

"I don't know. I don't have an answer. Maybe I will

one day."

Her blue eyes studied his, and she smiled. "You know something, J.J.?"

"What?"

"You're squirrel food."

The residents of the new Webber County abandoned everything that Wednesday morning and gathered in front of the sheriff's office in El Tejon. The town was to have its first trial by jury and it promised to be interesting.

When the court clerk, John P. Wilson, opened the doors to the courtroom, the crowd surged in and quickly placed claims on the available seats. There were some shoving and a few threats, but when the Honorable Judge Rutherford stepped in with his black robe and pince-nez spectacles, the crowd hushed.

"All rise," bellowed John P. Wilson. The crowd stood and waited until the judge climbed up on the podium and took his seat behind the high bench.

"Hear ye, hear ye," the clerk began, "the probate court of the state of Colorado is now in session. Be seated."

A low board fence had been built between the spectators' benches and the judge's end of the room, and two tables and a lectern had been placed in front of the judge's bench. The young woman from St. Louis, her attorney, and Alexander, acting as the chief investigator, sat at one table, and the assistant A.G., John Birdsell, and the St. Louis policeman sat at the other.

A small table and chair sat directly under the judge's high bench and that was occupied by the judge's court reporter, a small young man in a business suit. He opened a large book of blank pages, arranged a sheaf of pencils on the desk, and prepared to write down everything that was said.

The first order of the day was to select a jury, and all those called for jury duty were instructed to occupy the first row of spectator benches. Then the first six were instructed to sit in the jury box. And then began the voir dire, the questioning of prospective jurors.

The judge was the first to question the six to find out whether they were qualified and whether they might already favor one side over the other. Silas K. Cantwell was next. His questions were brief and he was satisfied. The assistant A.G. wasn't so easy to please.

"And now, Mr., uh, Johnson," the young lawyer began, looking at his notes, "were you acquainted with Mr. Frederick Dobbs?"

"Nope." Johnson was a tall man with chin whiskers and a bald head.

"Are you sure? He was a very well-known individual."

"Nope."

"You are a resident of El Tejon?"

"Yup."

"And you never heard of one of the area's most prominent citizens?"

"Who?"

Exasperated, the young lawyer shot his cuffs, unbuttoned his finger-length coat, and pulled down on the front of his vest. "Are you hard of hearing, sir?

I'm talking about Frederick Dobbs?"

The juror shifted uncomfortably in his chair. "Oh. Are you a-talkin' about Old Buckshot Dobbs?"

Birdsell threw a wooden pencil down on the table in exasperation. "Of course. Who did you think I was talking about?"

"Now, Mr. Birdsell," the judge said. "I will brook no badgering of the jury panel."

Shooting his cuffs and pulling down on the bottom of his vest, the young lawyer visibly forced himself to speak calmly. "All right, let me rephrase the question, did you know Buckshot Dobbs?"

"Nope."

"Well, what in thunder—? All right, all right." Birdsell studied his list of names and started to address the next man in the jury box.

"Knew of him."

"What? What did you say, Mr., uh, Johnson?"

"I said I knew of him. Ever'body knew about Old Buckshot Dobbs."

"Fine. That's fine, Mr., uh, Johnson. We have finally established the fact that you have heard of Frederick Dobbs. Now, may I ask whether you happen to be acquainted with Josephine Dobbs?"

"Yup."

"Yup? What does that mean?"

The judge answered. "It means yes, Mr. Birdsell."

"Yes? You are acquainted with her?"

"Nope."

Birdsell opened his mouth to speak, but no words came out. He walked around the table, picked up a pencil, threw it down, and finally squawked, "You just said yes. Which is it, if you please?"

"Yes and nope."

The young lawyer threw up his hands and looked at the judge in despair.

"Perhaps," the judge said, "you had better go on to the next prospective juror, Mr. Birdsell."

"Yes, Your Honor, perhaps that would be better."

"It's yes to the first question and nope to the next."

"What?" Birdsell looked with horror at Johnson, then at the judge.

"Mr. Johnson," Judge Rutherford said calmly, "would you please explain what you mean?"

Silas K. Cantwell interrupted. He cleared his throat, stood up, and said, "If it please the court, perhaps I can shed some light on the problem."

"Bully, Mr. Cantwell. Proceed."

"The confusion lies in the fact that Mr. Birdsell asked two questions. First, he inquired as to whether he 'may ask' about Mr. Johnson's knowledge of Miss Dobbs. Mr. Johnson answered in the affirmative, meaning that Mr. Birdsell may indeed ask. Next, Mr. Birdsell asked Mr. Johnson whether he is acquainted with Miss Dobbs, and Mr. Johnson answered in the negative."

"Bully. Do you understand that, Mr. Birdsell?"

The assistant A.G. dropped into his chair and answered reluctantly, "Yes, Your Honor."

"Bully. Go on with your voir dire."

It was a lengthy process. Alexander could see that the young lawyer was using every ploy and technique he had learned in law school. The jury panel was squirming in its seats, and even the judge was becoming impatient. The last man to be questioned was the saloon keeper, an employee of John Bokhauser. He had a handlebar mustache and garters on his sleeves.

"Did you know Frederick, er, Buckshot Dobbs?"

"Not too good. He came in a coupla times. Didn't talk much. I think he was a little loco."

"Never mind what you think, Mr., uh, Saloon Keeper. We are not interested in your opinions."

The saloon keeper leaned forward and glared at the lawyer but said nothing.

"Now then, did you know anything about his family?"

"Well, I heard he had a coupla daughters and a wife somewhere back East. Way I heard it, his old woman couldn't stand to live with him."

"I am not interested in anything you heard and I am not interested in anything you think. I ask you a simple question and I want a simple answer." The assistant A.G. yelled, "Now, just answer my question."

The saloon keeper jumped up, pointed a finger, and bellowed, "Don't talk to me like that, Mr. Lawyer. The last time a man talked to me like that I warped his skull with a bung starter. You yell at me again and I'll whip you till you bark like a fox."

An ominous murmur went through the spectators.

Bang, went the judge's gavel. Bang, bang. "Please sit down, sir." The saloon keeper sat, but he glowered at the young lawyer, daring him with his eyes to speak harshly again. The court reporter was writing furiously.

John Birdsell's face was red when he took his seat at the table and mumbled, "No more questions."

The saloon keeper was asked to please step out of the jury box and was quickly replaced by another man. Eventually, the assistant A.G. was satisfied.

"Bully," said the judge. "Now then, you six men are the jurors. I must ask you not to discuss the case with anyone until the trial is concluded, and do not, let me repeat, do not permit anyone to approach you on the subject outside the courtroom. Do you all understand? Bully. Now then," the judge pulled a gold pocket watch from under his black robe, looked at it, and continued, "it is approaching the noon hour. I am going to call a one-hour recess. Please be back at one P.M." He banged his gavel again, stood up, and left the room, walking between the spectators' benches to get to the connecting door.

Alexander et al. stayed at their table until the room was empty. "It looks," Alexander said, "as though we are ahead so far. Mr. Birdsell has made a serious mistake before the trial even gets underway. He has argued with the jury."

"It appears that way," said Silas K. Cantwell. "But remember, he's no dummy. He'll think it over and realize his mistake, and he won't make that mistake again. Not only that, I'm worried about what that detective from St. Louis might have to say."

"I never saw him before," said Miss Dobbs, "unless he was one of many police officers in the police station when I went there. I'm betting his testimony won't amount to a row of pins."

"I can't believe that, Miss Dobbs. The A.G. wouldn't have brought him here unless he had something incriminating to say."

Chapter Eighteen

The litigants in the legal proceeding had lunch at the New Windsor Hotel, but most of the spectators and the jurors ate lunch out of clean lard cans or syrup buckets or out of paper packages. They sat on the plank sidewalk with their backs against the buildings, and they sat cross-legged on the ground. When they saw the judge heading back to the sheriff's office and the courtroom, they all followed.

Sheriff Boyd Hutchins closed the door when all the seats were filled, shutting out a dozen or more citizens. He stood inside the courtroom with his back to the closed door.

The court clerk recited his spiel and the judge asked both lawyers if they had opening statements.

"No, Your Honor," said Silas K. Cantwell.

"Yes, Your Honor," said John Birdsell.

"Bully. Proceed."

The young assistant A.G. stood before the jury box, pulled down on his vest, buttoned his coat in the middle, shot his cuffs, and began.

"Gentlemen, what this litigation consists of is very simple. A man died intestate, that is, he left no will.

He apparently left valuable property. He was a man very few people knew and apparently no one knew him very well. The court appointed a Mr. Joseph Webber as executor, or administrator, of the estate. Mr. Webber engaged the Pinkerton National Detective Agency to try to find an heir. The detective agency sent Mr. James A. Alexander to El Tejon to screen all arrivals who pretended to be an heir."

All eyes turned then to Alexander.

"It was believed, gentlemen, that, when news of the situation reached the Eastern cities, there would be persons arriving in El Tejon pretending to be heirs and trying to lay claim to the deceased's, that is, Mr. Dobbs's, estate.

"What the state will prove, gentlemen, is that the young woman sitting over there is a pretender, an impostor, if you will. We will prove that she is not Miss Josephine Dobbs and that Josephine Dobbs died in a fire in St. Louis, Missouri. Now you all know the news of a wealthy man's death can attract vultures; vultures that hope to feed on his wealth by claiming to be his heirs at law. Gentlemen, we can't allow that to happen."

The jurors were listening, Alexander could see that. They were stealing glances at the young woman. John Birdsell had learned his lesson about antagonizing the jurors and was explaining everything in a language they could understand and appreciate.

"Bully. Now then, Mr. Cantwell, do you still wish to waive your right to an opening statement?"

Cantwell stood up. "Yes, Your Honor. We will prove our case without such grandiose speeches."

"Bully, Mr. Cantwell, call your first witness."

"I would like to call Miss Josephine Dobbs."

The young woman was wearing her white dress with the lacy collar and sleeves. Her blond hair had been brushed until it shone. She kept her eyes down as she walked with short, ladylike steps to the witness stand beside the judge's bench.

"Raise your right hand," the court clerk said. She did.

"Do you swear to tell the truth, the whole truth, and nothing but the truth, so help you God?"

"I do."

"Be seated."

Silas K. Cantwell buttoned his coat in the middle as he walked to the witness stand. "Would you state your name?"

"Josephine Dobbs."

"And where do you live, Miss Dobbs?" She answered. Her voice was clear and calm.

"Are you related to the late Frederick Dobbs, otherwise known as Buckshot Dobbs?"

"Yes."

"Would you tell the gentlemen of the jury how you are related?"

"He was my father."

"When was the last time you saw your father?"

"It was about thirteen years ago."

"What happened then?"

"My mother became weary of the frontier life and took me and my sister to St. Louis."

"Where were you living before your mother took you to St. Louis?"

"In a cabin on Antler Creek between here and Rosebud."

"How long had you lived there?"

"I don't remember living anywhere else prior to that, but my mother said we had lived there about ten years."

"What did your father do for a living."

"He worked at any job he could find. He cut timber, he was a teamster working a fresno when they built the road between here and Rosebud, and he prospected for gold."

"Did he find any gold?"

"Not until after my mother, my sister, and I went to St. Louis."

"Umm. I see." Under questioning, the lawyer got her to tell all about her childhood, the hardships, the schooling provided by her mother, and why she believed her mother had decided to leave her father and go back to the city. She told what she remembered about her father, that he was a kind and gentle but seemingly impractical man, full of dreams about striking it rich, that he was often gone for a week at a time on prospecting trips.

Her voice lowered as she told about receiving two letters from her father during the winter months, telling about his find and asking them to rejoin him at El Tejon, and about the letter she received later from Clarence Henshaw, also known as Bear Tracks Henshaw.

"Do you have the letters in your possession, Miss Dobbs?"

"I have the letter from Mr. Henshaw. The letters from my father were destroyed in a fire."

Silas K. Cantwell asked permission to present the letter as evidence. Permission was granted, and the letter was handed to the assistant A.G. to inspect.

"I have no more questions at this time, Your Honor."

"Bully. Mr. Birdsell, do you wish to cross-examine?"

"I most certainly do, Your Honor." The young lawyer stood, pulled down the front of his vest, shot his cuffs, and began.

"Now, Miss, uh, please forgive me if I do not refer to you as Miss Dobbs because I do not believe that you actually are. Now Miss, you say the alleged letters from your father were destroyed in a fire. Would you tell us about the fire?"

"It was—it was a terrible fire, I . . ." Her voice faltered and her eyes began to mist over.

"Go on."

"Please compose yourself, Miss Dobbs," the judge said.

She sat up straighter, folded her hands in her lap, and looked straight ahead over the heads of the spectators. The courtroom was quiet.

"I was walking home from a meeting of our theater group when I saw the fire wagons in front of our building, and I saw the smoke coming out of the windows. I ran to the front door but some fireman held me and wouldn't let me go in. I told them my mother was in there and I thought my sister was in there too. They said it was too dangerous.

"I—" she paused, swallowed, and went on "—looked through the crowd. Oh, the crowd was awful, so many people, and I didn't see my mother and sister and I knew they were still inside. I waited until the firemen were not looking, and I ran inside and tried to go up the stairs to our apartment, but—"

"All right, Miss, now you say the letters were destroyed in the fire and . . ."

A murmur went through the spectators, and some-one said in a loud whisper, "Let her tell about it."

Silas K. Cantwell jumped to his feet. "Your Honor, counsel asked her to tell about the fire, and now for some reason known only to him he doesn't want her to tell about it."

When he sat down, he whispered to Alexander. "His cross-examination is turning against him so far."

"The witness will continue," Judge Rutherford said.

"Your Honor," protested the assistant A.G., "what she is saying has no relevancy."

Bang, went the judge's gavel. "The witness will continue."

Birdsell shrugged. "Very well, go on, Miss."

She smoothed her dress over her lap, folded her hands again, and continued in a monotone. "The flames were so hot and the smoke, it was awful. I couldn't even see the stairs. My, uh, my dress was burning. I had to go back."

Her eyes were fixed on the rear of the room. "I—don't know exactly what happened after that. They told me later that pieces of the roof were falling off onto the sidewalk, and I was hit on the head."

"Was everything in your apartment destroyed in the fire?"

"Yes. The whole building was destroyed."

"Very well. Now, if you don't mind, Miss, would you tell the jury how you just happened to have the letter from Clarence Henshaw in your possession if the

213

other letters, the important ones from Mr. Dobbs, were destroyed?"

"I was carrying it in my dress pocket."

"Oh." The young lawyer threw up his hands in disbelief. "I see. You just happened to be carrying it in your pocket. Do you have a habit of carrying letters in your pocket?"

"No, but—"

"Yes or no, do you always carry letters around in your pocket?"

"Your Honor," Silas K. Cantwell stood up, "she has already answered the question."

"The witness will answer again," said Judge Rutherford.

"I started to say—"

"Yes or no."

An angry murmur went through the spectators again, and a man with a beard and a floppy hat in his hands stood up in the back row, shook a fist, and said, "Let 'er talk."

Bang, bang. "I will brook no interference from the spectators. One more outburst like that and I will clear the courtroom."

A few more angry murmurs came from the crowd, but eventually the courtroom was quiet again.

"The witness will answer the question," ordered the judge.

"The answer is no."

"I see. Umm." The assistant A.G. seemed to be pondering the answer. "I am going to ask you again, Miss, whatever your name is, do you have the aforementioned letters from Frederick Dobbs?"

"No."

214

"Oh, you don't have those?"

"I already said they were destroyed."

"Oh, they were? Somehow I knew you would say that. I knew you would say that the letters from Frederick Dobbs, something you need to support your case, were destroyed in a fire." The young lawyer turned to the jury. "How convenient."

Her eyes had turned green, and she met the lawyer's gaze eyeball to eyeball. "It's true, no matter what you try to make of it."

"I see. Umm. What do you do for a living, Miss whoever you are?"

"I'm an actress. At the time of the fire I had just finished a tour with a theater group."

"An actress?" The assistant A.G. feigned surprise. "Really?"

"Yes." She continued to hold his gaze.

Turning to the jury, the lawyer scratched his jaw and surmised loudly, "Well, isn't that interesting? An actress. Now then"—he spun around, facing her again—"tell the jury about Betty Blakely."

"Betty? What do you want to know?"

"Did she live across the hall from the Dobbs family in that tenement building?"

"Yes."

"How well did you know her?"

"Quite well. We were neighbors for a year or more."

"Were you intimate friends?"

"No, I can't say that we were."

"You shared secrets?"

"No. No, we were friends, but I don't recall sharing any secrets."

"Would you describe Betty Blakely?"

"She was a pretty girl, about my size, and blond."

"In other words the two of you looked something alike." It was a statement, not a question.

"Yes. I never thought of it before, but yes we did."

That brought a smile to the face of John Birdsell. He turned and smiled at the jury as he said, "Then, if the real Josephine Dobbs died in that fire, it would be easy for Betty Blakely to assume her identity, especially if Betty Blakely is a professional actress." He spun on his heels suddenly, scowled, and pointed an accusing finger at the witness. "Isn't it true, Miss, that you are in fact Betty Blakely?"

The witness was shocked for a second and blurted out, "No."

"Your Honor," Silas K. Cantwell was on his feet, buttoning the middle button of his coat, "the witness answered the question because she is being honest and has nothing to hide. But Mr. Birdsell knows full well that she didn't have to answer that question. However much Mr. Birdsell would like to, he still hasn't succeeded in doing away with the fifth amendment to the U.S. constitution."

"Your Honor," the assistant A.G. said, "I resent counsel implying that I am trying to destroy the constitution of the United States."

Said Cantwell: "It seems to me, Mr. Birdsell, that you are doing a great deal of implying here yourself."

Bang. "Gentlemen, the objection is sustained."

John Birdsell walked back and forth in front of the jury box and stopped in front of the witness again. He spoke quietly, "Would you mind telling the jury, Miss, just exactly who you really are?"

She compressed her lips, then with determination

met the lawyer's gaze. "I told you. My name is Josephine Dobbs."

"Oh, excuse me," the lawyer said with a sneer. "Miss Josephine Dobbs indeed." He pointed a finger at her again and shouted, "You are an imposter. You are in fact Betty Blakely."

"No, I—"

"That's all," the lawyer interrupted. He turned a scornful back on the witness and went to his table.

Silas K. Cantwell jumped up. "Well, I have more questions, Your Honor. This young lady has more to say than that."

"Very well, Mr. Cantwell, you may redirect."

John Birdsell interrupted. "If it please the court, it is getting late and I'm sure some of the jurors have chores to do at home. I would request a recess until tomorrow."

"But I would like to conduct my redirect examination of this witness before the court recesses."

"It can wait until morning, Mr. Cantwell." The judge banged his gavel and announced, "This court is in recess until nine A.M. tomorrow, and I must caution the jurors not to discuss this case with anyone in the meantime."

"Dammit," said Silas K. Cantwell after the judge had left the courtroom. "Now the jury will spend the next sixteen or so hours thinking about what just happened. They'll have that implanted in their minds and it will be hard to erase. Dammit."

He put his list of jurors' names inside his briefcase and closed it. "I told you the assistant A.G. wasn't stupid. He planned it that way."

Alexander put his hand on the young woman's

217

shoulder. "You did very well, Josephine. Don't worry. He hasn't proved a thing."

A worry frown wrinkled her forehead. "He was rather convincing. I had to answer his questions."

"You did exactly the right thing, Josie. You were entirely honest, and that was exactly what you should have been. Don't worry."

"I wish," said Silas K. Cantwell, "that we were through with your testimony, but we can't let it stop here. We'll talk more about the fire tomorrow and your injuries. We'll work on the jury's sympathy."

At dinner, she ate very little and excused herself and went to her room early. Alexander walked around outside awhile, then went to his room too. He lay awake in his bed for hours, wishing he had finished law school, trying to decide whether he wanted to go back and finish.

The crowd returned Thursday morning and had even grown. People were talking excitedly until they saw Miss Dobbs, her lawyer, and Alexander coming, then they fell silent and stepped back to allow them to enter the sheriff's office and then the courtroom. The jurors were already in the courtroom, seated in the jury box.

Spectators did a little pushing and jostling as they scrambled for the available seats, but they quieted when Sheriff Boyd Hutchins entered and glowered at them.

The Honorable Judge Rutherford got the preliminaries over quickly and directed the lawyer for the petitioner, "Mr. Cantwell, call your witness."

The lawyer stood up. "Miss Josephine Dobbs."

The young woman went to the witness stand, was reminded by the judge that she was still under oath, and took her seat, sitting erect, hands folded in her lap. Her eyes were the most beautiful blue that Alexander had ever seen.

"Now then, Miss Dobbs, just before the court recessed last evening you were telling the jury about a fire that caused the deaths of your mother and sister. You said you were apparently hit on the head by some falling debris and you don't know what happened after that. Will you please tell the jury what you remembered next?"

Her voice was clear and it carried easily to the back of the room. "I woke up in a bed at St. Mary's Hospital. It took awhile for me to remember what had happened and when I did I tried to get up but became dizzy and fell back on the bed. A nurse told me I had a bump on the head and a burn injury on my left, uh, lower limb. My, uh, the burn injury was painful." She paused and looked at her lawyer for instructions.

"Go on. How long were you in the hospital?"

"Two days the first time. The doctor advised me to stay longer, but I had to get out, to see if by some miracle my mother and sister had survived the fire."

"Did anyone come to see you during your stay in the hospital?"

"No. No one."

"No one came to ask your identity or anything?"

"No."

"Did you carry any identification papers?"

"No."

"Did they ask you at the hospital who you were?"

"Yes, a nurse asked me, but—I became dizzy and didn't answer right away."

"Were you asked again to identify yourself?"

"Yes, the next day. I told them all about myself."

"All right, now, tell the jury what you did when you left the hospital."

"I went back home, rather to what was left of it. I asked some of the neighbors if they had seen my family. They hadn't. I went next to the police station and asked about my mother and sister. I was told that they had died, and they—they showed me their bodies."

"Did the police ask your identity?"

"Yes. When I gave my name to an officer, he took the list of names of people believed dead and crossed my name off. He said that some of the bodies were—" her voice faltered and she looked down at her folded hands "—burned beyond recognition and they thought I was one of the victims."

"What did you do next?"

"My, uh, lower limb was hurting and I went back to the hospital. They kept me there two more days. When I got out, I stayed in a hotel until my burns healed and then decided to come to Colorado."

"How did you finance the trip?"

"I had just withdrawn most of the funds from my family's bank account and I carried it in a small purse on a chain around my neck. We planned to pay the rent six months in advance."

"Fine. Now. About that letter from Clarence Henshaw, how did you happen to have it in your dress pocket?"

She shook her blond head negatively and smiled

wryly. "I don't know, really. I just had it. To the best of my recollection, I took it with me to show to some of my friends in the theater group." She shrugged. "I don't really know."

"In other words, Miss Dobbs, it was just one of those things that people sometimes do without a reason."

"Objection." The assistant A.G. was on his feet again. "He is putting words in the witness's mouth, Your Honor. He is leading the witness.

"Sustained."

"I have no more questions, Your Honor." Cantwell took his seat at the petitioner's table.

"Any recross-examination, Mr. Birdsell?"

John Birdsell walked to the witness stand, bowed his head in thought, then asked, "When the nurse at St. Mary's Hospital first asked your identity, why didn't you tell her?"

"I became faint and was only barely aware of what was happening."

"And it was not until the next day that you were asked again?"

"Yes."

"How convenient. That gave you time to think things over, didn't it?"

"Don't answer." Silas K. Cantwell came around the table. "This kind of cross-examination is entirely out of order, Your Honor."

"Objection sustained."

"Very well. May I ask, Miss whoever you are, did you learn what became of Betty Blakely?"

"I was told that she died in the fire."

"When were you told that?"

221

"At the hospital, I think. A nurse told me that she was told that nobody who lived on the second and third floors survived."

"Were you told that the first day you were in the hospital or the second day?"

"It was the second day."

"I see. Umm. Well now, tell the jury this, was it before or after you identified yourself as Josephine Dobbs?"

"I, uh, I'm not sure. Things were a little confusing then."

"I see. Then it is quite possible that you knew who all died in that fire before you gave the hospital your name." It was a statement, not a question, and the witness said nothing.

"Now then," the young lawyer continued, "about that letter. Is it possible that Josephine Dobbs showed the letter to her friend across the hall and inadvertently left it there? And is it possible that Betty Blakely put it in her pocket, intending to return it? And is it possible that Betty Blakely heard the fire alarm and ran down the stairs to safety with the letter still in her pocket?"

Alexander whispered, "Why do you let him do that? That's pure speculation."

"Let him get it over with now," whispered Silas K. Cantwell. "He'll get it said sooner or later anyway, and if we're lucky we'll have a chance to counter it."

The young woman, also puzzled by the questions, looked at her lawyer for instructions. Cantwell shook his head and slowly stood up.

"Objection. I don't think I have to explain why."

"Sustained."

"No further questions," said John Birdsell.

The judge wasted no time. "Mr. Cantwell?"

"Your Honor," Cantwell said, buttoning the middle button of his coat, "I call Sheriff Boyd Hutchins to the witness stand."

All eyes followed the sheriff as he made his way to the front of the room and past the lawyers' table, hitching up his gunbelt on the way. He answered loudly to the usual questions and took the stand, sitting straight and maintaining a dignified air.

Preliminary questions were asked, establishing his identity and expertise. Then Cantwell asked, "Did you receive a complaint that persons as yet unidentified had made an attempt upon the life of Josephine Dobbs and her friend James Alexander at the Josey Mine?"

"Yeah, and I got the culprit, one of 'em anyways, in my jail."

"Objection, Your Honor." It was the assistant A.G. standing. "No one has been convicted of the crime."

"What you mean, Sheriff, is that you have a suspect under arrest, is that not correct?" said Silas K. Cantwell.

"Yeah. Yessir. That's right."

"All right then, did you investigate the complaint?"

"Yessir."

"Will you tell the jury what you found?"

Hutchins shifted in his chair so that he was partially facing the jury. He smoothed down his walrus mustache and began. "I went out to the Josey Mine and I could see where someone had to dig out of the tunnel."

"Go on."

"Wal, I could see that the entrance had caved in and someone had to of been trapped inside, and I could see that whoever it was had dug out."

"Were there any tools about?"

"Only a pickax and that was outside the tunnel."

"Would you say that whoever had to dig out had to use their bare hands to do it?"

"Yessir, it sure looked that way."

"Objection, Your Honor," the assistant A.G. said. "That is putting words in the witness's mouth."

"In the interest of saving time, Counsel, I will overrule that objection."

"Did you find anything that would cause you to suspect foul play, Mr. Hutchins?"

"Yessir. I found a keg of black powder missin', and I could see where it was set under some timbers that held up the roof of that tunnel."

"So, are you convinced, Mr. Hutchins, that the tunnel was sealed intentionally?"

"No doubt about it."

"And are you convinced that someone was inside the tunnel when it was sealed?"

"Sure as shootin' somebody had to dig out of there."

"Would you call that attempted murder?"

"Sure looks that way."

"Now, about that keg of powder, how do you know it was missing?"

"We took inventory right after Old Buckshot, uh, Mr. Dobbs and his manager were killed. I know exactly how much powder was stored in the powder shed."

"And are you satisfied that it was James Alexander

and Josephine Dobbs who were the victims?"

"Wal"—Hutchins pulled down on one end of his mustache—"they said they was, and they sure looked like a man and woman that'd been diggin' with their hands. Their hands was sure cut and torn up."

"Have you any idea, Sheriff, why anyone would want to kill them?"

"Objection, Your Honor. That is calling for a conjecture on the part of the witness."

"Sustained."

"Let me rephrase the question. Mr. Hutchins, in the course of your investigation, did you learn anything that would indicate a motive for an attempted murder?"

"Why sure. Somebody else wanted to claim that mine."

Leaping to his feet, the assistant A.G. shouted, "I object, Your Honor. That is conjecture on the part of the witness. He has supplied no evidence to support that assumption."

Bang. "Mr. Cantwell, you will refrain from eliciting suppositions. And you, gentlemen of the jury, will disregard that remark."

"Very well, Your Honor. I have no more questions of this witness at this time." Silas K. Cantwell sat down and winked at Alexander and Miss Dobbs. "By gosh if he can improperly plant thoughts in the jury's mind, so can I."

"Any cross-examination, Mr. Birdsell?"

"Yes, Your Honor." Birdsell stood up, pulled down on his vest, shot his cuffs, and walked over to the witness stand. "Now, Mr. Hutchins, you say a keg of blasting powder is missing. Do you by any chance have a copy of the inventory you took at the mine?"

"No. I did, but I mislaid it. I looked and I can't find it."

"Hmm. And now you say a keg a powder is missing. Let me ask you this, wouldn't a keg of black powder, when it explodes, make a large impression in the ground or rocks or wherever it explodes?"

"Yep. Yessir."

"Yet, apparently the damage to the mine entrance was light enough that two people, using only their bare hands, could dig out of the rubble?"

"Looks that way."

"I see. Let me ask you this, were the supporting timbers at the tunnel entrance new and strong?"

"No. They wasn't too strong."

"Could they have collapsed of their own volition?"

"Their what?"

"Volition, you know, of their own accord. Couldn't age and deterioration have weakened them until they collapsed?"

"That's possible, I reckon."

"Wouldn't a slight push or an accidental brushing against one of the supporting timbers cause it to collapse? And isn't it possible that if one collapsed, the others would follow?"

The sheriff pulled on one end of his mustache and pondered the question. "Naw, I doubt it. It would take a good hard push to bust one of them timbers."

"But I ask if it was possible. It is possible?"

"I reckon."

"Then is it possible that the collapse of the tunnel entrance could have been accidental?"

"Wal—"

"Yes or no."

"Wal—"

"Your Honor, I request that you direct this witness to answer the question yes or no."

"The witness will answer the question."

"Wal, I'd have to say yes."

"Very well. Then what you are saying is you are not absolutely certain that any blasting powder is missing. And you are saying that if the tunnel entrance had been blown up with blasting powder, a good deal more damage would have been done. And you are also saying that the collapse of the entrance could have been an accident."

"Wal—"

"That's all. No more questions." The young lawyer turned his back on the witness and walked to his table.

"Wal, I'd like to say—"

Bang. "That's all, Mr. Hutchins."

Silas K. Cantwell stood and buttoned the middle button of his coat. "I have a couple of redirect questions, Your Honor."

"Bully."

"Mr. Hutchins, when you took inventory at the mine, was anyone with you?"

"Sure. Mr. Webber was there."

"Then does he have a copy of the inventory?"

"Objection, Your Honor. Saying what someone else has in his possession would be hearsay."

"Sustained."

"Very well. Mr. Hutchins, can you explain why the powder didn't do as much damage as it might have?"

"Wal, the powder was old and some of it was damp.

227

I wouldn't of been surprised if it didn't go off at'all."

"Then the blast wasn't as strong as the assailants expected it to be?"

"I'd say it wasn't."

"But it was strong enough to seal the mine and trap two people inside so they had to dig their way out with their bare hands."

"Objection."

"Sustained."

"I have no more questions of this witness, Your Honor."

"Any recross-examination?"

"No, Your Honor."

"Bully. Before we go any further," the judge scowled at the spectators, "I want that man in the third row to quit expectorating. You there, you with the can in your hands, will you put that can away and quit expectorating or shall I have you removed?"

Chapter Nineteen

A husky timberjack wearing red suspenders and a two-day growth of beard suddenly sat up straight in the courtroom and stopped chewing. A large lump was stationary in his left cheek. "Huh?"

"You," the judge pointed a finger, "I warned you, all of you, that I would brook none of that sort of thing. Now, if you expectorate one more time I will have the sheriff remove you."

"Huh?" The timberjack looked first at the spectator on his left and then at the spectator on his right.

A woman whispered loudly, "Brook what?" It was Ma Blessing.

"That skunks me," answered her nearest neighbor.

Bang, bang. "Spitting. Stop that spitting. One more spit and one more outburst and out you all go."

Another timberjack snickered and said, "Old Jethro never expect'rated in his life, but don't never work downwind of 'im on a windy day."

Bang, bang. "Any more of those smart-aleck remarks and I'll have the sheriff clear the courtroom. I have authority under the law to maintain decorum and I will maintain decorum."

"He's gonna do what?" asked Ma Blessing.

Bang, bang. "Quiet."

"Well, all right," said Ma Blessing, her voice lower now, "but I wish he'd say what he means."

The timberjack with the cud in his cheek swallowed suddenly—and looked sick.

Judge Rutherford waited until the spectators quieted down and said, "Mr. Cantwell, do you have another witness?"

"Yes, Your Honor. I call Clarence Henshaw to the witness chair."

"Bully."

Silas K. Cantwell looked over the spectators and shouted, "Clarence Henshaw?" When he got no answer, he shouted the name again. Still no answer.

A spectator said, "Old Bear Tracks? I seen him a-leadin' his jackass out of town this mornin'."

"He ain't here," said another.

"Thank you," said Silas K. Cantwell. To the judge, he said, "Your Honor, I have one more witness, but it looks as though he is not here. I request a continuance until he can be located."

"Mr. Cantwell," the judge looked down from his high bench, "I have a busy schedule. Can't we go on with this? I will send the sheriff to look for your witness in the meantime."

"If it please the court, Mr. Henshaw is an important witness. We would request a continuance until he is found."

"Mr. Cantwell, it is your responsibility to see that your witnesses are subpoenaed. I will brook no delays in this hearing. Now, do you have another witness?"

The lawyer's features pulled together in a tight

frown. "I didn't subpoena anyone because I didn't think it would be necessary." He shook his head sadly. "No, Your Honor, I have no more witnesses."

"Very well, then I will ask the state to present its case. Mr. Birdsell, do you wish to call a witness?"

"Yes, Your Honor, I call Mr. George McMann."

The detective from St. Louis scooted back his chair, stood up, and walked to the witness chair. He was stout, with a dark suit and vest, a wide colorful necktie, and a row of cigars sticking out of his breast pocket. He raised his right hand, said "I do," and sat.

Under questioning, he said he was an investigator with the St. Louis, Missouri, police department and had investigated the tenement house fire that killed fourteen people.

"Were you able to identify the deceased?"

"Most of the bodies we were able to identify, but there were three that were burned too bad."

"Did you identify the bodies of Mrs. Margaret Dobbs, Ettie Dobbs, and Josephine Dobbs?"

"We made out Mrs. Dobbs, all right, and the young woman named Ettie Dobbs, and there was another body with theirs at the head of the stairs that looked to be the body of Josephine Dobbs."

"Did you identify the body of Betty Blakely?"

"No."

"When were you aware that a young woman claiming to be Josephine Dobbs was alive?"

"Two or three days later. When that young woman there," he pointed at Miss Dobbs, "came to the station."

"Did you believe her?"

"Well, we weren't convinced, but we had no reason

231

to think she was lying."

"Did anything happen to make you change your mind?"

"Yeh. The Pinkertons came around and started asking questions. They told us about Mr. Dobbs dying intestate in Colorado and leaving some valuable property, and we put two and two together."

"Did you draw any conclusions?"

"Yeh. The way we see it is this. The bodies of three women were found at the head of the stairs. They tried to go down the stairs, but the fire and smoke shot up the stairs so fast they they fried in their tracks. One body was Mrs. Dobbs and another is her oldest daughter, we are sure of that, and the other has to be her youngest daughter."

"You say the flames shot up the stairs?"

"Yeh. That's what the firemen said could have happened. When the front door was opened, air rushed in and fueled the fire and it had the effect of an explosion."

"They had no chance to turn back?"

"Not much."

"What other evidence do you have?"

"There was no body found in Betty Blakely's apartment nor anywhere near it."

"I see." The young lawyer was deep in thought for a moment, then said, "I have no more questions of this witness."

"Bully. Mr. Cantwell?"

Buttoning his coat, Silas K. Cantwell walked to the witness stand and stared at the detective a moment. "Did you have any positive way of identifying all those bodies, Mr. McMann?"

"Well, some of them were recognizable. We got the neighbors and relatives to identify them."

"But three were burned so badly that they could not be identified?"

"That's right."

"All right, let's assume, Mr. McMann, that the body of either Josephine Dobbs or Betty Blakely is one of those three. That would leave two other bodies unidentified. Who could they be?"

"There were two other women missing. They lived on the third floor. We don't know which body is which."

"Where were those bodies found?"

"In the hall on the third floor. Looked like they tried to get to the stairs and were overcome by smoke and couldn't get back to their apartments."

"All right, now let's see." The lawyer walked slowly to his table, head down, and walked slowly back. "There were three bodies at the head of the stairs on the third floor, and two of them have been identified. The question is this: Who is, or was, the third body?

"Now then, Mr. McMann, let me ask you, could it be that Betty Blakely was in her apartment when she heard the commotion and the alarm, and could it be that she ran from her apartment, joined Mrs. Dobbs and Ettie Dobbs at the head of the stairs and all three died there?"

"Well, that's possible, but—"

"And," interrupted Silas K. Cantwell, "could it be that Josephine Dobbs wasn't even at home when the fire broke out and arrived later and was injured trying to save her mother and sister?"

"Yeh, but—"

233

"That's all, Mr. McMann." Cantwell sat at his table.

"Any redirect before we recess for dinner?"

"Yes, Your Honor." The assistant A.G. went to the witness. "Mr. McMann, let me ask you two very simple questions. Based on your experience and expertise as a police detective, do you believe that any of those bodies found on the second floor of that tenement building was that of Betty Blakely?"

"No, sir."

"And do you believe that Betty Blakely is alive and sitting here in this courtroom?"

"Yes, sir."

A loud murmur went through the spectators, and the six jurors stared hard at the young woman petitioner.

"Any recross-examination, Mr. Cantwell?"

"Just one question, Your Honor. Mr. McMann, have you any proof of what you just said?"

"No, no proof, but—"

"Let me ask you again in a different way, do you have any solid, and I do mean solid, reason to believe that that young lady sitting there is not Josephine Dobbs?"

"Well, I—"

"No more questions."

"Very well," said Judge Rutherford. "Gentlemen of the jury, it has been a long morning and I apologize for allowing this testimony to continue past noon. We will now recess for one hour, and I hope to be able to conclude this hearing this afternoon." Bang. "The court is in recess."

"All rise."

Everyone stood as the judge stepped down from his podium, gathered his black robe, and walked down the aisle to the sheriff's office.

Chapter Twenty

"How does it look," asked Alexander as he, Silas K. Cantwell, and the young woman petitioner walked out of the courtroom.

"It's anybody's guess," the lawyer answered. "We need that other witness. Where could he be?"

"He may have left for his cabin," said Josephine Dobbs.

"Sheriff"—the lawyer approached the desk of Sheriff Boyd Hutchins—"have you sent anyone to look for Mr. Henshaw?"

"Yep. I sent a man on a fast horse up to his cabin under Thunder Butte, and another east toward Rosebud. But it's hard tellin' where he might be. Old Bear Tracks comes and goes."

"Dammit," exclaimed the lawyer. "Dammit all anyway. I should have had him under subpoena. It just didn't occur to me that he would disappear."

Outside, the sky was threatening another mountain rain squall, but as yet the ground was dry. Spectators were sitting on the ground and on the plank sidewalk eating out of a variety of tin buckets. A large hand-drawn sign hung on the door of Ma Blessing's cafe. It read: CLOSED BE OPEN FOR SUPPER.

Silas K. Cantwell fidgeted with his lunch of im-

orted salmon at the New Windsor Hotel. Josephine
Dobbs picked at her food. Alexander ate his lunch but
t formed a large lump in his stomach.

"Do you think we have a chance?" she asked.

"We have a chance, a small chance. I had hoped to
wing the odds in our favor before the case goes to the
ury. We need that witness."

"Neither side has offered any real solid proof of
nything," said Alexander. "The assistant A.G. has
rought out sufficient cause for suspicion, but no
roof. If only we had something solid to offer."

Silas K. Cantwell put down his fork and wiped his
nouth with a linen napkin. "Let us go back to court
nd hope."

The crowd followed them into the courtroom and
he six jurors took their seats. Alexander studied their
aces, trying to read something in them. Their faces
evealed nothing, and they seemed to be trying to
void looking at the young woman.

The Honorable Judge Rutherford came in, folding
is black robe around him. Everyone stood until he
as seated, and the usual ritual was quickly com-
leted. "Now then," said the judge, "has the state any
ore witnesses?"

"None, Your Honor."

"Then has the state rested its case?"

"Yes, Your Honor."

"Bully. Now, has the petitioner anything to add?"

Silas K. Cantwell looked hopefully over the specta-
rs. Alexander and the young woman looked too.

"Well, Mr. Cantwell?"

"Your Honor, I respectfully ask again for a contin-
ance. Just until tomorrow morning, Your Honor.

Surely, Mr. Henshaw, our last witness, will be located by then."

"Mr. Cantwell," the judge looked down from his high bench, "seeing that your witnesses are present is your responsibility, and I have a busy schedule to maintain, your motion is denied. Now, do you have anything more or do you rest your case?"

Cantwell stood slump-shouldered. "I'm afraid I'll have to—"

He didn't finish his statement. The door between the sheriff's office and the courtroom opened. All heads turned that way, and a loud murmur went through the spectators. Clarence "Bear Tracks" Henshaw stood there.

A collective sigh came from Cantwell, Alexander and Miss Dobbs. The old prospector stood in the door, his sad eyes roving over the spectators, looking for a friendly face.

"Mr. Henshaw," shouted Silas K. Cantwell, "please come forward."

Henshaw walked down the aisle slowly, hesitantly. He appeared to be ready to bolt and run at the slightest provocation. His extra-large boots made thumping sounds on the wooden floor.

"Please, Mr. Henshaw. We're all friends here. Please step up to the witness chair." Henshaw clumped his way to the witness stand, raised his right hand as directed, and mumbled his "I do."

"Please be seated, Mr. Henshaw."

The first questions were to establish his identity and his occupation. He answered: "Miner, prospector, cowpuncher, timber cutter, gambler."

"Mr. Henshaw, may I ask, why did you disappear

today?"

The old prospector's sad eyes roved over the crowd again, still searching for a friendly face. He still had a week's growth of salt-and-pepper whiskers. "I dunno. I reckon I jest didn't want to set up here."

"What brought you back?"

"I dunno. I reckon I got to thinkin' and I thought mebbe Ol' Buckshot'd want me to." He talked with a painfully slow drawl.

"Very well, Mr. Henshaw, how long have you lived in this area?"

" 'Bout fifteen yar, I reckon."

"Did you know the deceased, Mr. Dobbs?"

"Shore did."

"How long did you know Mr. Dobbs?"

" 'Bout fifteen yar, I reckon."

"Did you know Mr. Dobbs's family?"

"Seen 'em."

"I see." Silas K. Cantwell rubbed his jaw thoughtfully. "I take it then that you saw them from time to time but weren't very well acquainted with them, is that correct?"

"I knowed 'em when I seen 'em. The woman and two girls."

"When was the last time you saw them?"

" 'Bout twelve, thirteen yar ago."

"Where did you see them last?"

"Seen the girls at the dance over to Rosebud."

"I see." The lawyer paced back and forth in front of the jury box, head down, looking at the floor. "What do you remember about Frederick Dobbs?"

"Ol' Buckshot? I knowed 'im 'bout as much as anybody, I reckon." The witness was feeling more at ease now. "He was a man that played the cards as they come up. He wasn't always knockin' down and skinnin' the next gent."

"Are you saying he was fair and honest?"

"Shore am. The Ol' Lady dealt 'im a mean hand for many yars, but he kept playin' and finally drawed aces."

"The old lady?"

"Shore. Ol' Lady Luck."

"Do you mean to say that he had no luck prospecting for years, then finally struck it rich?"

"Shore am. But he was a onhappy man. Wanted his family. Sent fer 'em. But the Ol' Lady spun the wheel and he crossed the Big Divide afore any of his family come."

"I see." Cantwell paced slowly in front of the jury box, looking down, pulling at his lower lip. "Now then, Mr. Henshaw, where did the Dobbs family live?"

"On Antler Crik, 'bout four mile this side of Rosebud."

"What was Mrs. Dobbs like?"

"Objection, Your Honor. We're straying from our purpose here."

"Sustained."

"Very well, Mr. Henshaw, can you describe Mrs. Dobbs and her daughters?"

"Purty. Mighty purty females. Purtiest in the territory. Ol' Buckshot was a peaceable man till somebody said somethin' 'bout his family, then he got meaner'n a muskrat. One time he throwed down on a feller with a shotgun, and that's when we called 'im Ol' Buckshot."

240

"How old were the daughters when you saw them last?"

"I'd cal'clate the eldest was around sixteen and the young 'un was twelve or thirteen. The eldest was just buddin' into womanhood and the young 'un was almost as tall."

"Then the younger daughter would be about twenty-six years old now?"

"I reckon."

"What did the younger daughter look like?"

"Tow-headed. Tall, like I said, and kinder skinny. But she looked to be the kind that'd fill out with a little more age on her."

"What did the other daughter look like?"

"Black-headed. They was both purty and about the same size, but other than that you wouldn't a knowed they was sisters."

"Did you know their names?"

"Ettie and Josey. That's what Ol' Buckshot called 'em. He named his mine after the young 'un."

"Would you recognize either one of them if you saw them today?"

"I dunno. Been a long time."

"Would you look at the young lady siting at the table over there, and tell the jury whether you recognize her?"

Henshaw turned his sad eyes toward Miss Dobbs.

"Shore do. That's the lady I run onto up at my shack at Thunder Butte. Her and her friend was tryin' to outrun some Injuns."

"Had you ever seen her before?"

"Dunno. Could of."

"Could she be Miss Josephine Dobbs?"

241

"Could be, I reckon." Henshaw squinted at her. "Could be Josey all filled out."

"All right now, you say you last saw the two daughters at a dance at Rosebud?"

"Just outside Rosebud. In the schoolhouse on Antler Crik."

"They attended a dance?"

"Shore did. One at a time."

"One at a time?"

"Shore did."

"Would you explain that?"

Henshaw rubbed a callused hand over his chin whiskers and looked over at Miss Dobbs with his sad eyes. "I don't know if I should say it. She wouldn't want me to tell about it."

"Tell about what?"

" 'Bout that dance. 'Bout her and her sister."

"Your Honor," John Birdsell was on his feet. "Can't we get on with this? If he has anything to say, will you instruct him to say it?"

"The witness will answer the questions."

Silas K. Cantwell pulled at his lower lip. "Mr. Henshaw, the jury needs to know what you know about the daughters of Frederick Dobbs. Would you please tell us about them?"

The witness's sad eyes seemed to be even sadder now, and he talked with an even slower drawl. "Wa-al, I don't mean to tell no tales out of school and I don't mean to hurt nobody's feelin's."

"Go on."

"Wa-al, they only had one purty dress twixt 'em and they taken turns goin' to the dance."

"They took turns, you say? How did they manage

242

that?"

"Out back. In the willers. The willers that growed on the crik." Henshaw paused and looked at Miss Dobbs. "I shore am sorry, ma'am. I wouldn't tell if I didn't have to."

The assistant A.G. was on his feet again. "Your Honor, will you direct the witness to get on with his testimony?"

"The witness will proceed."

"Wa-al, they taken turns wearin' that dress. They changed in the willers. First the young 'un put on the dress and went inside whilst the eldest waited in the willers, then the young 'un came out and the eldest put on the dress."

Silas K. Cantwell stopped his pacing. The jurors and spectators were listening carefully.

"Do you mean," Cantwell said, "that the two girls changed clothes in the willow bushes and took turns going in to the dance?"

"Shore do."

"Well . . ." The lawyer had to pause and think a moment. "Are you certain that who you saw in the willows in the dark—I'm assuming it was at night— were the two Dobbs sisters?"

"Shore am."

"How could you be certain?"

"Full moon. You could almost read a newspaper."

"Then you saw them clearly?"

"Shore did."

"And they actually changed clothes standing in the willow bushes? How did they manage that?"

"I seen the young 'un skin that dress off over her head and stand there in her bare hide shiverin' and huggin' herself to keep warm."

"Didn't they have on any underclothes?"

"Some. But they had to trade stockin's too."

"Your Honor," The assistant A.G. talked like a man running out of patience. "Must this continue?"

"Mr. Cantwell, if all this is relevant, would you explain why?"

"Yes, Your Honor. I am eliciting this testimony as a means of identifying Josephine Dobbs. In the interest of prudence, let me explain that a party dress is cut full and when a dancer spins and pirouettes, the dress sometimes flares up and exposes the, uh, stockings. Now, it is apparent that the girls had only one pair of, uh, attractive, uh, stockings, and, when they changed dresses, they changed stockings too."

"Very well, Mr. Cantwell, but do not dwell on this subject any more than is absolutely necessary."

"Now then, Mr. Henshaw, what else happened?"

"Wa-al, they was seen. I seen 'em and purty soon another feller came out in the willers ta—he seen 'em too. And purty soon the girls got wise that they was bein' seen and they stampeded."

"They ran?"

"Shore did. It was kinder pitiable. The elder 'un let out a holler, and they hauled their freight out'n thar, and the young 'un was runnin' 'thout much on."

"Where did they go?"

"They cut fer home, I reckon."

"Did you ever see them again?"

"Shore didn't. I heered that Missuz Dobbs loads 'em in a wagon next day and quits the country."

Chapter Twenty-one

Silas K. Cantwell walked the length of the jury box and back. "Mr. Henshaw, are you literate?"

"Shore am, and I b'lieve in the hereafter too."

"No, no, that's not what I mean. Let me rephrase the question, can you read and write?"

"Shore can."

"Did you write a letter to Mrs. Dobbs in St. Louis, Missouri, telling her about the death of her husband?"

"Shore did."

"Why did you do that?"

"Wa-al, I figgered somebody ought to. Ol' Buckshot and me, we was partners sometimes, and I knew about his family and I knew he had their address wrote down and I knew where it was."

"So you took it upon yourself to do what you thought ought to be done?"

"Shore did."

Silas K. Cantwell picked up the letter and handed it to the witness. "Would you look at that letter and tell the jury if you wrote it."

"Shore did."

The lawyer paced the floor again, head down, then

looked up at the judge. "No more questions."

When Cantwell sat down, Alexander whispered, "Is that all? Don't we need more from him?"

The lawyer winked. "In due time, in due time."

The assistant A.G. stood up, pulled down on his vest, shot his cuffs, and walked over to the witness stand. "Mr. Henshaw, why did you write that letter?"

"I jest tol' why."

"Why didn't you leave it up to the authorities to notify the next of kin?"

"The 'thorities didn't know 'bout the next of kin."

"Why didn't you notify the authorities?"

"Why ast somebody else to do what I oughta do?"

"I ask a question, Mr. Henshaw, and I expect an answer, not another question."

"Your Honor," Cantwell stood and buttoned his coat. "The witness has answered in his own way. Counsel is merely trying to badger the witness."

"Counsel will not badger the witness."

"Very well. Now, Mr. Henshaw, where were you when the sheriff's department was looking for the next of kin?"

"Over to Rosebud."

"Did you know the authorities were searching for heirs?"

"Didn't think much 'bout it."

"Why didn't you cooperate with the authorities, Mr. Henshaw?"

"Didn't want to. Don't want no traffic with the 'thorities."

"Why?"

"Your Honor," said Silas K. Cantwell, "all this is irrelevant. The important fact for this jury to know is that the next of kin were notified. Although they were not notified by the authorities, they were notified."

"Sustained."

"All right, all right. Now, Mr. Henshaw, you said you haven't seen Josephine Dobbs for twelve or thirteen years, is that correct?"

"Shore is."

"And you wouldn't recognize her if you saw her now?"

"Wa-al, I might."

"You might? But you said you doubted you would recognize her. Would you explain?"

"I ain't forgot what she looked like standin' there in the willers."

"All right, now about seeing her in the willow bushes. You said it was nighttime?"

"Shore was."

"How could you see anyone or anything clearly enough at night back in the willow bushes to recognize them?"

"Full moon. Light as day."

"Oh, come now, Mr. Henshaw, the light couldn't have been that good."

"Shore was."

John Birdsell shook his head in disbelief. "Come now. Are you trying to tell this jury that you could see her clearly enough to recognize her?"

"Shore am. She wasn't more'n five feet away from me onct."

"Umm. I see. Tell us, Mr. Henshaw, what were you doing out there in the willow bushes? Peeping?"

The witness's face grew red and his eyes weren't sad anymore. "Wasn't no such a thing."

247

"What were you doing then?"

"I went out to the willers to, uh—"

Silas K. Cantwell interrupted. "Your Honor, I think I can help clear up this point, if I may."

"Bully. Proceed, Mr. Cantwell."

"Mr. Henshaw," Cantwell said, "is it safe to assume that you went out to the willow bushes to relieve yourself?"

"Shore is."

A couple of the spectators tittered. Cantwell sat down.

"All right," John Birdsell said, "now explain how the young girl came to be so close to you?"

"I heered 'em and seen 'em comin', and I didn't want to scare 'em so I stayed still. They changed dresses and the young 'un came over close to whar I was to get in the light so she could see to unbutton the dress and them stockin's."

"And she didn't see you?"

"Not then. I was in the shaders, and I didn't want to scare 'em. And she was turrible busy gettin' them clothes undone."

"All right, but you have said already that you didn't know whether you would recognize her again. Would you or wouldn't you?"

"Wa-al—"

"Yes or no. Would you or wouldn't you?"

"Wa-al, I—"

"Yes or no."

Henshaw stared hard at the assistant A.G. His face was growing redder by the minute. "What I'm tryin—"

"Your Honor, would you instruct the witness to

answer my question yes or no?"

"The witness will answer the question."

Henshaw half-turned to face the judge. His eyes were hard and his stubble-covered jaw was set. "Your Honor Mr Judge, afore I set in this here chair I swore to tell the whole truth and a bunch of other stuff, and I can't tell the whole truth with one word."

Bang, bang. The Honorable Judge Rutherford pointed his gavel at the witness. "The witness will do as instructed, and one more outburst like that and I will have you jailed for contempt of court."

Almost as one, the spectators were on their feet.

Angry voices shouted a jumble of threats. One male voice came through loud and clear: "You ain't gonna jail nobody, Mr. Judge. All he wants to do is speak his piece."

Another husky voice came through. "I fought in the war fer to keep this country free and I ain't gonna stand here and see some godalmighty gov'ment big shot lock up one of us citizens jest 'cause he wants to speak his mind."

Bang, bang, went the judge's gavel. The spectators shouted louder. "This is s'posed to be justice and he wants to lock a feller up for tellin' what he knows."

The spectators were in the aisle, making threatening gestures toward the front of the courtroom. "Ain't nobody gonna git locked up 'less it's the judge and lawyers."

Sheriff Boyd Hutchins was trying to push his way through the crowd but was getting nowhere.

"Gentlemen, gentlemen." It was Silas K. Cantwell shouting. "Gentlemen." He stood on a chair and waved his arms to get their attention. "Gentlemen, please. Please be calm."

Bang, bang.

"Your Honor," Cantwell shouted, "will you please stop doing that? Gentlemen," he shouted at the spectators. "Please be quiet. Let me speak. Please."

Gradually, the crowd quieted, but a few threats still came through.

"Gentlemen, nobody is going to be locked up. I can promise you that. Please be quiet."

The crowd quieted.

"Now," Cantwell turned to the judge, "it is getting late, Your Honor, and I request a recess."

"This court is in recess," the judge said. He raised his gavel but changed his mind and laid it gently on top of the bench.

"All right, gentlemen," Cantwell shouted, still standing on his chair, "the court is in recess. No one is going to jail. We'll reconvene court first thing in the morning, and I promise you that Mr. Henshaw will get to say everything he wants to say. Now will you please leave?"

Slowly, reluctantly, the spectators turned and filed through the door, shaking their heads and grumbling. Cantwell stepped off his chair and approached the bench.

"Your Honor, if the court pleases, I would like to offer some advice based on my years of experience dealing with frontier citizens."

The judge started to speak but changed his mind.

"Your Honor, citizens in Denver are conditioned to allowing the authorities to take care of justice, and they seldom voice an opinion. But here, Your Honor, the citizens are accustomed to dealing with matters of justice in their own way.

"Now, I have practiced law in Ute County for more than ten years, since the city of Rosebud was a one-street city, and I think I know these folks. They are honest, hard-working, God-fearing citizens and they want justice. Yes, Your Honor, I truly believe that they sincerely want justice.

"But, Your Honor, if they think for one minute that the law has become unreasonable and if they think for one minute that the courts are unfair, they will revert to taking the law into their own hands."

As an afterthought, Cantwell added. "And I'll bet Theodore Roosevelt would agree with me."

"Mr. Cantwell." The judge took off his pince-nez spectacles, put them back on, and looked down at the lawyer. He opened his mouth to speak further and again changed his mind. Bang. "This court is in recess until nine A.M. tomorrow."

"Just a minute, Your Honor. If it pleases the court." The assistant A.G. stood before the bench. "Due to all the commotion, I would at this time move that a mistrial be declared."

That was when James J. Alexander stepped up and got into the fray. "Oh you would, would you? That's just another one of your dirty little courtroom tactics, getting a mistrial, causing a delay. You're losing your case and you know it, and this is your way of punishing everyone involved."

The assistant A.G. spun around, facing Alexander. His face was red and his voice was loud. "Who in hell are you?" He pushed a stiff forefinger against Alexander's chest.

"I am James J. Alexander, and I have an interest in

this case. I have watched you bully and insult witnesses and try to make everyone think you are some kind of superior animal just because you went to law school. Well, I went to law school too, and if you don't take your finger off my person I'm going to resort to some frontier justice and knock you on your pompous ass."

"Gentlemen, gentlemen." Silas K. Cantwell got between the two men and gently pushed at Alexander. "This is not the way to settle disputes. Gentlemen, please."

Bang. "There will be no mistrial as long as there is a chance that this hearing can continue properly." Bang, bang. "Now clear the courtroom or I will have the sheriff arrest you for loitering."

Reluctantly, the two combatants turned and went their separate ways. Alexander forced himself to calm down. He turned to Miss Dobbs. "I want to apologize for my language. I don't usually talk that way among ladies."

She smiled widely. "You were wonderful, James. You were just abso-bloody-lutely wonderful."

At the hotel desk, the lawyer asked whether there were any messages and was handed an envelope. He opened it, read the message, and smiled. "It's from James B. Wiltheimer, Attorney at Law. His client, the young man who calls himself Charles Dobbs, is withdrawing his petition for probate. And"—he handed the note to Alexander—"he wants to retain you to investigate his client's criminal case. He believes his client is innocent of anything other than possibly attempted fraud."

Alexander read the note. "I believe he's right.

There's more to all this than meets the eye."

"What do you mean, James?" Miss Dobbs's eyes were puzzled.

"I don't think he's responsible for what happened to us."

"Now that you mention it, neither do I. I've been so involved in this trial that I haven't given much thought to it."

The lawyer interrupted, "What are you two talking about? Didn't you say someone hired those two hoodlums to murder you?"

"Yes, but—" Alexander looked at the floor and shook his head.

"Whoever it was," said Miss Dobbs, "was probably the same man, or men, who arranged the murder of my father."

"Well, will you forget that for now?" the lawyer asked. "We haven't won this trial yet."

"O.K.," Alexander said, "but if you send a message back to Mr. Wiltheimer, tell him that I will be happy to take the case."

"I'll send a message on the stage tomorrow."

After supper, Alexander and the girl walked hand in hand down one side of Main Street and back up the other side. At her hotel room door, she allowed him to kiss her gently on the lips. Then she said, "I must rest. Tomorrow I will have to give what could be the most important performance of my life."

"You'll knock 'em dead, Josie."

It was Ma Blessing who brought Clarence "Bear Tracks" Henshaw to the courtroom next morning. "I

253

didn't let 'im out of my sight all night," she said. "I fed 'im and kept 'im sober and brought 'im back here to finish what he has to say."

Henshaw looked around the courtroom with his sad eyes. He hadn't shaved but his beard hadn't grown either.

The assistant A.G. stood before him as he sat on the witness chair. "Now then, Mr. Henshaw, as I recall, you said you could not recognize Josephine Dobbs if you saw her today. Is that correct?"

"Wa-al, yes and no."

John Birdsell stomped back to his table, picked up a pencil, threw it down, and turned to the judge. "Your Honor, must we go through this again?"

Silas K. Cantwell cleared his throat and stood up. "If it please the court, perhaps I can help."

"Bully. Proceed."

"Mr. Henshaw," Cantwell rubbed the back of his neck, "if you will answer yes or no, I will see that you have an opportunity to say what you want to say later. I promise you, you will get to speak your mind." Cantwell sat down.

"Bully. Mr. Birdsell?"

The young lawyer walked back to the witness stand. "I repeat the question, would you or would you not recognize Josephine Dobbs if you saw her today?"

"Shore would."

"What?" John Birdsell couldn't believe his ears. "But you already said you couldn't."

"I'd know the scar."

"The scar? What scar?"

"On her laig. Right above her left knee. I seen it."

"Josephine Dobbs has a scar on her left leg? Just

above the knee?"

"Shore does."

"How do you know?"

"Seen it."

"When?"

" 'Bout twelve or thirteen yar ago."

"Where?"

"In them willers."

"Oh, I see now. When you saw her changing dresses in the willow bushes you noticed a scar on her left leg just above the knee?"

"Shore did."

"What sort of scar?"

The old prospector held up two fingers. "It was 'bout this big and whiter than the rest of her hide."

"I see. Are you telling this jury that you could see that small a scar at night in the willow bushes?"

"Shore am."

"That's hard to believe, Mr. Henshaw."

"It's so."

Shaking his head in wonderment, the young lawyer went back to his table, stood there a moment with his head down, then said, "No more questions."

"Bully. Any redirect?"

"Here we go," Cantwell whispered to his client. He took his time walking to the witness stand. The jurors were fully alert, watching, listening. The lawyer rubbed the back of his neck, studied the floor and said finally, "Mr. Henshaw, are you certain that Josephine Dobbs has a scar above her left knee?"

"Shore am."

"There is no doubt in your mind about that? You saw it clearly that night?"

"Shore did. She had them stockin's held up with suspenders and I seen it when she was fiddlin' with 'em."

"No further questions."

"Bully. Mr. Birdsell, any more questions from you?"

"None, Your Honor."

"Mr. Cantwell, any rebuttal?"

"Yes, Your Honor, I would like to recall Miss Josephine Dobbs."

Alexander gave the young woman's hand a squeeze as she stood. With her head up and back straight, she went to the witness stand and took her seat. Again, the judge reminded her that she was still under oath.

Silas K. Cantwell got right into the subject. "Miss Dobbs, do you have a scar on your left leg just above the knee?"

"Yes."

"Would you tell the jury how you happen to have it?"

"Well, actually, the first one was caused by a severe cut. My sister and I were—let me begin again. We had a picket fence around a garden that we all worked, and my sister and I were trying to walk on top of the plank that held the pickets in place. We had seen pictures of circus performers and we were pretending that we were walking a tightwire. I lost my balance and fell across the top of the fence and one of the pickets gouged a length of flesh out of my, uh, limb."

"No more questions." Cantwell went back to his table.

"Mr. Birdsell?"

"So you have a scar on your left leg, Miss whoever you are?"

"Yes."

Birdsell waved his hands in a hopeless gesture and turned to the judge. "Your Honor, I know that what I am about to suggest will bring forth a strenuous objection, but I believe the jury has the right to see for itself."

"Objection," shouted Cantwell. "That would be extremely improper, Your Honor. Mr. Birdsell is asking a young lady to show an intimate part of her anatomy to the jury." When he sat down, he winked again at Alexander.

"Gentlemen, would you approach the bench?"

The two lawyers stood before the judge, and all three whispered among themselves for several minutes. Then Silas K. Cantwell took his seat and John Birdsell went back to the witness.

"Miss whoever you are, I must ask you to raise your dress and show the scar to the gentlemen of the jury."

Loud voices came from the spectators section, and a few sounded outraged. Judge Rutherford started to bang his gavel, but remembered what happened the last time he had tried to gavel the spectators into order. "Please," he implored. "Please control yourselves. Believe, me, ladies and gentlemen, we are not asking the young lady to do anything improper. But we simply must determine whether she is or is not Josephine Dobbs. There seems to be no other way."

The spectators quieted but sat on the edge of their benches, mouths open, breathing shallowly.

"Well, Miss," said the assistant A.G.

Chapter Twenty-two

The young woman turned hurt eyes to her lawyer, asking for help. He went to her and put a consoling hand on her shoulder. "I'm very sorry, Miss Dobbs. I tried to find another way to convince the jury, but—" He shrugged helplessly.

"Well, Miss."

Moving slowly as if in a trance, she took hold of her skirt with both hands and started raising it.

The six men in the jury box leaned forward. Spectators in the back rows stood up and gathered at the front of the spectators' section.

Judge Rutherford picked up his gavel, shrugged, and put it back down.

The young woman's ankles were bared now, and she continued raising her skirt.

One of the jurors leaned so far forward to see it all that he lost his balance and had to grab hold of the railing around the jury box.

With tears rolling down her cheeks, the young woman raised her skirt until her stockinged knees were uncovered.

Spectators let out a collective "Ooh."

She raised her skirt higher and stopped. Her dark stockings came to just above her knees and were held up with suspenders.

Alexander, remembering the plain cut-off union suit she was wearing when he—never mind that, he scolded himself—was pleased to see that she was now wearing lacy knee-length underdrawers.

"Please, Miss Dobbs," her lawyer implored, "show them the scar."

A tear dripped off her chin. But with determination, she unhooked the stocking on her left leg and rolled it down a few inches. A scar was visible, beginning at her knee.

She pulled the leg of her underdrawers halfway up her thigh.

"Ooh," said the spectators.

The scar was wide and white, tinged with pink in places, and it extended up the outside of her thigh.

"Gentlemen of the jury, have you seen enough?" the judge asked.

The jurors bobbed their heads. The witness quickly shoved her skirt back down to her shoe tops.

"Well, Mr. Birdsell?"

The young lawyer had a smug look on his face as he stood in front of the jury box. "I call Mr. Clarence Henshaw."

"You may step down, Miss."

She was replaced by the old prospector and she went to her seat with her head up.

"Now, Mr. Henshaw, did you see the scar?"

"Shore did."

"Is that the scar you saw that night in the willow bushes?"

"Shore ain't."

"No more questions."

"Mr. Henshaw," Silas K. Cantwell stood before him now, "is the scar you saw just now in the same place as the scar you saw that night, years ago?"

"Shore is. Only it was littler."

"That's all. Thank you, Mr. Henshaw. Your Honor, I would like to recall Miss Dobbs."

"Very well."

Back on the witness stand, the young woman sat composed, her ankles crossed and her hands folded in her lap.

"Would you tell the jury how you got that scar, Miss Dobbs?"

"In the fire that took the lives of my mother and sister. My dress caught fire when I tried to go into the building. I had a bad burn."

"Did you have a scar just above your knee before you were burned?"

"Yes."

"Then the burns you suffered caused another, larger scar that covered the old one?"

"Yes."

"Let me ask you one more very important question, Miss Dobbs, and then I will be through. Will you look at the gentlemen of the jury and state your name?"

Her blue-green eyes met the gaze of each of the six jurors, one at a time. "My name is Josephine Dobbs."

"Your Honor, the petitioner rests her case."

"Bully. Now, Mr. Birdsell?"

"We have nothing more, Your Honor."

"Bully. Now, will counsel for both sides approach the bench?"

The two lawyers stood before the judge and another

whispered conversation ensued. When the lawyers went back to their tables, the judge asked, "Mr. Cantwell, do you have a closing argument?"

"Yes, Your Honor." Silas K. Cantwell buttoned the middle button of his coat and stepped up to the jury box. For a long moment, he stood with his head down, rubbing the back of his neck. Everyone in the room was quiet, waiting, listening.

"Gentlemen," the lawyer began, "there is no use going over all the evidence in this case. This has been a trying experience for you, and I'm sure you all have good memories, so I'll be brief. What we have here is a young lady who claims to be Josephine Dobbs of St. Louis, Missouri, and an assistant attorney general who says she is someone else. If you find in her favor, she takes possession of the Josey Mine. If you find for the state, the state will take possession of the mine.

"Mrs. Margaret Dobbs, wife of the late Frederick "Buckshot" Dobbs, separated from her husband about thirteen years ago and took their two daughters with her to St. Louis. Later, Buckshot Dobbs discovered gold and became wealthy. And still later, he died, and Mrs. Dobbs and her oldest daughter also died in a fire in St. Louis. Josephine Dobbs survived although she suffered burns.

"Later still, Josephine Dobbs, with no family left, came by herself to El Tejon. As soon as the word got out that she was the daughter of Buckshot Dobbs an attempt was made on her life. Obviously by someone who did not want her to take over Mr. Dobbs's estate. Someone believed she was the real Josephine Dobbs and wanted her out of the way.

"She has in her possession a letter written to her

mother by Bear Tracks Henshaw. Mr. Henshaw has identified the letter. He could not positively identify her, but he said it has been thirteen years since he saw her last and then she was only twelve or thirteen years old. He did, however, describe a scar on her left leg, a scar that should identify her.

"Sadly, Josephine Dobbs had suffered a severe burn while trying to save her mother and sister in that fire, and the new scar covers the old one. But, gentlemen, the burn scar is in exactly the place where the old scar was. It was merely unhappy circumstances that covered the only positive means of identification.

"Now, gentlemen, you are all fair-minded citizens. That young lady over there has suffered terribly. First the loss of her father, then the loss of her mother and sister, and then an attempt on her life, an attempt that caused her and her companion to suffer even more while lost in the mountains.

"She is a very plucky young lady. In fact, gentlemen, she is one of the most courageous women I have ever had the pleasure of meeting. Did you hear how she drove away a band of marauding Indians?" The lawyer chuckled. "She had never fired a gun in her life, yet she picked up an old Civil War army pistol and drove them away, thereby saving herself and her companion.

"Miss Josephine Dobbs has not only suffered physically and mentally, she has just now suffered the pain of humiliation, having to display an intimate part of her body."

Silas K. Cantwell walked slowly away from the jury box, then returned, head down, rubbing the back of his neck. He looked up at the jury and concluded with, "What more can I say, gentlemen?" He turned his back on the jury and took his seat.

The assistant A.G. was on his feet before his opponent sat down. He shot his cuffs and began.

"Gentlemen of the jury, this litigation is the result of a petition for probate, the litigants being a young woman who calls herself Josephine Dobbs and the state of Colorado represented by the Colorado Attorney General's office. Your function is to determine whether the petitioner is the heir at law of one, Frederick Dobbs, deceased, who died intestate, or whether she is a fraud and merely pretending to be an heir at law.

"Now, there are criminal statutes concerning fraud and attempted fraud, and if you find for the state, we most certainly will file criminal charges against the petitioner."

John Birdsell pulled down on the front of his vest and went into the evidence presented, starting with what the petitioner said, then going into testimony by the sheriff, Clarence Henshaw, the St. Louis police officer, and back to Henshaw and the petitioner. He went over it all in detail, reminding the jury of every point that he considered relevant to his case.

The jurors were getting tired of sitting on the hard benches and were beginning to squirm.

"Gentlemen," the young lawyer went on, "Betty Blakely was told while she was in a hospital suffering a burn on her left leg that the Dobbs family had perished in the tenement house fire, and she was an opportunist who tried to take advantage of the situation. She is a professional actress and had every reason to believe that she could get away with it.

"And that burn scar on her left leg, how fortunate. It was just what she needed to assume the identity of the dead Josephine Dobbs. Well," the assistant A.G. smiled a slow, wry smile, "I find all that incomprehensible."

On he went while the jury squirmed uncomfortably. After describing as an outrageous lie the testimony about an attempt on her life at the mine, the assistant A.G. concluded.

"Her entire story is a lie, beginning with the tenement house fire, what she was told in the hospital, what she told the police in St. Louis, what she told the sheriff about the attempt on her life, and the scar on her left leg."

Dropping his voice to a low, serious tone, John Birdsell said, "Don't let her get by with it, gentlemen. Don't let her get rich with a series of lies." Then he pointed a finger at the young woman and shouted.

"She is Betty Blakely. She is an imposter."

With that, the assistant A.G. turned on his heels, stomped over to his chair and sat.

A low murmur went through the spectators but quieted when the Honorable Judge Rutherford cleared his throat and started to speak.

"Usually, gentlemen of the jury, the attorneys and the presiding judge meet in the judge's chambers to find some area of agreement on the judge's instructions to the jury. We have decided in a brief consultation here to forego that step in the trial.

"There is only one question to be resolved here, and you, gentlemen of the jury, have already been told what it is. Now, I don't know where you will retire to deliberate, possibly in the sheriff's office or wherever you choose, but you will now retire, elect one of your members as foreman and begin your deliberations."

The six men in the jury box looked questioningly at each other and began whispering among themselves.

"Gentlemen," the judge said, "it is customary for the jury to retire to a private place to deliberate."

The jurors ignored him and continued whispering. They gathered around the man named Johnson, the juror with the chin whiskers and bald head, and one of them jabbed him in the chest with a finger. "Who, me?" Johnson was heard to ask. More whispering and then an affirmative shake of their heads. They resumed their seats and waited for Johnson to speak.

The tall, thin Johnson stood up, cast a quick look at the spectators and at the other jurors. The jurors nodded at him. "Go on," one of them whispered. "Uh, Your Honor," Johnson began, hesitantly.

"Have you reached a verdict already?" the judge asked.

"Yeah. Yessir, Your Honor. We're done deliberatin'."

"Very well, what is your verdict?"

The jury foreman scowled and pointed a work-gnarled finger at the young woman. "We think that she is, uh—"

The courtroom was deathly quiet. Spectators held their breath. Alexander clenched his fists and ground his teeth.

"Go on, sir," the judge said.

"We think she is Josephine Dobbs, the daughter of Old Buckshot Dobbs."

A roar of approval came from the spectators. Alexander jumped up and hugged Miss Dobbs. Spectators pushed through the gate between the spectators' section and the court and gathered around the young woman. They patted her shoulders and all tried to talk at once.

"When you gonna open the mine?"

"Yeah, when?"

"I don't really know," she answered. "I'm afraid I know nothing about mining. I'll have to sell it to someone who does know."

"Get 'er open. We need the work."

Judge Rutherford banged his gavel once, started to do it again, then yelled, "Court's adjourned." He stepped off the podium and made his way through the crowd, holding his black robe about him. His court reporter scribbled the last of his notes, folded his book, gathered his pencils, and followed. The assistant A.G. picked up his papers, shoved them into his briefcase, and pushed his way outside.

The probate court was adjourned.

Champagne flowed at the dinner table in the New Windsor Hotel that night. Alexander ordered the best in the house and kept his glass and the glasses of Miss Dobbs and Silas K. Cantwell filled.

"Tell me, Mr. Cantwell, did you ever at any time believe we had the case won?"

"Never. I knew we had a good chance, but I was never certain. You can't second-guess a jury."

"You know, Mr. Cantwell, we never put on any real solid proof, yet not only the jury but the spectators too favored Josephine. Can you tell me why?"

"There is one very good reason, James. It's something you won't read about in the law books, and you probably won't ever hear one of your law professors talk about it either."

"What? I'm all ears."

"Stupidity."

"What?"

"I mean exactly that. It's stupidity on the part of the jurors. Let's be frank. Most people are followers. They aren't capable of thinking for themselves. If you put on a good show for them in the courtroom, they'll give you anything you want. All trial lawyers are aware of that, and the smart ones take advantage of it."

The lawyer took another sip of his champagne. "We put on a good show. You're right, we had no real proof, but we did have what every trial lawyer dreams of. I'm talking about a pretty girl." He smiled at Miss Dobbs. "And a sad tale, a very sad tale to tell. And to top it off, a pretty girl who was forced, and I do mean forced, to show her legs to the jury. You'll recall, James, that I got the other side to demand that she show her legs.

"Now," Silas K. Cantwell sat back in his chair and beamed, "in the absence of incontrovertible proof, what more could a trial lawyer ask for?"

Instead of smiling with him, Alexander was shaking his head sadly. "What you're saying is that the jury system is a failure because of the stupidity of the jurors."

"No, I'm not saying it's a complete failure. More justice comes out of it than injustice. But I am saying it is far from perfect. When you have jurors who are not capable of clear, logical thinking, then there is going to be some injustice."

"It's too bad." Alexander was still shaking his head sadly.

"What will happen in the future, James, is that the judges and lawyers will try to alleviate the problem by withholding certain information from the jury, you know, the kind of information that might unfairly prejudice the jury."

"In other words," Alexander said, "the judges and lawyers will take it upon themselves to separate the grain from the chaff, so to speak, because they don't think the jurors are smart enough to do that."

"That's exactly right."

"And then we will have jurors rendering verdicts based on incomplete information, based on whatever information the judges think they are capable of handling."

"I'll tell you one thing, James, the future for lawyers looks extremely good. The more civilized society becomes, the more complex the law becomes and the more demand for lawyers. Why," Silas K. Cantwell smiled over the rim of his wine glass, "every time the U.S. Congress meets they pass more laws and create more business for lawyers. And every time the Supreme Court hands down a batch of rulings, it makes it easier for someone to sue someone.

"The time will come, James, when the way to get rich is not to work hard, invest wisely and all that, but to bide your time, watch for an opportunity, and then sue someone.

"If you're smart, and I know you are, you'll go back to Harvard and finish school. With a sheepskin from Harvard you would get offers from law firms all

ver the nation. Or you could hang your own shingle.
'ou've been on the frontier now and had some
rontier experience, you could open a law office right
ere in El Tejon."

"I don't know," Alexander said, shaking his head
gain. "I don't know."

Silas K. Cantwell took the stage to Rosebud and
aid he would figure out his fee and send it by mail.
Ie also promised to find a reliable mining engineer to
nspect the Josey Mine and make an estimate as to its
alue and to place an ad in the *Rosebud Journal*,
aying the mine was for sale.

There was just one more thing Alexander had to do.
Ie had to find out who wanted Josephine Dobbs
nurdered.

First, he talked with Sheriff Boyd Hutchins about
t, reminding him of what he and Miss Dobbs had
eard the two hired killers say. "It's obvious that
uckshot Dobbs and his employee Bertrum Wingate
ere murdered and the murder was made to look like
n accident," he said. "What we have to find out is
vho arranged it."

"We?" the sheriff asked, smoothing his walrus
nustache.

"Yes, we. You as the official law enforcement
fficer in Webber County and me as an operative for
he Pinkerton National Detective Agency." He fibbed
little about that, but he hoped the sheriff wouldn't
now it.

"Oh yeah, they said in court you're a Pinkerton."

"Yes. I've been working undercover."

"Wal, I'll be a donkey's uncle. I thought you aske[d] too many questions for a businessman."

"Anyway," Alexander went on, "I'm convinced tha[t] your prisoner, the man who called himself Charle[s] Dobbs, is innocent of attempted murder."

"I'll keep him locked up till the next time the judg[e] gets over here and then I'll turn him loose and see tha[t] he gets out of town."

"The question is, Mr. Hutchins, who would prof[it] from the death of Buckshot Dobbs? You'd think [it] would be someone who claimed to be his heir, bu[t] only two people have submitted that claim and the[y] were both far from here when Dobbs and Winga[te] died."

Sheriff Boyd Hutchins stroked his mustach[e] thoughtfully. "I just can't even make a guess withou[t] knowin' more about everything."

The next event was disappointing. Miss Dobb[s] came to Alexander's room right after he returned to i[t] and she was puzzled. "I took over my father's ban[k] account and, would you believe it, James, he had [a] balance of only six hundred and twenty dollars."

"Really? Did anyone at the bank have an explana[a]tion?"

"Oh, sure. Mr. Webber showed me the papers. M[y] father took out a loan to buy supplies, and th[e] balance on it was four hundred dollars. He als[o] showed me a record of deposits and withdrawals and [I] could see that the deposits became fewer and smaller[.]"

"Strange. I wonder why?"

Both Alexander and the young woman soon foun[d]

out why, and they were disappointed again.

A mining engineer in green corduroys, lace boots, and a campaign hat arrived on the stage, and, when he met in the hotel lobby with Miss Dobbs and her constant companion James J. Alexander, he immediately started shaking his head negatively.

"I have already inspected the Josey Mine, Miss Dobbs, and I can tell you right now that it's not worth much."

"What?" The word came from Alexander and the young woman simultaneously. "But," said Alexander, "everyone said it is a very rich gold mine."

"Not everyone. I knew some time ago that the vein was thinning out. A Mr. Wingate hired me to estimate whether it would be profitable to continue working the mine. I had samples of ore assayed at Rosebud and advised Mr. Wingate that it was very low in gold content."

"Are you saying it's worthless?" Alexander couldn't believe what he was hearing.

"No, not entirely worthless. Some of the ore already taken out but not processed yet is probably worth a few thousand dollars. And the equipment is worth something."

"Are you sure about this?"

"Sadly yes." The engineer produced a folded sheet of paper from his inside coat pocket and handed it to Miss Dobbs. "This is a copy of the written report that I gave to Mr. Wingate and Mr. Dobbs."

She read it over and handed it to Alexander who read it. "This is dated June eighteen. Did you give copies of this to anyone else?"

"No. A railroad official named, let's see, uh, Rivers, I believe, asked to see it but I refused to show it to him."

"A railroad official? Why would he want to see it?"

"I don't know. I do know, however, that the Denver & Rio Grande was considering laying rail to El Tejon."

"Was?"

"That's all I know about that."

"But you didn't show this to anyone with the railroad company?"

"No. I wouldn't do that. It was strictly confidential. Oh, an attorney named Cantwell asked to see it just this morning, and I told him I would have to have your permission, Miss Dobbs. Do you want him to receive a copy?"

"Yes. He's my attorney."

Alexander was silent. Then Miss Dobbs spoke again. "My father was an experienced prospector. How could he have been fooled?"

"He wasn't fooled. He knew there was never a vein that didn't end. But Mr. Wingate wanted a professional opinion."

"And you are sure that this," she waved the written report, "was strictly between you, Mr. Wingate, and my father? No one else knew about it?"

"As far as I know. If anyone else knows it, they didn't get it from me. I'm sorry, Miss Dobbs. It was a good discovery and a lot of high-grade ore was taken out of that mine. Generally, values get better as depth is gained, but in this case the opposite was true. It got so the ore wouldn't pay expenses. It has happened to other mines in this vicinity."

"I just can't believe it," Alexander said.

They went to Ma Blessing's cafe for supper and sat at a corner table. Alexander had disappointment written all over his face.

"You look like your favorite horse died," Ma Blessing commented when she came to serve them, "only you ain't got no horse."

Miss Dobbs was in better spirits, and she quipped, "He didn't know what kind of joker he was drawing when he took over my case." She smiled at Alexander and then at Ma Blessing. "He's got the low-down blues, but he'll get over it."

"How can you be so cheerful considering what you just lost?" he asked.

She punched him on the shoulder with a small fist. "J.J., you're enough to make a cat laugh. I didn't lose anything. I just didn't win a whole heck of a lot. It's all right. I'm young and healthy. And I'll get something out of all this, enough to go wherever I want to go and do whatever I want to do."

Ma Blessing couldn't contain herself. "Will you tell me what in the popeyed world you're talkin' about. You just inherited a gold mine, young lady."

Shaking her head, Miss Dobbs said, "What I inherited isn't worth much, Mrs. Blessing. We just found that out."

"You're jobbin' me."

"No, I'm not. The gold has petered out."

"Well, now." Ma Blessing rubbed her forehead with the back of her left hand and studied the floor. "Come to think of it, I heard someone say once that the Josey wasn't as good as some people think she is."

"Who told you that?" Alexander asked.

"I don't recollect, right now. One of the miners, I

reckon. I thought he was just talkin'."

"But," Alexander was puzzled, "everyone here thought the mine was a rich one."

"Not ever'body. I heard little rumors that some of the rocks comin' out of her didn't look like much."

"But it wasn't common knowledge, was it?"

"No. I'd say it wasn't. When they had that engineer feller pokin' around out there last spring, some people got suspicious, but when the mine kept on operatin', they figured the rocks must of assayed out pretty good."

"I would think," said Miss Dobbs, "that it would be hard to keep a secret in a small town like this."

"It's pretty hard, all right," said Ma Blessing. "People like to talk."

"There was one way," Alexander mused.

"How?" Miss Dobbs wanted to know.

"Dead men tell no tales."

"What do you mean, James?"

"Oh, nothing. Just thinking out loud." He looked up at Ma Blessing and smiled a grim smile. "Pay no attention to me, I'm just disappointed that Miss Dobbs didn't get rich. She deserved to."

He picked at his supper and finally put down his fork and wiped his mouth with his handkerchief. The young woman ate heartily. "When you have to scrabble for a living the way I have, James, you learn to live with disappointments."

"I suppose so. But this thing is a real puzzler. I just can't figure it out."

She put her hand on top of his. "Do you just have to figure it out, James?"

Meeting her blue-eyed gaze, he said, "Yes, Josie, I

do. I wish I could be happy-go-lucky like you, but I just have to figure it out."

Sleep didn't come to James J. Alexander that night. He couldn't get it out of his mind. He lay wide awake in bed for hours, then got up and walked the floor in his pajamas. He tried to recall everything that had happened since he and the young woman arrived in El Tejon, and he tried to recall everything that was said.

The town fathers, the triumvirate, as someone once called them, were highly optimistic about the economic future of the town. They were just brimming over with optimism. But some of the working class suspected that things were not going so well. Hell, they knew things were not going so well. But apparently most of them believed what the triumvirate was saying, that when the Josey Mine reopened the town would boom again. Only, it turned out that the mine was next to worthless.

What would happen to El Tejon when the news got out?

That was when a thought that had been incubating in Alexander's mind began to hatch. He felt that he could almost reach out and grab the answers. Almost but not quite. The answers were on the periphery of his mind but wouldn't come into focus.

He walked across the room and back in the dark, carefully avoiding the furniture. The thought grew, and suddenly he exclaimed out loud. "Yes, by George, I believe I have it."

And that was when he heard the terrifying scream come from the room next door.

Chapter Twenty-three

For two or three seconds Alexander was stunned. He had been deep in concentration, and it took that long for his mind to adjust to the fact that someone was in danger. It was Josie.

Hastily, he ran across the room, bumped into a chair, shoved it aside, grabbed the doorknob, twisted it open, and ran into the lamp-lighted hall. The scream came again.

The door to Josie's room was standing open, and he could see the dim figure of a man bending over, reaching for something under the bed. When he heard another scream, he knew it was Josie under the bed, trying to stay out of the man's reach.

In two long, quick strides, Alexander was behind the intruder, grabbing at him, wrapping his arms around his head, pulling him back away from the girl.

The man managed to twist around and straighten up. Alexander hit him in the face with a left fist and followed with a hard right cross. The girl was still screaming. Another left-hand blow knocked the intruder down, and Alexander, trained to always be a gentleman, danced away from him.

It was a mistake.

The man came up swinging, and what he was swinging was a long-bladed knife. When he lunged forward, Alexander backpedaled in the dim lamplight from the hall and stumbled over a chair. He fell onto the floor. The man swung the knife in a wide arc, stumbled over Alexander's feet, and fell onto his knees.

Alexander no more than hit the floor than he was rolling and scrambling up. He grabbed the wooden chair that he had fallen over, and, when the man got up and lunged again, he shoved the chair into his middle.

Now they were facing each other in the semidarkness. The intruder held the knife in front of his body, moving it slowly back and forth, watching for a chance to strike.

Backpedaling again, Alexander kept the chair between him and the intruder—and the knife. But he tripped again, this time over some bedclothes that had been thrown onto the floor, and he fell on his back in the hall.

He lost his hold on the chair when he hit the floor, and when he tried to get up he found he couldn't. The intruder was sitting on his legs, holding him down.

The knife rose.

In desperation, Alexander grabbed for the arm and hand that held the knife. He got them and pushed up with all his strength, teeth bared, grimacing with the effort.

But the intruder put all his weight on the knife hand, forcing the knife down, slowly but surely. The point was only a few inches from Alexander's chest.

Alexander saw the man's lips skin back in a cruel grin as they struggled. The man knew he was winning. Alexander knew it too.

And then the man was yanked over backward.

When Miss Dobbs had awakened in the night and found a man leaning over her, she screamed and rolled off the opposite side of the bed, then rolled under the bed. Now she crawled out and heard the struggle in the hall. She saw the intruder sitting on Alexander, pushing the knife down. She had to do something and she had to do it immediately.

Without thinking about it, the young woman did the first thing that came into her mind. She grabbed the bottom of her billowy nightdress and flung it over the man's head, pulling him back.

The intruder fell over backward with the girl's nightdress over his face. She fell onto her knees, straddling his face. Alexander jumped up, grabbed for the man's knife arm with both hands, forced it to the floor and held it there with his knees. It was easy then to twist the knife free.

The racket brought other hotel patrons out of their rooms, and Alexander yelled for them to grab the man. "Hold him," he shouted breathlessly. "He tried to kill Miss Dobbs."

Two men dropped onto the intruder and pinned him on his back to the floor. Another ran up with a lighted lamp in his hands. The girl crawled back, pulling her nightdress off the man's face.

"Who is he?" someone asked.

The intruder, instead of being angry or scared, wore a smile.

"I done died and went to heaven," he said, looking up at the girl.

She too was breathing hard and strands of her blond hair were hanging over her face.

"Yessir," the intruder giggled, "that was the softest, nicest—"

"It's him," Alexander exclaimed. "The giggler, one of the men who tried to kill us before."

The girl realized then that she was standing in the light before a group of men in her nightdress and she hurried back into her room and slammed the door. Alexander realized he was in his pajamas, but he stayed where he was.

"Somebody go fetch the sheriff," one of the men said. "I'll go," said another as he buttoned his suspenders.

Sheriff Boyd Hutchins was puzzled. "I searched him and found a few dollars and this." He held up a piece of paper, and Alexander could see that it was the engineer's report on the Josey Mine. "Now what I can't figure out is why he broke into that young lady's room and tried to kill her. He didn't touch the money she had."

"I can tell you, Sheriff," Alexander said. He sat in the sheriff's office, which was brightly lighted with three coal-oil lamps. "Miss Dobbs is getting dressed and she'll be here in a minute. I think between the two of us we can tell you things about El Tejon that few people know."

Hutchins sat in his desk chair and tilted it back on its hind legs. He stood up when Miss Dobbs opened the door and came inside, then sat again. "All right, you two, tell me everything you know about all this."

The girl occupied the only other chair in the room. She had on her dark wool skirt and a white blouse buttoned up to her throat. She looked at Alexander and he looked at her. "Do you have it figured out, James?"

"Yeah, I believe I have. I'm just trying to decide where to start."

"I'm listening." The sheriff had an impatient look on his face.

"Sheriff," Alexander began, "have you heard of the triumvirate?"

"Sure. I've heard Calvin Stewart, John Bokhauser, and Joseph Webber called that. Why?"

"Correct me if I'm wrong, Sheriff, but the way I heard it they founded the town of El Tejon. They platted it, got it incorporated, and used their political influence to have it designated a county seat. They believed the town would boom and their investments and efforts would pay off handsomely.

"For a time it did boom. Rich ore was being taken out of the ground, the lumber industry was going full blast, and cattle and sheep were getting fat on the mountain grasses. And to top it all off, the Denver & Rio Grande was planning to extend its rails to El Tejon. The town was destined to become another Cripple Creek. The triumvirate was so convinced the boom would continue that they built a fine hotel, a bank, and a mercantile and encouraged others to invest and build."

Alexander paused, then said, "Pardon me for changing the subject, Mr. Hutchins, but did you get any information at all out of your prisoner?"

"Not a word. He won't talk a'tall. Won't even tell his name. All he does is grin. Go on with your story."

"Things started to come apart in El Tejon. The mines were petering out. Shipping lumber by wagon train was too expensive. Mr. Steward had to compete with sawmills near the railroads. And the board of directors of the D&RG began wondering whether it would be wise to extend their line to El Tejon. I learned that much by talking to some railroaders in Rosebud and to the engineer who made out that report there.

"The triumvirate became desperate. They could see their investments slipping away. But if they could convince the D&RG to go ahead with plans to lay rails here, everything would be saved.

"Mr. Stewart could expand his sawmill and ship lumber by rail, cattlemen and sheepmen would use El Tejon as a shipping point, and, who knows, a packing house might be built here. All sorts of good things could happen if the railroad came here.

"But if the railroad company knew that the Josey Mine, the last working mine around here, was peter-

281

ing out too, they probably wouldn't build here. Now—"

The sheriff interrupted, "Did you say the Josey was peterin' out?"

"Yeah, Sheriff. Take a look at that paper there. It's a report from a mining engineer. The Josey was going the way of other mines around here."

"Well, I'll be a donkey's uncle," Boyd Hutchins exclaimed.

"Getting back to my story, the triumvirate hit upon a scheme. If they could keep the railroad from knowing about the Josey Mine, then maybe they could still persuade the railroad to come to El Tejon. They are excellent salesmen, you know, and they obviously have political influence.

"But to do that, they had to keep the mine owner and his manager quiet."

He looked at the girl, and she locked onto his gaze with her blue-green eyes. "I think I know the rest," she said quietly.

"You tell it, Josie."

"It occurred to me some time ago. But I thought they wanted the mine. It occurred to me when I got to thinking about that attempted bank robbery the day after I arrived here. The more I thought about it, the more I believed that it wasn't an attempted robbery at all but was instead an attempt to kill me."

"What?" the sheriff asked. "What gave you that idea, Miss?"

"It was Mr. Webber at the bank, the way he acted. He was very nervous. And when someone shouted that the bank was being robbed, he grabbed a pistol from his desk and started shooting. But he wasn't taking aim. He was shooting high as though he didn't intend to hit anyone.

"And later I saw the bullet hole in the chair I had been sitting in. If Mr. Alexander hadn't pushed me to the floor, I most certainly would have been shot in the back.

"But," a puzzled frown creased her forehead, "I thought it was Mr. Webber's idea and I thought he wanted the mine. Now that James, Mr. Alexander, has mentioned it though, I'll bet all three of them are in it."

"Why didn't you tell me about this before?" Hutchins asked.

She folded and unfolded her hands in her lap. "I had no proof. I couldn't really believe it myself. Mr. Webber seemed so nice and so professional."

The sheriff pulled out a drawer of his desk, tilted his chair back, and parked his booted feet on the open drawer. "So you think Mr. Webber, John Bokhauser, and Calvin Stewart wanted you dead? And you think they had somebody kill your dad and his manager?"

"That's exactly right," Alexander put in, "but not to take over the mine. They wanted the mine and its secret closed long enough for the railroad to commit itself to laying rail to El Tejon. They believed Buckshot Dobbs had no family, and it would take many months, maybe years, for the state to take over his property, unravel his affairs, and sell the mine to someone who would reopen it."

Miss Dobbs was shaking her head. "It's hard to believe that three men, men of financial means, would arrange three, no four, murders."

"People have been killed for less," the sheriff said.

"And if we needed further proof," Alexander put in, "what happened tonight is it. That knife wielder in there," he nodded toward the jail in back, "wasn't after money, he wanted that report. And he wanted Miss Dobbs dead. They're still trying."

"It's gonna be hard to prove in court." The sheriff shook his head sadly.

"Maybe it won't be. You said, Sheriff, that he wouldn't talk?"

"Naw."

"Maybe, just maybe if you tell him what we just told you, you know, let him know that you know all about it, he might confess and implicate the others."

"It's worth a try." Hutchins let his feet down from the desk drawer and let his chair down on all four legs. "I think I'll go back there and have another little conversation with him."

The dark sky was turning pale on the eastern horizon when Alexander and Miss Dobbs went back to their hotel. They went to their separate rooms, then met again in the lobby. By then the sun was showing itself, and the town was stirring to life.

Ma Blessing was just unlocking her front door when they arrived there and she invited them to "Come on in and set while I fire up the skillet. Java'll be ready in a minute."

The coffee was hot and strong and good, and the strength of it bore through the weariness in Alexander's body. The girl was quiet, as if in deep thought, and Alexander asked what she was thinking about.

284

"Oh, nothing much." She smiled a weak smile. "Well, to be honest, about everything that has happened. I wonder what will become of this town now. It's sad, really. I kind of liked it here."

"It is sad. El Tejon will probably become a ghost town like some of the other mining towns, towns that were once alive and happy. People here will go to Rosebud or Cripple Creek to find employment. Ma Blessing will have to close up and move too. Yes, it is sad."

Sheriff Boyd Hutchins came in just as they finished eating and occupied another chair at their table. He hitched his gunbelt around to a more comfortable position. "It worked. At first he wouldn't say nothin', then I told him everything that happened and why and who did it. I could see he was thinkin' about it. Then I hit him with the full blame. I made out if he didn't turn state's evidence, he'd hang all by hisself. And I promised him if he'd tell his story to the district attorney over at Rosebud and to a jury he wouldn't be hung. I believe I can get the D.A. to agree to that."

"Did he talk then?" Alexander asked.

"Talk? He brayed like a jackass. You two guessed right. It was them three, and now I've got the goods on 'em. They won't get by with it."

They were silent a moment, each with separate thoughts, then the sheriff added: "It's too bad. I wish it hadn't happened. This town will die on its feet now. I want you two to do somethin' for me, I want you to promise you'll keep all this to yourselfs till I can get that jasper to the county jail at Rosebud and get him to tell his story to the D.A. Will you do that? And I need some time to get some warrants for them three too."

"We'll do it, Sheriff."

At the hotel, Alexander and the girl were quiet as they sat in the lobby. There were things he wanted to say to her but he didn't know exactly what. Several times he started to say something and changed his mind. Each time she looked at him expectantly and was disappointed when he clammed up again.

They were surprised to see Silas K. Cantwell dismount from the stage when it arrived.

Cantwell and two other well-dressed men got out of the coach and stretched their legs on the plank sidewalk. When the lawyer saw Alexander and the girl, he motioned to the two men and they all headed directly for them.

"I've got two prospective buyers for the Josey Mine," he said. "I know about the engineer's report. I persuaded the engineer, as your legal representative, to show it to me and tell me all about it. These two gentlemen are mine owners who are interested in buying the equipment at the Josey."

He introduced the two men. They all shook hands, and Miss Dobbs said, "You seem to be a good business manager too, Mr. Cantwell. I would like to turn the whole affair over to you. I'll pay your fee, of course, but I would like to pay it out of the proceeds from the sale of the mine."

"It might take a few weeks, Miss Dobbs, to conclude an agreement and collect the money."

"Take your time. I have enough cash from my father's bank account to go wherever I want to go. I'll keep in touch."

"Very well, if that is what you wish. I'll charge you five percent of the proceeds and bill you too for my attorney's fees."

"That will be fine."

The three left Alexander and the girl alone again.

He wanted to touch her, to replace that wisp of blond hair that had fallen across her forehead. Instead, she touched him. She put a hand on his arm and turned toward him. Her eyes were the clearest blue he had ever seen.

"J.J., James," she began, "I, uh—"

He didn't let her finish and blurted out, "Where—where are you going from here, Josie?"

"I don't know, James. Where are you going from here? Back to college?"

"Naw. I thought it over and I still don't want to be a lawyer. But I don't know where I'll go."

He paused and looked at her speculatively. "I've heard that San Francisco is an exciting place."

"Yes." Her blue eyes sparkled. "They say San Francisco has more spunk, sparks, and sports than any place in the world."

He smiled. "Well—" And then he turned serious again. "Will you tell me something, Josie, will you tell me whether you really are Josephine Dobbs?"

She chuckled and her blue eyes met his. "What time is it, James?"

"Time? Why, uh." He looked at the clock over the clerk's desk. "It's twelve twenty-five. Why?"

"What is the date today?"

"Why, it's uh, August twenty-eight, 1899. Why?"

"Well, I'll tell you, J.J." A mischievous gleam came into her eyes. "At twelve twenty-five o'clock on August twenty-eight in the year 1900, I'll tell you everything you want to know."

"But that's a year from now."

"Uh huh."

"That means we'll, uh—"

"Uh huh."

A slow smile spread across his face. He stood up and pulled her to her feet.

"Come on. Let's go pack."